THE
OXFORD MURDERS

BY

ADAM BROOME

Ostara Publishing

First published By Geoffrey Bles 1929

ISBN   9781906288082

A CIP reference is available from the British Library

Some of the words used and views expressed in this text, in common
usage when originally published, could be considered offensive today.
The Publishers have reproduced the text as published but would wish
to emphasise that such words and terms in no way represent the views
and opinions of the Publisher.

Printed and bound in the United Kingdom

Published by   Ostara Publishing
                    13 King Coel Road
                    Lexden
                    Colchester
                    CO3 9AG

CONTENTS

THE OXFORD MURDERS

CHAPTER I

The "Fresher"

IT was certainly unusual—most unusual. The old grey face of St. Antony's College, nestling in the quiet square behind "The House," had witnessed many strange scenes in its honourable seven hundred years of history. But not St. Antony's, not perhaps any college in all Oxford, had formed the background for such a spectacle as was being enacted that grey and damp October evening which ushered in the Michaelmas Term of 192—.

Many of the sights were familiar enough. One after another the hard-worked taxis followed each other up from the station and down King Edward Street to the Lodge of the College. Each was piled higher than the last with the luggage of returning undergraduates and freshmen.

One little knot of young men clustered under the gas lamp outside the College gates, another in the cosy Porter's Lodge. Freshmen from the same schools formed their own little cliques. Second and third year men, *their* schools almost forgotten in the newer ties which bound them to Saint Antony's, discussed the adventures of the past long "Vac," the fate in store for the College on the football field and on the river.

The dark grey quadrangles were dotted with lights on every stair, as the men again took possession of their old rooms, or made their first acquaintance of the new.

Reggie Crofts, a short, dark, handsome youth, who had taken his Schools the previous term, and was up now taking a year's course before going out to a Government post in West Africa, was chatting with a group of third year men whose trials lay before them. They lounged against the scouts' pigeonholes in the ante-room to the Porter's Lodge proper.

"Well, perhaps you're right—" the speaker was a tall fair, broad-shouldered young man who captained St. Antony's Soccer team, and was to be tried for his "Blue." "Building the Empire and all that—bushwhacking, thrashing Africans, having a pot at a jolly old elephant. Topping sport—if you like it, no doubt. But me for a stool in the governor's office—if ever I come through the Law School alive—raking in the perfectly good shekels he collects. Lots of cricket in summer and lashings of footer in the winter. *You* can do all my 'outpost-of Empire' stunt for me, basking in the tropical sunshine with a dusky short-frocked flapper——"

"*If* she wears frocks *at all!*"—a voice completed the sentence for him.

A laugh went round the little group at this sally. Before Reggie could retaliate, "Tubby" Crayford exclaimed.

"I say! What's all that row outside? Shall we go out and have a dekko?"

"Let's!" shouted twenty or thirty voices.

There was a general rush for the entrance gates.

Outside stood a four-wheeler—such a four-wheeler as Oxford only can produce. A crowd of urchins and loafers, who seemed by their puffing and panting to have followed it up from the station, stood around it in the roadway, and on the narrow pavement between it and the College porch. On the top of the cab was a miscellaneous collection of objects, strange even in Oxford on the first day of term.

At the back, almost falling off the roof, so great was the con-gestion in front, was a large bass drum of somewhat battered aspect. The remaining space was cluttered up with an assort-ment of ancient coloured tin hat-boxes, brand-new cow-hide trunks, bundles clumsily tied up with rope and wrapped in coarse white and blue homespun cloths, and round multi-coloured baskets.

The horn of a large, old-fashioned gramophone hung down in a drunken-looking way over the door of the vehicle, and a large concertina, balanced precariously on the top of a new Madeira wicker table, jolted unsteadily to and fro as the momentum of the cab was checked as it came to a standstill.

"Cripes! Wonder if 'e's going to give a show 'ere!"—a small ragged urchin, his eyes ablaze with excitement and anticipation, nudged his companion as the vehicle finally stopped.

"You bet yer life!" came the answer. "I see'd two gals inside, all dressed up and wiv blacked faces, better than them lidies up at St. Giles's fair. The drum and all's the same!"

"Garn!—they don't have no St. Giles's fair down 'ere by the Colleges." The rebuke was given with all the self-satisfaction of superior wisdom, tinged with the faint hope that, after all, its speaker *might* be wrong.

Interest now focussed on the swarm of undergraduates which, headed by "Tubby" Crayford, poured through the huge oak gates of St. Antony's, thrown wide open to receive the returning members and their goods and chattels.

Crayford, Reggie Crofts and their friends, followed by a good many more young men, who had got wind that something out of the ordinary was afoot, were at first unable, in the gloom after the brightness of the Porter's Lodge, to make out what all the hubbub was about.

"What's all this blinking row about?"—it was Crayford who spoke. "I can't see any reason for all this fuss about a perfectly good 'fresher' rolling up to Alma Mater."

"I can't see what's *inside* yet," said Reggie Crofts, elbowing his way through the rapidly growing throng. "But just look on the top. Has this feller mistaken the College for the Coliseum? Look, you chaps."

The door of the crazy cab now opened, and one of its occupants stepped out. The clothes were the clothes of Savile Row— no mass-production, multiple shop had turned out those immaculate boots. But the features of the wearer were the features of a coal-black, broad-nosed, thick-lipped African negro. He looked around him with an expression in which timidity and disdain were equally mingled. Transferring his gold-topped malacca cane from one yellow-gloved hand to the other, a large solitaire diamond pin in his silk tie flashing brilliantly in the lamplight, he turned to "Tubby," the nearest figure to him, and said, in a nasal, drawling voice:

"Can you tell me, sah, if this is St. Antony's College?"

"It's Regent's Park *he* wants!"—the voice came from the back of the crowd in front of the College gates.

"Stow it!" cried another voice. "He's a week late for the Vac. two houses a night variety show at the theatre!"

An outburst of laughter greeted the remark. When it had subsided, "Tubby," with becoming gravity said:

"Yes, this is St. Antony's."

"Thank you, sah," said the African. "Can you tell me, sah, if there is someone here to help me with my luggage?"

From a dozen lusty throats went up the shout,

"Barker! Barker! Forward!—Job for you!"

Barker was the St. Antony's porter. For twenty-five years he had served the College, and to hundreds of men gone down, he, more than even the three Wardens whom he had seen come and go, and than the fourth whom he now served, stood for St. Antony's and all that it meant for them.

As the occupant of the cab awaited his arrival, he turned back towards its door and spoke to someone inside.

"*Now* we shall see 'em!" cried the urchins, and an excited murmur ran round the crowd of ragamuffins and loafers which grew with every minute.

"Can't make it out at all," said Crofts.

"Anyway, we'll stop and see the fun," cried Crayford. And the mob of undergraduates surged forward and pressed the small boys back.

From the cab, assisted by the immaculately tailored negro, stepped an unexpected figure. It was a woman—a young woman—

but of a race but rarely seen in Oxford. For she was obviously a full-blooded negress. She was, of her kind, comely. Short and slender, her woolly head covered by a bright light blue silk handkerchief, her ears resplendent with heavy gold ear-rings, a confused smile in her dark eyes, her white teeth flashing in contrast with her black skin, she stepped to the ground. She was dressed in African style, in a black silk, long-sleeved *buba* or loose native blouse, a yellow velvet wrapper or *lappa* swathed about her waist. She wore no stockings, and her feet were shod with a pair of barbaric looking native-made red leather sandals.

"Cheers!" cried a voice in the crowd. "Good old Cambridge— first again!"

There was a chorus of groans, a scuffle and a short diversion as the disloyal onlooker was chased off. Meanwhile, as the dusky beauty continued to smile in rather a bewildered way on the crowd before the College gates, the negro once more approached the door of the vehicle.

A delighted murmur broke from the assembly, from undergraduates, urchins and loafers alike, as the second figure emerged from the darkness of the cab's interior into the glare of the College gate lamp. As the ponderously built negress who now appeared put her foot upon the step of the carriage, the vehicle gave a lurch, and the bass drum, gramophone, concertina, Madeira table and a few miscellaneous bundles and boxes came hurtling to the ground with an ear-splitting crash.

"All hands to the pump!"

"Save the women and children first!" the facetious cries of the undergraduates rang out as the crowd salved the scattered objects and bore them in triumph to the College gates, and turned for a closer inspection of the unwitting cause of the disaster.

She was a plump African woman of medium height, of maturer years than her companion, and was dressed in what she apparently intended to be the latest European mode. A short starched white muslin skirt stood stiffly out around her. A white silk blouse enveloped her voluminous bust, and a black silk sash encircled her ample waist. Her sturdy legs were covered by black silk stockings. A pair of smart, high-heeled shoes, two sizes at least too small, encased the feet upon which she stood so awkwardly. A large floppy black hat, weighed down with ornaments of sparkling jet, prevented a clear view of her features.

"Bravo, Auntie! All's well!" shouted a voice in the throng, which was now in high good humour. Barker, the porter, had now arrived on the scene, and the crowd fell back to await developments. The portly Barker, his hair still scarcely greying, his moustache yet a dark brown, looked younger than his sixty odd years. He approached the African with his usual deference.

"Might you be Mr. Konti, sir, that we're expecting?"

"Yes," replied the negro in his slow, drawling tones, "I *am* Mr. Konti. I want you to get my baggage in and show me my rooms."

"Very good, sir," said old Barker, eyeing the luggage and the two sniggering women with some suspicion. "I'll get your cabman and the under porter to give me a hand."

"Thank you," said Mr. Konti with condescension. Beckoning to his female companions, he made for the College entrance as the crowd fell back to let him pass. Barker turned round scandalised.

"Excuse me, sir," said he, following the negro, "but who might these ladies be?"

"These ladies," replied the African, drawing off his gloves and standing aside to let the women pass, "are two of my *wives*."

Barker had seen active service in his younger days in the Army. But no bursting shell had ever shattered his composure as much as the negro "fresher's" words. Getting in front of the three figures before they could enter the porch of the College, he held up a protesting hand.

"But surely, sir, the Warden told you when you were admitted that ladies are *not* allowed in College!"

"Indeed he did not," said the indignant Konti. "It is true I did not ask him. But you forget that I am a Prince in my own country. And a Prince may do what others may not."

"I'm very sorry, sir. But it's against the College rules, against the Statutes of the University, and cannot be allowed."

"But," said the negro, becoming heated in his righteous indignation, "do I not tell you that I am a Prince in my own country?"—and he tried to pass the resisting porter.

Oxford College porters are a race apart. Their tact is a byword. Barker had never had to face a predicament like this before. But he did not lose his head, and did his best to uphold the rules of the institution which he served without, at the same time, wounding too deeply the feelings of the new undergraduate of St. Antony's.

"I am sorry, sir. And sorry indeed for the ladies" (he hesitated on the word, for Barker was a staunch supporter of the ethics of the Christian religion). "But if you were the King of England himself, the College rules would have to be obeyed."

The immovable attitude of the porter at last caused the black man to pause. He had come up against, in the person of Barker, the consolidation of the laws and rules of College and University for generations past. The new civilisation bowed before the old and admitted defeat.

"Where can I take the ladies for the night?" he asked, subdued.

"There are many hotels in Oxford, sir. I suggest the Mitre, the Clarendon, or the Randolph. Your cabman will take you to one, and if that is full, you can try the others."

The luggage was by now all stowed in the College porch, and, somewhat crestfallen, the self-styled "Prince" went back to the cab which still waited outside. He got in, followed by his wives, and as the cab drove off, the crowd burst into cheers. Two undergraduates, taking charge of the bass drum, thumped it with rhythmic vigour. The cheering group at the College gates sang lustily:

"For he's a jolly good Mormon!" as the back of the vehicle vanished into the gloom of "Teddy" Street.

CHAPTER II

Human Leopards

MR. COMMISSIONER PRESCOTT finished his leathery sardine omelette with a relish which he would have found hard to explain had he been in Europe. But after five hours of listening to native witnesses on the cramped veranda of a hut in a West African village, hunger is as good a sauce as any. And was there not a bottle of cool lager waiting in the canvas water-bag swaying before him in the breeze? Mrs. Prescott had gone home two months before, and her husband could indulge in a few luxuries which she, had she been present, would in no wise have permitted.

Prescott was a disappointed man. Nearer fifty than forty, rotund, bull-necked and going bald, he was hardly an attractive figure. In the Army, years before, he had attained the rank of Quartermaster-Sergeant. A commission had followed, and his time expiring whilst he was on service with his regiment in West Africa, he had secured an appointment in the political service of the Colony.

His position was now that of District Commissioner. But his mental equipment remained that of the Quartermaster-Sergeant. The previous year he had been still an Assistant District Commissioner. But the assassination of Edmund Cargill, District Commissioner,* had caused an unexpected vacancy in the Baoma District of the North-West Province which Prescott had been promoted to fill.

* See *The Porro Palaver.*

Prescott was the victim of many delusions. The chief of these was the conviction that he was the only really honest European officer in the Colony. Even the Governor, when not present, came in for a share of the District Commissioner's innuendoes. That visit to a man-of-war in the Government launch. Was not the occasion strictly speaking a private one? Was not its object attendance at a cocktail party? Yet was it likely that the Governor had (as Prescott himself said *he* would have done), separated it from the official accounts and paid for the petrol used out of his own pocket? Prescott would shake a melancholy head at the idea of such dishonesty in high places, the setting of so much lower a standard of morality than he himself observed.

So keenly did he feel on the matter that he sent long letters to *The Times* deploring the lax morality of the Colonial Government service. He wrote these letters under a pseudonym, with a Government typewriter, on Government paper, and enclosed in envelopes officially supplied. But had he been taken to task on the subject he would doubtless have replied hotly that he was justified as his writings were, as his signature proclaimed, "*Pro Bono Publico.*"

Prescott made work where no work normally was. But his hands were now more than full of supremely important tasks. Much trouble had been experienced in the Baoma District in the past, owing to the activities of the native secret society known as the Porro. The measures taken by his predecessor, Cargill, had succeeded largely in their object, the breaking of its power. But the West African native, unable to read or write, with no football matches, cricket or the cinema yet to absorb him in his many leisure moments, revels in intrigue. Active membership of the Porro Society now being a somewhat difficult and dangerous proposition, native yearnings for subterranean intrigue were turning in another direction. The number of cases reported to Prescott during the past few months of wounding and death, alleged to be the result of attacks by leopards, were getting rather alarming. And the D.C. at last determined that the time was ripe for a personal visit to the regions in which the outrages were being committed.

He had not yet definitely brought a charge against anyone—too prompt action in such cases may easily do more harm than good. But suspicion was beginning to focus on certain individuals. An informal enquiry had been begun. Prescott, whose limited education and narrow vision had made him almost inclined, with the natives, to suspect the working of supernatural agency in some at least of the cases which had been brought to his notice, had spent a long morning interrogating witnesses from villages near or in which the incidents had occurred. He was feeling very weary and hopelessly at sea.

There was only one person remaining to be questioned in the afternoon, but her testimony, he had been able to see from the statements already made, would either make it possible for him to proceed to action or force him to abandon hope of any concrete results.

His lunch finished he threw himself into a battered deck chair, which accompanied him on all his travels, and prepared for a comfortable doze. This was easier to plan than to achieve. There was no Rest House in the village. The March afternoon was stiflingly hot. A herd of lean cows was sheltering under the thatched eaves of the opposite hut, only a matter of ten yards off. The effluvium arising was far from gratifying to European nostrils. The flies chased off by the tails of the cattle found the white man's face and arms a more comfortable rendezvous. The chatter of the groups of natives, lying in hammocks or squatting on the floors of the adjacent huts, was not a little irritating as they told and re-told the incidents of the morning's hearing.

Prescott sent out a police orderly to stem the tide of talk within reasonable limits. But the altercations which arose as the result of this manœuvre made him begin to wish that he had left things as they were. As he tried once more vainly to compose himself for the forty winks which he had promised himself, the figure of a European appeared around the corner of the hut, followed shortly by a second.

"Hullo, Prescott! How do? How do? Having a cushy time?" The

first man shouted his greeting in a jovial tone. The geniality of the speaker was not reflected in the D.C.'s frigid reply.

"Is that you, Doctor Mahaffy? What brings *you* this way?" he got out. Then, turning towards the second white man. "Ha, Grigson; so you're here too. Thought you were up at Baoma checking the Police stores. They're in a pretty confused state. Shouldn't wonder if somebody didn't lose a little *copper* (money) over it."

Prescott's main purpose in official life seemed to be to get inventories of stores correctly checked and entered. Another throwback to his former calling. Nothing delighted him more, on taking over a district from a fellow officer, than to check the usual impedimenta of a bush station so meticulously as to be able to send in a neatly typed list of deficiencies to headquarters, and to get his predecessor surcharged with the cost of an office ruler, two wastepaper baskets, one feather pillow, two bentwood chairs (clerks, for use of), and the like. This sort of thing represented to his ordered mind what he was pleased to term "hundred-per-cent efficiency." It enabled him, too, to make covert references to the dishonesty of European Government officials. For how, he would argue, could a whole Government ruler come to be missing unless the unscrupulous officer in charge had (*a*) used it for his own private purposes, or (*b*) sold it?

"No," said Mahaffy, "we've come to pay you a professional visit. I represent the famous firm of Cascara, Salts and Co., the eminent drug firm. My friend here (he waved to his companion), "travels in handcuffs and warrants of arrest. Anything doing in either of our lines?"

The flippancy of the genial Irish doctor was distasteful to the serious-minded Prescott. But Grigson, the young Police Officer, burst into a hearty laugh. His main inclination at the moment was to give the pompous District Commissioner a good sound kick where he would feel it most. Fortunately for the dictates of official decorum he suppressed his desire.

"I'm afraid," said Prescott, frowning, "that the business I'm engaged on is rather serious. Sorry I can't offer you chairs. I've only this one I travel with," he indicated the steamer chair from which he had risen.

"Don't mind us," cried Mahaffy. "Here's a perfectly good wall." And he and Grigson dumped themselves on the low mud wall facing their host. Each was dressed in khaki bush-shirt, shorts, stockings and marching boots.

"Phew!" said Mahaffy, mopping his streaming red face and his partly bald head with a genuine old Woolworth bandana. "It's a damned hot day, and those twelve miles from Baoma are pretty warm going."

He eyed the canvas water-bag swaying temptingly overhead.

"Yes," said Prescott, refusing to see the thirsty gleam in the other's eye. "It's pretty hot to-day, anyway."

"Have a gasper," said the Doctor, extending a battered nickel-silver case as a hint that hospitality of another nature was expected from his host.

"No thanks," replied the other primly. "I find that too much smoking in the day affects my throat in court. Single-handed as I am I *must* keep as fit as possible." Prescott spent a lot of time in placing himself upon pedestals of one kind or another.

"You haven't a glass of water handy I suppose?" ventured Grigson. "We're devilish thirsty you know."

"Boy!" called the D.C., "fetch dem watta!" The servant would equally well have understood the order in correct English. But one of Prescott's many slogans was "When in Rome do as the Romans do," and he had painfully and conscientiously, and albeit quite unnecessarily, acquired a voluble fund of "pidgin" English.

To the disgust of Mahaffy and Grigson they were soon confronted with a tray on which stood a terracotta water cooler and a couple of tumblers.

"Sorry if the water's not *quite* cool," said Prescott. "Can't be too careful—dysentery you know. Always see my water boiled myself, and what they did this morning is still a bit warm."

"I didn't want a *bath*—I wanted a *drink,*" said the Doctor. He managed to raise a smile, but it was rather a grim one.

Giving up hopes of a beer, the policeman and the Doctor politely declined the proffered refreshment and lighted up their pipes.

"And how are you getting along? Any nearer catching any of these murderer fellows yet? I'll swear that the last selection of dead babies and things you so kindly packed off to me in gin cases was cut up by *men*—not chopped by leopards, whatever your African friends may say." The Doctor's tone was flippant and was immediately resented by the solemn Prescott who, however, feared the lash of Mahaffy's tongue too much to administer an open rebuke.

"I don't know *what* to think yet," said the D.C. "I've still got one more witness to hear—the most important of the lot. A good deal depends on what she has to tell me. If human agency *is* at work, destroying the lives of these innocent young children, no punishment can be too great for the dastardly criminals responsible." Prescott's tones were an excellent imitation of those of the admirable Methodist divine under whom he and his wife sat Sunday by Sunday when they were at home.

"Yes," concurred the Doctor. "Black as their hides may be, I suppose they're entitled to a square deal." Mahaffy's cynicism in discussing the natives as if they were no more than brute beasts was largely superficial. But he knew that it irritated the smug D.C. And he was himself annoyed at the substitution of the nauseous lukewarm water for the welcome cold beer he had half expected, despite the well-known meanness of Mr. Commissioner Prescott.

"I do not like," continued Prescott, "to cast suspicion on *anyone* until I can get hold of really convincing evidence. But everything points to Paramount Chief Konti as the instigator of these outrages. Even if he is not guilty himself, he *must* know who are. And if he won't tell the Government, he stands at least in the shoes of a conspirator."

"This," put in Grigson, the sturdy, good-humoured Assistant Police Commissioner, "is the first time I've been up against these Human Leopards. It seems that the Porro Society is a kind of Sunday school affair compared to them. From what I've heard from a pal of mine in Sierra Leone, the rough idea is this. A number of the local 'bright young things' form themselves into a secret club, with a special 'medicine' as the object of their devotion. This 'medicine' increases the manliness of its keepers. But it must be anointed afresh from time to time with fresh human blood, or it loses its efficacy."

"You're right," said Mahaffy, who knew as much about the natives of the district as most people. "That's the big idea. Finding that they're not getting 'the goods,' the members of the gang hold a secret meeting in the bush. Lots are drawn. The unlucky one has to provide the next victim. The easiest way is for him to leave one of his own kids where his pals can find it at a given time. Somebody dresses up as a leopard—claws and all complete—grabs the 'piccan' when it's having its beauty sleep, yanks it off into the bush where his friends are waiting. They kill the poor brat, each take a snack, anoint their old 'medicine' with its blood and carry on until it needs a fresh dose. When you've got half a dozen wives, each producing a kid a year, I suppose you kind of begin to lose the ordinary fatherly feelings."

Every line in Prescott's features expressed the strongest disapproval of Mahaffy's flippant speech. Yet he knew, from his own experience, that the summary was a fairly correct one. He could have wished however, that the other could have couched it in somewhat different terms.

"The worst of it is," said he, "is that, as the acts of the Society are in the nature of *religious* performances, it's very hard to stamp it out. The natives themselves do not think of it as they would of an ordinary murder. And those who are not members are firmly convinced that the author of the crimes is a sort of supernatural leopard. They all believe that the ordinary leopard *won't* attack a human being, and the moment a case of wounding by a leopard occurs, they at once jump to the conclusion that the Leopard Society is at work. It's all arguing round in a circle."

"Did you say that old Chief Konti was supposed to be at the bottom of it? The old devil's as rich as be damned. And hasn't his poisonous stiff of a son just gone home to Cambridge?" It was Grigson who spoke.

"Oxford," corrected Mahaffy, "so his father told me, in one of his more or less sober moments."

"Well," said the policeman, "Oxford's gain is Cambridge's loss. Or the other way about if you like."

"I'm sorry, Doctor—sorry, Grigson," said the D.C., rising from his chair. "But I adjourned the enquiry till half-past two, and it's now a quarter to three." Then to his orderly, "Saidu! Tell dem people and the Chief for come—'*one time*'!"

The village where the D.C. was holding his investigation was a very small one, consisting of not more than a dozen or so huts. The one which he himself was occupying was the largest. There was the usual native "barri" or court-house in the centre of the place, where the headman adjudicated upon the weighty matters brought daily to his notice by the rank and file. But it was very small and in very bad repair. Furthermore, having been used, apparently, for many months as a sort of communal stable for the livestock of the inhabitants, its suitability for Europeans presented other distinct disadvantages. So the court met on the tiny veranda of the Commissioner's own hut.

As soon as the villagers saw signs of activity on Prescott's veranda—the policeman putting the small travelling table with its books and papers in position, the orderly bustling off to summon the Chief—they began to swarm round the hut as thickly as the flies around the cattle.

Chief Konti, only too obviously under the influence of palm wine or some more potent liquor, in a resplendent red velvet gown, white-turbaned ceremonial fez, and holding the brass-headed staff which is the symbol of a Paramount Chief's authority, was assisted to his chair facing the D.C.'s table by two of his hammock-bearers.

When the preliminary turmoil had subsided and an air space had been cleared near the veranda wall by the policemen, to prevent the three white men from being completely stifled, the last witness was summoned. The court was informal—a mere enquiry—and there was no witness box.

"Titi! Titi!" cried the court orderly. From a place on the floor, close to the knees of the Chief, arose a young woman. She was of lighter complexion than the throng around her. Her nose was less flat than that of the typical West African. Her lips were less thick and full, and her dark eyes stared dreamily ahead of her as she stood to face Prescott at his table. In her short-sleeved indigo blue *buba*, her white *lappa*—with silver bracelets flashing in the sunlight and her silver ear-rings glistening as she moved, she had an attraction which was a little uncanny.

The policeman interpreting asked her her name. Looking right over the heads of the three white men before her, she spoke in a quiet, rather hesitating voice. Her tale, told partly direct, and partly as answers to the D.C.'s interpreted questions, was as follows:

"My name is Titi. I live in the village of Mano. I have no man. I work for my father and my mother. My father is one of Chief Konti's 'big men.' One night, about a week ago, we had had chop (*food*). My father and my mother, my brothers and sisters, went to bed. I was alone on the veranda of our house. The pots had not been washed after 'chop.' So, to save myself trouble the next morning, and as the moon shone bright that night, I got them together and went down to the water-side. I began to wash them. Then I heard low voices—men's voices. I was afraid. For it was late and all the people of the village were sleeping. I feared any man who would walk about so late at night. I hid in a clump of elephant grass close to the water-side. I saw six men come down the path from the village. In front was Margai, the Chief's head hammock-boy. He held a bundle of banana leaves. I saw blood dripping from the bundle. He went down to the stream and sat down on a stone by the bank. The other five men were Suri, the Chief's big brother, Momodu, one of his sons, Gegba, another son, Brima, his brother-in-law, and Kangaju, his speaker (*chief counsellor*). They all sat down. The hammock-boy unwrapped the bundle and spread the contents on two banana leaves in their midst. I could see red meat, but I did not know what animal it was. All the men put their hands towards it, and each took a piece of meat and ate it. The hammock-boy wrapped up part of what was left in a small parcel, and threw the rest into the bush on the other side of the road. Then all six washed their hands in the stream and went back up the hill to the village. I was frightened. I waited a little while and went home. Next morning, when I woke up, I heard all the people in the village crying. I heard that a leopard had caught a little girl, Sentu, the daughter of Momodu, the Chief's son. That is all I know."

The auditors, the white men included, had listened spellbound to the black girl's story. She spoke as if in a dream, sometimes closing her eyes, and looking, even when she opened them, always before her, over the heads of the Europeans.

This was indeed evidence, if it could be substantiated. A silence which could be felt came over the gathering. It was the voice of Prescott which broke it.

"Look here, my girl. Had I myself been there with you all the time, I should have seen all you saw?"

There was a pause. The answer came and was translated by the orderly.

"No sah. The girl say, if you be there, you no able for see dem things she say. She say—all the time—when she see dem things— she *sleep!*"

CHAPTER III

Tea for Two

REGGIE CROFTS had taken the precaution of reserving a small table for two in a cosy corner of the Moorish Tea-Lounge. His tea appointment with Barbara Playford was at four-fifteen. But he knew something of the punctuality of the fair sex, and of one of its members in particular.

Having booked his table, he went down to the door of the café and up towards Carfax, to await his guest. "The Corn" was, as usual, a seething mass of activity. Amongst the crowds hurrying North Oxfordwards were young men in shorts and blazers, returning from "tubbing" practice on the river. Towards Carfax, in the reverse direction, came muddied figures returning to their Colleges from football and hockey on grounds up the Woodstock Road. There was a fair sprinkling of feminine members of the University, but he looked in vain—it was now four-twenty—for the particular one he sought. He pondered, as he watched, on the attachment of the girl undergraduate for her academical dress. Surely the women were not *always* going to or returning from lectures, especially at such an unearthly hour of the afternoon. Possibly, he mused, the secret was to be found in the undeniably becoming nature of the feminine counterpart of the men's "mortar-board." He had heard gibes at the expense of the women under-graduates. He had even been guilty of uttering them himself. But he argued, as men will when they are forced to abandon a cher-ished illusion, that Barbara Playford was not as other girls were.

She might be a girl undergraduate, she might be a scholar of Somerville, she might have taken a better class in "Mods." than he had himself. But she was, for all that, a woman—a delightful, feminine, lovely woman; he did not care what her academic attainments might be.

It was certainly annoying to have to wait out in the street like this. It was now, undeniably, four twenty-five, and the appointment had certainly been for four-fifteen sharp. But then, he knew little of the idiosyncrasies of female dons. Perhaps *they* did not watch the clock. Perhaps *they* did fix tutorial hours at times when their unfortunate pupils would have been better occupied on the river or on the hockey field. Anyway, whatever they did, it was distinctly chilly waiting about on a cold November afternoon, with an appointment with the most charming girl he had ever met, when the said delightful maiden showed no sign of having even remembered the engagement.

The word "engagement" occurring in his thoughts gave them a different direction. But that did not alter the fact that it was now half-past four. A noisy bus from Wolvercote was momentarily held up by a traffic jam at Carfax before it reached its appointed stopping-place. A passenger, taking advantage of the few yards thus saved, stepped nimbly off the platform and threaded quickly through the traffic and pedestrians.

"Hullo! Reggie! *So* sorry! Miss Durnford *wouldn't* let me go till she was quite sure that I really *did* understand the last chapter of Aristotle's *Ethics!*"

So that *was* it. These modern Minervas *did* compel attendance in the afternoon—and at teatime at that! Reggie could cheerfully have smacked both Aristotle and Miss Durnford very heartily indeed. But there were compensations for the chilly wait. Reggie had to admit that the girl's "cap" was decidedly becoming, and he could not imagine Barbara looking as sweet in anything else.

She was tall, well-made, radiantly pretty, and her brown curls, peeping out beneath her demure academic headgear, were simply *too* adorable. The open jacket showed a bright Fair Isle jumper, and the short tweed skirt did ample justice to a pair of shapely legs in pink silk stockings. There was no room for cavilling at her slender ankles and little feet, though Barbara Playford was an athletic girl.

"Doesn't matter a scrap," said Reggie. "I've had nothing special to do this afternoon. The Tropical Course people don't seem to be as exacting as the Somerville dons, thank goodness. Let's go up and have some tea. I should say you were a bit dry if you've been having a whole afternoon with Aristotle!"

They sank into their comfortable chairs and forgot their past troubles over deliciously crisp hot crumpets and steaming China tea. In another six or seven months Reggie would be setting out for West Africa. But he had made up his mind, before he went, to ask Barbara to be his wife. He had a pretty good idea that his chances of success would be, ordinarily, fairly good. But whether the girl would care to accompany a husband to "The White Man's Grave" was quite another matter.

She was a clever scholar—her uncle was the distinguished Master of St. Thomas's College—and she had every chance of a prosperous career at home. None the less, he was determined to risk a proposal that very afternoon.

"And how's St. Antony's these days?" asked Barbara, who made a charming picture as she lay back in her chair in the corner of the softly lighted tea-room. Her finely moulded features glowed with health. Her pretty red lips were supremely tempting, and the soft tendrils of her dark hair, now that her cap was removed, played coquettishly around a pair of dainty ears.

"Oh, so so," answered Reggie. "There've been some *frightfully* funny rags with this African fellow, Konti. I believe his full name is Athanasius Septimus Konti—'Septic' for short! For he's a full-blown Christian, though the son of a pagan potentate."

"I thought you told me he turned up with a whole cabful of wives?" said Barbara.

"Aha! So he did," returned the young man. "But he's a Christian for *all* that. You know our Greats don, Brightwood—the thin, lank bird who babbles about Plato and Free Will and Determinism, and all that tripe?"

"I know him," the girl nodded. "Been to his lectures. Shining light of the Seventh Day Adventists or Holy Rollers or something like that in his spare time—frightfully saintly I believe."

"Yes, that's the bloke. He got to hear about the wives incident. Didn't believe it at first. Thought somebody was pulling his leg. For 'Septic' had joined up with some sort of 'pi' outfit of which 'Brighters' was the secretary or something. He spoke to the African about it after chapel one evening and there was a most frightful row. The black fellow seemed to know the Scriptures all backwards, and hurled great chunks of them at poor old 'Brighters'' head, showing that monogamy was all an invention of St. Paul and the Early Fathers, and was never laid down in the Bible proper at all. Oh, there was the very devil of a row, I can tell you. And old 'Brighters,' with all his logic and stuff, got most frightfully tied up, and left old Konti cock of the walk!"

"And what's he done with these wonderful wives?" laughed his companion.

"Found them digs—or a harem I suppose you'd call it—somewhere in St. John Street or Wellington Square, I believe," replied Reggie. "To think that, in only a few months now, by Jove!—I shall be out in Africa myself amongst millions and billions of Kontis!"

"And how does he get on with the other men in College?" asked Barbara.

"Never see much of him," said Reggie, "except in Hall. Looks as if he's more used to chopsticks or something of the sort in spite of his posh clothes. He came in search of the true light of learning and all that junk. Going back to instil education into his brother blacks. He's son of some Chief or other in the very colony I'm going to. But as he only passed 'Smalls' after six shots and looks like taking a bad toss in Pass Mods. I don't think I need fear his coming any intellectual superiority over me! He can hardly try to put it across me after that!"

"I should say not," laughed Barbara. "It's difficult to think you're going away so soon"—her voice was a shade softer as she spoke the last words.

"Lots of other fellows to take my place," said Reggie with an assumed levity which he was very far from feeling. He leaned across the little table which separated them, and looked straight into Barbara's eyes. "I say, you know; I hope you won't think me most frightfully sentimental and soft and all that. But do you mean that perhaps you'll—you'll *miss* me—just a little?" The girl's fresh colour deepened slightly. She lowered her gaze from his. Just the least suspicion of a sigh escaped her lips. She liked this frank, good-looking, energetic young man who was not content to look forward to a cramped, dull existence at home on a secure pittance—was not afraid to break all the ties which bound him to home, but, taking his courage in both hands, was going to face a new, ambitious life in a new country. A country which, if a particle of what she had heard was true, had not for nothing earned the title of "The White Man's Grave." Barbara Playford was not, she would proudly proclaim, sentimental. It was a charge to which few girls of her generation would plead guilty. She had danced, played bridge, played hockey with scores of undergraduates during her three years at Oxford. She had said good-bye to young men off to India, to Australia, the Continent, not thinking nor caring whether she would see them again or not. Such a feeling as came over her now, when she realised that in a month or two she must say farewell to Reggie Crofts on his departure for West Africa, she had never experienced before. And it troubled her.

She had thought a good deal about Reggie lately, but never, till she now realised that he was to pass out of her everyday life once and for all, did she suspect that her liking for him had any deeper foundation. That last look of his, as his eager, handsome face bent forwards towards her over the little table, had told her one thing. It had told her, with a voice as loud and as clear as if he had spoken the very words, that Reggie Crofts loved her, and loved her dearly.

As the realisation came to her, she knew that, from the very bottom of her heart, she loved him in return.

"Oh—yes—of course I shall miss you," the words sounded forced and strange. "But after all—it's not for very long—eighteen months I think you said?"

Her eyes met his again. But she felt that she could not bear to see the gleam of passion in his frank, straightforward gaze. She turned a little aside. The tea-shop had slowly emptied. No one could see them in their corner.

The young man motioned to the chair beside him. Barbara rose, came round, and sat in it.

Before she could realise what was happening his arms were round her, and she did not resist him. His face was almost touching hers.

"Barbara! Barbara! I love you," his voice was hoarse with emotion. "Do you love *me*—just—just—only a little, darling?"

The girl made no effort to restrain him. Her arms were soon about his neck, and he pressed her breast to his. Their lips met in a long, passionate kiss. He knew the answer to his question. And it was the one that of all he desired.

They came again to earth. An Oxford tea-shop, in term time, is no paradise for lovers. Though other customers had gone, the waitress must soon be coming with the bill. Barbara resumed her seat. It was tiresome to have to quit Elysium just because a company must have its dividends! But Barbara and Reggie were commonsense young people and knew that facts must be faced.

"So that's that," said Barbara Playford, her manner natural and prosaic now that the storm of passion and emotion in her had found an outlet.

"Did you have *two* cream buns or three? And was it China tea or the other? I suppose an engaged man is apt to forget these little details—but the waitress won't!"

"Engaged!" cried the girl, in mock astonishment. "And to whom are you engaged I should like to know?"

"Oh, come! I *say!*" said Reggie. "I thought it was, once, anyway, the inevitable consequence of a girl's kissing a man!"

"Good Lord!" cried Barbara, laughing. "I must have a good many *fiancés* knocking around the world if that's the case!"

It might be wrong to assume that a tinge of jealousy entered Reggie's mind at these words. But before he had time to frame a suitable retort, the waitress, long overdue, arrived upon the scene, and the reckoning began.

CHAPTER IV

Konti of St. Antony's

THE hall of St. Antony's College was a scene of bustle and hurry. The bell had sounded for dinner. The crowd of undergraduates on the old steps leading to the porch, came pushing through the line of scouts waiting at the oaken doors. Those same doors had been rubbed by the elegantly clad shoulders of the courtiers of Charles the Second when he sojourned in Oxford City.

Every variety of men's dress was displayed by the throng which awaited the entry of the Warden and dons before taking their seats on the old uncomfortable wooden benches, which had served the College for three or four hundred years, and were like to endure for at least as many more. The Oxford commoner's gown, not as long as an ordinary lounge coat, is never very imposing. Torn into a mass of ragged strips hanging to a woebegone square collar—the prevailing fashion with the freshman who hopes to be mistaken for a second or third year man—it loses what dignity or significance its original designer may have intended.

But there was one at least amongst this term's "freshers" who displayed his academic gear in all its pristine glory. It might have come straight from the window of the tailor's shop in the "High" at which he had bought it. It was Mr. Septimus Konti—"Septic" for short—who thus stood out amongst his fellows.

Had Mr. Commissioner Prescott, Doctor Mahaffy or Captain Grigson been present in St. Antony's Hall that evening, they would have found it hard to believe their eyes: that the sedate young man in grey flannel trousers, Fair Isle jumper, blue silk collar and the College tie, decorously gowned, sedately waiting for grace to be said, was the son of the dissolute, drunken old Chief Konti of Batkanu. Son, if it came to that, of a cannibal, no less, if half the Commissioner's suspicions were true.

The Warden was late to-night. Only one of the dons, Brightwood, the Senior Tutor, who had been worsted in the scriptural argument of a few days back, had arrived at the high table. The undergraduates were getting restive, for they were hungry. There was a buzz of conversation, and, presently, some stamping and shuffling of feet. Tired of standing waiting not a few of them sat down on the benches.

At last the Warden appeared. Every man was at once on his feet. Dr. Pelling, in earnest conversation with another of the dons, walked gravely through the serried ranks like a general reviewing his army.

There were few dining at the high table; only half a dozen covers were set. The doors of the Hall were closed. The Warden struck the table with a little silver-bound oaken mallet. When silence reigned, he bowed towards the Senior Scholar, who returned the courtesy and reeled off the aged-old Latin grace without stops or pauses, as if he had been literally quoting some ancient Codex.

The dons of St. Antony's were a curiously heterogeneous collection. Doctor Pelling, the Warden, perhaps the finest Greek scholar of his day, was certainly the rudest of the contemporary Oxford Heads of Colleges. Tall, spare, with hooked nose, white hair, thick spectacles and a stooping walk, he was like some bird of prey for ever on the look-out for a victim amongst the smaller fry around him. He took his seat before the massive silver goblet, the pride of St. Antony's plate, which always graced the Warden's place at table.

On his right sat Andrew Brightwood, the Christian-minded Greats Tutor, whose rout on the matrimonial question had been retailed by Reggie Crofts to Barbara. No love was lost between the Warden and the Senior Tutor, whom all expected to step into the vacant Headship when Doctor Pelling either died or resigned. The latter eventuality was not in the least likely to occur. Pelling was over eighty—a hardy eighty which foreshadowed an almost certain ninety—his intellect as keen as it had ever been.

On his left was the Rev. Otto Bland, the Dean, a man of fifty or so, and of no particular scholarly attainments, but an excellent disciplinarian and very popular with the younger members of the College. His Christianity, which was genuine enough, was rather of the muscular, breezy order, and Mr. Bland had been known to come out with an occasional "damn" with an air of challenging the early Fathers to do their worst. The Warden did not like him: but he feared him, for he always had the feeling that, in downright rudeness he might easily meet his match in the Dean of St. Antony's.

A loquacious member of the little group was Mr. Samuel Taylor, Professor of some abstruse branch of moral Philosophy. He had written voluminous tomes on his subject, whatever it was, which might be found, "Published at Two Guineas" and remaindered at sixpence in dusty boxes in the Charing Cross Road. He was tall and slim, and gave vent to criticisms of things in general in a suavely cynical manner. Never having had any dealings with them in their own countries, Professor Taylor was a great advocate of equal treatment for the coloured races.

Of the remaining two, Adrian Barnes, for many years University Reader in Criminal Law, a plump, rather apoplectic-looking, bald little man, was so occupied with his food and his wine that the rest hardly ever troubled to address a remark to him. And even if they did, it was rarely that they received any reply.

The junior member of the company, Alec Ferguson, had only taken his degree a couple of years before. He had been a Fellow of the College for less than a year. He would not have relished being reminded that, in point of fact, he had scarcely emerged from the undergraduate stage. He was pale, fair-haired, sturdily built, distinctly good-looking. Ferguson appreciated the good things of life, sartorial and otherwise. If he could not afford an early settlement of his bills, what did it matter? Hang it all, these Oxford tailors and wine merchants were damned well-off, and if *he* didn't pay *his* bills, the fellows didn't lose. They covered his tardily met accounts by the high overcharges they inflicted on the chaps who *did* pay promptly. And, anyway, a figure like his was a good advertisement, for *any* tailor. And so that was that. Ferguson, under a pseudonym, had published a novel which he had hoped was sufficiently daring to incur the pain of being banned. But it had passed unnoticed, except by one obscure reviewer in a country paper, who had dubbed it "dull, tedious and immature." The bound copies had mostly been remaindered. The surplus unbound sheets had been resold by the pound, as wrapping paper to a firm engaged in business as bottle packers close to the printers'. Mr. Ferguson was excessively modern, and was always on the look-out for opportunities of shocking the susceptibilities of his older colleagues.

"I hear that our friend Konti is settling down very nicely to College life," said the Dean in his suavest and oiliest manner.

"I should have thought," snapped the Warden, looking more like a bird of prey than ever, "that that was scarcely an appropriate adverb to apply unless Mr. Konti's intellectual efforts were slightly more successful than they are. I understand that he only succeeded—and even then with the greatest difficulty—in passing Responsions after *five* vain attempts. And his tutor informs me that he will probably take at least two years, if not more, to negotiate Pass Moderations."

"I'm afraid that's so, Warden," continued Mr. Bland, quite unruffled. "But I think you will admit, sir, that his is a case in which some allowance must be made."

"I always consider," put in Professor Taylor, in his urbane tones, "that we of the white races, who consider ourselves civilised, are never quite able to put ourselves in the same position as our coloured fellow men—never quite appreciate *their* point of view."

"Can't manage quite so many wives, or acquire the charming habit of squirting betel nut juice all over the place, Professor," said the rebel Ferguson.

"I have been considering lately," interposed the Senior Tutor in mild tones, "a good deal the question of polygamy—I——"

"And what are *Mrs.* Brightwood's views on the subject, might I ask?" said Ferguson.

The Dean laughed openly—even the Warden's eyes twinkled—Mr. Barnes swallowed part of a glass of sherry the wrong way, and the Professor gave vent to an audible grunt of displeasure.

"I would not," went on the Senior Tutor, when comparative calm again prevailed, "wish to imply that I had myself any personal inclination to adopt the habits of a polygamous state of society. But I must confess—ah—that—on mature consideration—if I may say so—I have—ah—reached the conclusion that—strictly speaking—the practice is not entirely incompatible with Christian principles, as far as we know what they were in the earliest—the *very* earliest—days of that creed."

"Do you mean to imply, sir," croaked out the Warden in his most crushing manner, "that you intend to sacrifice a lifelong conviction—break up a happy home—and enter on a course of loose and immoral living, because your logical training is inadequate to meet the arguments of a newly matriculated African freshman?"

The worthy and respectable Brightwood looked as though he would have liked the earth to open and swallow him up. Before he could develop his theories further, or produce, a plausible explanation, Ferguson renewed the attack.

"I think," said he, "that you will be the first to agree that a man should have the courage of his convictions. I do not think that there's any recorded rebuke to King Solomon on account of his somewhat extensive—I might almost say his *all-embracing* matrimonial policy."

"I am afraid," said Mr. Barnes pompously, the lawyer in him coming to the surface as the excellent wine began to course through his veins, "that in the state of society at present existing in this country—any attempt on your part, sir," he inclined towards Brightwood, "to put your theories into practice might involve you in a serious breach, as much of the established canons of the Church of the present day as of the law of the land. No doubt legislators—like Homer—occasionally nod, and their rulings may appear, to the untrained mind, a little arbitrary. But the fact remains that the Statute eyes with no little disfavour the practice known as bigamy, on which subject, indeed, I was—ah—engaged in lecturing this morning."

"I think," ponderously announced the Warden, who was beginning to feel a little sorry for the perplexed and nonplussed Senior Tutor, "that the conversation is taking a trend which is scarcely consonant with the dignity of such a gathering as this."

Brightwood heaved a sigh of relief, the Dean gave a chuckle, and Ferguson, who had been preparing a further onslaught, checked himself in a mock serious problem which he was about to propound, on the rights to property of the children of the various wives of a polygamous husband.

The innocent cause of the dons' conversation, at his place at the freshmen's table, was chatting quite at his ease with his new-found companions. The Michaelmas Term was half-spent, and he had become a not unpopular figure. His rawness was wearing off. He had begun to learn that it was not necessarily good form to order champagne at every meal, just because you happened to have a pretty substantial allowance. On "the Coast," in the big towns, amongst the native intelligentsia, it had been considered the best possible good taste to wear diamonds, either real or imitation—in conspicuous places on the person at important gatherings, festive or otherwise. But his reception the first time he had dined in Hall, when he wore evening clothes, complete with boiled shirt, with a diamond stud in the front as big as a sixpence, and gold cuff links, set with enormous rubies, had convinced him that something was amiss. He had proved adaptable, good-natured and anxious to please. And when he had learned on the Soccer field, that it was not in accordance with the strict rules of the game to give an opponent a straight left-hander on the jaw, or to kick him violently in the shins when you wanted to get the ball from him, he began to shape as quite a useful player. A possible "Blue" was even hinted at in the future. He was certainly extremely lithe and agile, and his keenness and desire to do the best for his side were not to be denied. Even Barker the porter, who had looked askance at him at first after the incident which had occurred on the night of his arrival at St. Antony's, began to melt. The negro's tips were on a more lavish scale than those of any undergraduate he had ever known. The members of his chapel had consulted with him, and pointed out to him what a chance he had of trying, in his humble way, to rescue a pagan soul from the outer darkness in which it was groping.

Konti was reticent on the subject of his wives. They were kept very much to themselves away in their lodgings in St. John Street, and the visits which they were longing to pay to their lord and master in college were firmly discouraged. Occasional screams from their apartments had indicated to passers-by that at least one West African idea, that the best way to deal with a refractory woman is to give her a sound thrashing, had not yet been eradicated by a close contact with Western civilisation.

For the negro freshman, life on the whole passed pleasantly enough. He found, with some surprise, that here, in the white man's own country, a black man was looked upon as at least an equal. Things went even further than that at North Oxford tea-parties. He found himself, as often as not, the lion of the hour, and the dons' wives vied with one another to secure his attendance at their entertainments. Very differently had he been treated at home in far-off Africa, by the few Europeans he had chanced to meet. In particular had he been slighted by the white Medical Officer, Dr. Mahaffy of Baoma, even in the very village of Batkanu where his father was Paramount Chief.

But there *was* a fly in his ointment. "Smalls," after five vain attempts, and many weary hours of cramming by a London tutor, he had eventually managed to pass. But Pass Mods. rose like some unscalable wall before him. Not the thick elephant grass bush of his native land was more impenetrable than this intellectual barrier, which cruel white men had erected between him and his chance of a degree. One of the subjects which he had decided to take was Latin. His own college tutor had expressed himself unequal to the task of, unaided, getting him through the ordeal which awaited him next term in the Schools. He had therefore enlisted the services of a Mr. Day, a private tutor, who lived in Norham Gardens. And it was at his house that he spent a good deal of the time that his fellow undergraduates employed on the fields or on the river. That evening when Hall was over, he went straight back to the old oak-panelled rooms in the second quad to wrestle once more, with the aid of a "crib" with Cicero's devastating *Philippics*. The old room had witnessed some strange scenes since the time when it was built when Elizabeth was queen. But never had it seen one more incongruous than that of the swarthy West African negro, whose not far distant forbears had been running naked and wild in the tropical jungle, studiously poring over the polished polemics of the greatest orator of ancient Rome.

Soon after he had settled himself comfortably in his Minty chair before the blazing fire a knock sounded on the door. His scout, Hanslope, came in for his last visit before going home to ask for any orders. There were none to be given.

"Well, good-night sir," said he. "I found these letters in the Lodge—came by the six o'clock post."

He left the room and Konti examined the letters. One was from a London bookseller—obviously a bill. He threw it aside. The second bore the postmark of Baoma, the headquarters of the district in which was his father's chiefdom. It was dated about three weeks before. He tore it open eagerly. News from home was welcome in this strange, far-off land. Old Chief Konti could not write. Even had he that accomplishment, it was doubtful whether his sober moments would have been of sufficiently frequent occurrence for him to be able to hold a pen. Neither did he know much English. What he wished to say had to be translated and transcribed by his clerk, whose education was of the sketchiest. But the understanding of the effusion presented no difficulty to the negro freshman.

> "Batkanu,
> "31 *October* 1928.
>
> "*My Dear Son,*
> "*Your letter in hand. I had already sent you Money Order*

for Forty Pounds, and the time is so hard. The D.C. done take the tax, and as so many wicked persons have not paid in time, I have had to pay for them so as not to make palaver. Long time I send plenty plenty *copper for you so you may learn at Oxford college and be B.A. Now, my son, you tell me you think you no able for pass the mods quickly. If that be true, I do fear that you must leave and come home. You must leave Oxford college without B.A., which will bring much shame on your father and make the D.C. and the other white men laugh me. I, your father, tell you now that if you cannot do the pass mods as you call them by next year you* must *come home. I no able for pay all that copper for nothing. The D.C. presses me hard. He even goes so far as to say he think that I, the Paramount Chief, know about these leopard murders which my people have been doing to bring trouble on my head with the Government. How are Miatta and Regina? Your other three wives send you plenty plenty 'how-do.' Isatta had twins last week. Remember that if you no able for pass the mods by next year latest you will have to come home.*

"yours loving father,

"Momodu Konti.

"His X Mark.

"Written by Z. Ezekiel Moses,
"Paramount Chief's Clerk."

This letter was a blow to Septimus Konti. His dream of going back to his father and his people, resplendent in white rabbit fur and an imposing gown, were vanishing into thin air. Such a catastrophe, after the way he had talked, must not, could not be allowed to happen. Something decisive must be done, and must be done quickly. And yet, in the face of the reports of his College tutor and of Mr. Day, it seemed that the odds against his passing Mods. next term were very, very remote. Cicero, "crib" and all, were flung on to the floor. Septimus Konti set himself to think, and to think very seriously.

CHAPTER V

The Murder in Wellington Square

WHO knows Oxford City knows Wellington Square. A rather depressing place at the best of times. In summer the rows of houses, each exactly like its neighbour, in dingy yellow brick, open their windows behind cork-decked boxes of wilting flowers, and assume, during Term, a gaiety which scarce becomes them. The Square re-echoes to the clashing strains of gramophones and wireless. Young men shout in lusty baritone and throaty tenor to the accompaniment of hired pianos, Parties bent on river excursions pass hurrying through en route for Tims's boat-house. But winter sees the Square in very different guise. The open space in the centre, the gates of which remain for ever closed, is a mass of fallen leaves and damp rank vegetation. An itinerant "singer"—for Wellington Square is off the wonted beats of the men in blue—wails disconsolately on the curb. The windows are inhospitably fastened, and muffins and toasted tea-cakes are the order of the day behind the foliage of the sagging aspidistras.

The Michaelmas Term had progressed, and the first week in December heralded the approach of "Collections," those colourless counterfeits of the "real thing" in the Schools.

It was about a quarter-past eleven on a rainy night. The theatre had emptied but a few moments before, and Reggie Crofts, in a dripping mackintosh, was seeing Barbara Playford home to Somerville before returning to his own digs in St. Michael Street.

Down St. John Street they passed together and into Wellington Square.

"Pretty putrid show I thought," said the young man.

"*Frightfully* boring," replied Barbara. "But I bet in a few months' time you'll be aching for a show even as bad as that."

"Horrible thought! But from a letter I've had this mail they seem to put up a few quite jolly stunts of their own out there at times. A chap I knew at the Course is now in the Police in Sierra Leone, and we've been corresponding a bit. *He* seems to be having a pretty cheery time, anyhow. Chasing amiable cannibals who dress up as leopards and eat raw babies so far as I'm able to gather. *Frightfully* exciting I should think. Might do with some of these fellows in jolly old Oxford, what? Better than some of the junk that comes to the theatre these days, anyway!"

But to Barbara the idea of cannibalism, and in the very country to which Reggie was so soon to go, conjured up visions which were scarcely reassuring. His tone was flippant, but she could not repress the slight suspicion of a shudder.

"But surely, Reggie, they don't go in for man-eating *now* do they? Why all those Government pamphlets you showed me are full of figures about schools and education and things. And then, look at Mr. Konti."

"Yes—look at him indeed. But I should say *his* civilisation was pretty much on the surface, and his religion too. What about his harem? The fair damsels live somewhere up this way I believe."

They turned into the Square. As they passed from Little Clarendon Street out into the Woodstock Road on the last lap to Somerville, they almost ran into a hurrying figure under a dripping umbrella as they turned the sharp corner.

"I *beg* your pardon, madam—I am *indeed* sorry! Quite my fault."

The gamp was raised and the girl saw the face of the man who held it.

"Why!" she exclaimed. "It's Professor Toogood! I'm quite sure it's as much our fault as yours!"

"Not a bit of it, my dear young lady! Not a bit." The thin ascetic face of the old Professor lighted up in a beaming smile. "It's quite a long time since I've seen you or your uncle. I don't often go out nowadays, especially on such an evening as this. But I've been dining with some old friends of mine up the Woodstock Road. How is it you never come to see us now?"

Mr. Toogood was the Regius Professor of Latin, and lived with his wife in Beaumont Street. The girl was about to answer when the Professor caught sight of her companion.

"Ah—I think," said he, smiling roguishly through his spectacles, "that I can—ah—divine the cause! I had heard of your engagement. May I, sir, congratulate you?"

Reggie reddened slightly, but so obviously genuine was the old Professor's greeting that he shook the proffered hand with vigour.

"Well, well," said Mr. Toogood. "I don't think that this is the kind of night for folks to linger about. But we must all meet again—and soon. I will get my wife to write to you. Good night. Good night."

The Professor disappeared round the corner, and the couple went on to the gates of Somerville where Reggie left Barbara, who had had permission to accompany her *fiancé* to the theatre.

.   .   .   .   .

The notes of Great Tom died faintly away in the distance. It was one o'clock in the morning. As Police-Constable Merrilees turned into Wellington Square he shivered under his streaming cape. The rain had ceased, some time, it was true. But it had left uncomfortable traces behind it. The air was humid and chilly. He had found nothing worthy of note in St. John Street; but then, he never did. The iron railings of the dank empty garden of Wellington Square rose up menacingly before him. He cast the rays of his lantern on the pillar box. There was nothing there to excite his attention. He never thought that there would be. But duty was duty and he was a policeman. Other folk might sleep comfortably in their beds of a night and in the early morning. His eyes must be awake and alert to see what theirs could not. Slowly he plodded round the Square, flashing his lantern into the areas of the houses. Now and again, from force of habit rather than from any real attention to what he was doing, he turned the rays of his lamp towards the inner side of the Square, flashing it mechanically upon the dingy green-painted railings which enclosed the gloomy garden. Something caught his eye. Anything at all unusual came as a relief to Police-Constable Merrilees on his dreary beat. Yes—the otherwise unbroken line of the railings was interrupted at one point. The object looked like a hat—a dark hat. Some undergraduate's joke he supposed. The fifth of November was past. But these young gentlemen were for ever up to some lark or another. It was hardly worth while investigating. He flashed his lantern back down the areas of the surrounding houses, and completed the round of the Square. He was about to turn off into Little Clarendon Street to complete his patrol. But it was not yet time for him to report back at the Police Station. He determined to have one more look—at closer quarters—at the object which had arrested his attention.

Slowly crossing the road to the railings near one of the closed gates which for ever bar access to the desolate patch within, he once more turned his lantern towards the hat. Yes—it *was* a hat: a grey soft hat. He thought they called it a Homburg; anyway when it was in green or mauve or purple and worn by the young.

Reaching up his left hand, unencumbered as was his right with his lamp, he released the object from the spike which held it and proceeded to examine it at his leisure.

It was a fairly new hat. Inside was, in gilt letters, the name of a tailor in "The Broad." But there was nothing to show to what private owner it belonged. It was wet—of course it had rained earlier in the night. Police-Constable Merrilees decided to take it back with him to the Station. It was lost property—very little doubt of that. It was in much too good a condition to have been abandoned permanently by the person who had worn it. Very likely a part of some practical joke.

As the policeman folded it up, the easier to carry it, his lantern poised on the low wall in which the railings were set, he felt his hand all wet and rather sticky where it was in contact with the hat. He stuck it between the railings and produced a handkerchief with which he wiped his hand. He took the lamp, seeking a drier portion of the hat by which he might hold it. In doing so he noticed a dark stain on his handkerchief. His wife had given him a clean one when he left his home for duty. He had—till now—he was sure of it—had no occasion to use it—certainly no chance of making it dirty like that. And it was one of a new lot—white with a lovely coloured border—that he had bought at Woolworth's in "The Corn" only last Saturday.

Taking the lantern again he examined the article further. Yes—there was no doubt that when he had wiped away the moisture which had got on his hand from the hat, the handkerchief was smeared with a dark red stain which looked as if it were blood.

This was curious. He took the hat and examined it again. Yes, there was a large dark patch on the leather lining. It was wet: it *was* blood. He also noticed a jagged hole or cut in the hat, near the stain. The hat was, otherwise, in very good condition.

Police-Constable Merrilees stopped and began to think. This did not look like a practical joke. This might be something much more serious. Replacing the hat between the railings, the police-man took his lantern and flashed it through into the darkness beyond. He saw a gleam or sparkle on a twig of one of the bushes within. The bushes were still wet with the rain. But this did not look like merely the answering reflection of a wet twig alone. He put his hand carefully through the railings to the twig. His fingers closed around some object, whatever it was, that had seemed to shine. Withdrawing his hand again he opened it and, lying on his palm, revealed by the rays of his lamp, was a pair of gold spectacles. One lens was missing—the other cracked. The frame was all twisted and bent.

His interest was now thoroughly aroused. Placing the battered frame in one of his front pockets and carefully buttoning it in, he prepared to make a further search. On the green-stained path on the other side of the sparse bushes—and partly on the bed of earth which ran around the garden—lay a black huddled heap—a heap which looked like a human body.

Merrilees was now entirely on the alert. Outside the fiction he was accustomed to read he had never come upon a situation like this. The railings did not look too hard a proposition for an agile man. He took off his belt and cape and hung them on the railings. In a few seconds, somewhat to the detriment of his uniform, he was inside the garden of Wellington Square—a distinction—in itself, which he could have shared with few. He carefully approached the form, inert upon the garden path. He touched it. There was no movement. A little further investigation showed that it was, without doubt, a human body.

He remembered his police training in first aid, and the restoration of life in the apparently dead. But mindful of a regulation to the effect that in suspicious cases, as little as possible should be disturbed, without moving the body he felt for the region above the heart. He could detect no movement. The limbs were stiff and cold.

Flashing his lantern on the face he saw that the body was that of a scholarly looking elderly man with white hair. Blood had been flowing from the back of the left side of the head. The man had on a black overcoat, and when he had been trying to ascertain if the heart were still beating, Merrilees had noticed that the man was wearing a stiff starched shirt and evening clothes. He was sure that he had seen the man before, in life. But he could not remember exactly where, and was quite sure that he did not know him personally, nor even his name. Looked like one of these University dons.

He was as sure as a layman could be that the man, whoever he was, was quite dead. The body was lying on its stomach, the head being turned round as if the victim before death had tried to see the assailant who had struck him down from behind. The constable felt that, in any case, there was little else that he could do without assistance. The Sergeant in charge of the beat had met him an hour or so ago, in Beaumont Street, and it was extremely unlikely that he would meet him again until he reported for relief at the Police Station.

The first thing he must do was to get a doctor. Hurriedly scrambling back over the palings he determined first to run to the house of Dr. Raymond in Beaumont Street. It was getting on for half-past one. Quickly he ran down St. John Street and reaching the doctor's house, rang the night bell. It seemed an age before the Doctor, an elderly man, appeared in person.

"Sorry sir," said the constable, "for troubling you so late as this. But I've just found a man—dead, I think, in the garden in Wellington Square. I should like you to see the body. The Police Surgeon lives a long way from here, and I'd no means of getting in touch with him."

"By all means, my good man—by all means. The worthy Doctor, doubting at first, as often, the real urgency of a message at so unearthly an hour, was fully convinced by the man's words and manner of the need for his services. "Just wait till I've slipped on some clothes and I'll be with you almost at once."

"And Doctor," cried Merrilees, as Raymond hastily remounted the stairs, "May I use your telephone to make my report to the Station?"

Permission was at once given, and the Doctor had appeared again by the time the policeman had established communication with his superior.

"That's lucky, sir," he said. "The Chief Constable was visiting the Station, and he'll be round in the Square in his car in a jiffy."

The Doctor and the policeman set off at a smart pace down St. John Street and on into Wellington Square. By the light of Merrilees' lamp they could easily make out the tragic heap in the deserted garden. The next problem which arose was how to get the elderly Doctor inside it, for his examination. It was one thing for the young athletic constable to climb the railings into the enclosure. It was a very different matter for the Doctor to accomplish the feat, and he flatly refused to attempt it.

"I'm quite willing," said he, "to do all that I can to assist the course of justice. But it is humanly impossible for me, at my age, and with my rheumatic joints, to climb those railings. Who keeps the key of this gate?"

As well, almost, to ask for the keys of Heaven as for those of the sacrosanct garden in Wellington Square! As the two men were deliberating the new difficulty, the sound of a car heralded the approach of the Chief Constable. A smart two-seater drew up. The Chief Constable of the City Police, leaving the constable-chauffeur at the wheel, stepped briskly out.

"Good morning, sir, for it is morning," said he to Dr. Raymond. "Sorry you should have been called out so early. But from Merrilees' message over the 'phone just now it seems that something pretty serious has happened. Have you seen the body?"

"No, Foster, I've not." He explained the predicament.

"I'm sure *I* don't know who keeps the key of this pleasure spot," said the Chief Constable. "And I hardly think it's worth asking everyone in the Square. I think this is an occasion for taking the law into our own hands. Smith!"—he called to the chauffeur—"bring me the biggest spanner you can raise!"

Before he received the tool, Merrilees, who had advanced to the railings to recover the hat which he had found and left there, exclaimed:

"Excuse me, sir. But I found a hat hanging on these railings. I left it here when I ran for the Doctor. It was stained with blood. But now it's gone!"

Without waiting to hear further explanation, Chief Constable Foster, a tall, muscular, well-built ex-officer, armed with a useful looking weapon, was not long in forcing the lock of the garden gate.

Followed by the Doctor and the policeman, he approached the inert dark mass sprawled on the path before him. As he bent to make an examination he started back as if he had been shot.

"My God!" he cried. "It's Professor Toogood!"

CHAPTER VI

In the Settling Room

OXFORD was appalled when the news of the tragedy in Wellington Square became known. The late Professor had been popular with all. The City had been quite as much a centre of his activities as the University. The benevolent grey-headed, gold-bespectacled figure had been familiar at meetings connected with the social welfare of the town's poorer citizens. No local charity to which his limited means allowed him to subscribe had ever appealed in vain to the kindly Mr. Toogood. His fame as a Latin scholar was European, nor was America behindhand in adding its share of praise for his outstanding contributions to the knowledge of his subject.

If *The Times* deplored in no measured terms his death at an assassin's hand, the *Oxford Times* did not lag behind in pouring forth its tribute to the dead man's memory. His last appearance in public had been to deliver a lecture on "The Literature of the Augustan Era" to a crowded audience at the Schools—an audience which had included some of the most distinguished scholars not only of England, but also of France and Germany and a score of other countries. When next the public took notice of the dead Professor it was in very different circumstances.

"Gloucester Green" has a sound that is almost romantic. It suggests, somehow, the merry frolics of an age long since past. One seems to hear in it the jingle of the horses' bells, the merry jig of the travelling fiddler, the country dances of the stalwart men

and buxom maidens of a time we know no more except in song
and story. But alas! for fancies. In reality Gloucester Green in
Oxford City has no such pleasing associations. A cobbled, con-
creted square, shut in by dull red brick houses and other buildings. The greater part of its space is cut up into divisions, each
within iron rails, where sheep and cattle each Wednesday morning change hands at the weekly market. In the very centre of the
unlovely square stands a small low block of buildings. Amongst
them are the City mortuary and the Settling Room. An ominous
name this. For although its ordinary use is as a place in which
the farmers square their debts when the day's transactions are
closed, it is also the usual venue for inquests in cases of death
by violence.

The late Professor had been a resident member of the University. And though his body had been found by a constable of the
City Police, the University Coroner, as in all such cases, claimed
cognisance and was to hold the inquest. The mortuary is so near
the room used as a court that the usual agreement had been
reached with the City authorities for the use of the building.

It was a sad little scene that was enacted that dull December
day in the bare little Settling Room in Gloucester Green. The
University jury had viewed the body in the near-by mortuary. The
Coroner had taken his seat at the plain, bare wooden table. Chief
Constable Foster was, by the courtesy of the Coroner, present in
uniform, for whatever the result of the deliberations of the jury,
the City Police would have work to do anon.

The witnesses to be examined were Mrs. Toogood, the
Professor's widow; Police-Constable Merrilees, who had found
the body; Reggie and Barbara, who had seen the victim so soon
before he met his death in Wellington Square; Dr. Raymond and
Dr. Haywood the Police Surgeon; and Mr. Sarson, a University
don, with whom Toogood had been dining that night.

No statements had yet been taken by the Coroner's Officer.
The procedure was in this detail different from an inquisition before the City Coroner. The Coroner was in ignorance of what the
evidence of the witnesses would be. The rain pattered drearily

and persistently down on the high glass windows of the Settling Room, as the first witness stepped forward before the Coroner's table. The oath being administered, the inquest began.

Mrs. Toogood, the widow of the dead Professor, was a faded little woman in the late sixties. She was dressed in deep black and it was hard to see her face. For she held constantly before her a handkerchief with which she dried her ever-running tears. Her evidence was punctuated by distressing sobs. Her statement, given with the assistance of the Coroner, amounted to this:

"I am the widow of Alexander Grotius Toogood of St. Paul's College. He was Regius Professor of Latin in the University. We live at 152, Beaumont Street. I remember the night of the 3rd of December. My husband had arranged to dine with a friend of his, Mr. Sarson up the Woodstock Road. I had a bad headache so I did not feel up to going with him. He left the house at a quarter-past seven. I never saw him alive again."

At this juncture the poor frail little woman broke down completely. The Coroner, with a few words of sympathy, stayed the proceedings until Mrs. Toogood was able to continue. She described her identification of the Professor's body at the City Mortuary in Gloucester Green, whither it had been removed by the police with the consent of the University authorities. As she recalled the last ghastly scene, the unfortunate woman again broke down. When she had to some extent recovered, the Coroner, gently, and obviously disliking the unpleasant duty—for the duties of a University Coroner have happily but rarely to be performed—asked her a few questions.

"My husband," she said, "was sixty-four years of age. He was very healthy. He and I had been married over thirty years. Since I knew him he only had to call in the doctor twice. Once it was owing to an attack of influenza. The last occasion was about three years ago. He had stepped on a rusty nail when going to his bath and got a poisoned toe." In answer to further questions, in a voice in which pride in her husband's eminence was mingled with grief at his terrible fate, the widow continued:

"My husband had no enemies. He was friendly with his colleagues in the University and with every one in the City who knew him. He was not in the habit of carrying much money with him and I don't think he had much that night."

It was with genuine relief that the kindly Coroner, the jury and the few spectators saw the conclusion of the examination of this pathetic witness.

Her place was taken by her husband's host of the evening, Montague Sarson, a tutor of St. Paul's College. He deposed:

"I knew the late Mr. Toogood intimately. He reached my house on the 3rd of December at about half-past seven. My wife was away on a visit to London and we dined together alone. The Professor was in very good spirits and joked and laughed as much as usual. He left my house at about a quarter-past eleven. It was raining. He was joking and laughing up to the last moment that I saw him."

The Coroner asked a few more or less formal questions, and Reggie Crofts and Barbara Playford deposed to their having met the deceased at the corner of the Woodstock Road and Little Clarendon Street at about 11.20 p.m. There was nothing in his demeanour to show that there was anything unusual on his mind. On the contrary, he seemed in the best of spirits.

The next witness was Police-Constable Merrilees, who described the finding of the Professor's body in Wellington Square at about 1 a.m., and his summons to Dr. Raymond and the Chief Constable. He was positive that there had been a soft felt hat stuck between the railings surrounding the Square garden when he had left the spot to call the Doctor. It was the presence of this very hat not long before, on a spike on the railings, close to where he had found the body, that had first drawn his attention to it. He concluded that it belonged to the victim. He had seen the name of a tailor in Broad Street stamped in gold on the leather lining, but there was no indication of its private owner. As far as he could say there was no one else about in the Square when he left to fetch the Doctor. Of course he would not be able to see the far side of the Square. Many windows overlooked the spot where the body was found. About twenty minutes had elapsed between the time he had left the spot and the time at which he had returned with the Doctor. There had been heavy intermittent rain during the night and in the early morning, and no footprints could be observed.

Dr. Raymond was next called. The only fact to which he could testify was that he had ascertained, when he reached the body, that life was extinct. It was not feasible, at that time, to make any very thorough examination as it was still dark, and the only illumination obtainable was that from the constable's lamp.

Chief Constable Foster described his recognition of the dead man's body as that of Professor Toogood. The Professor had, some years before, served the office of Senior Proctor, and they had been officially related on several occasions, notably upon one fifth of November, when the City and University Police had been in co-operation in quelling the exuberance of a large number of festive undergraduates who had been celebrating the historic date. The body had, with the consent of the University authorities, been taken to the City Mortuary in Gloucester Green, which was convenient as the inquest was to be held in the Settling Room The Professor's pockets had been found to contain a note-case with two one-pound notes and one ten-shilling note in it, a private diary and a few old letters. There were also about ten shillings in silver in the left-hand trouser pocket, and a bunch of keys in that on the right-hand side. There was no sign of the pockets or the clothing having been rifled or disturbed in any way. The Professor was not known in the City as being by any means a wealthy man. There was congealed blood on the back of the left side of the head.

The last witness to be called was Dr. Haywood, the Police Surgeon.

"I examined the body of the deceased first of all between 1.30 and 2 a.m. on the 4th of December last, in the garden of Wellington Square. My examination there was superficial as the light was bad. I was able, however, to ascertain that the skull was fractured in two places. The hair on the left side of the back of the head was clotted with blood, which had issued from a small wound. I formed the opinion that death was due to very severe concussion and shock, due to a blow delivered on the back of the deceased's head by a heavy and blunt instrument. On a further and more detailed examination later I ascertained that there was a small hole in the left occipital bone at the base of the skull. The hole was neatly made in the bone and there was grey matter around its edges, which was undoubtedly due to the extrusion of part of the material of the cerebellum."

A few more technical descriptions concluded the evidence of the Police Surgeon.

"In your opinion," asked the Coroner, "death was due to severe shock or concussion of the brain, due to a heavy blow on the back of the left side of the head, and not to the hole which penetrated to the brain and which was probably made by some sharp instrument?"

"I think there can be no doubt of that," replied Doctor Haywood. "The drilling of the hole—and I should say it had been carefully and skilfully drilled—would in itself, in so vital a spot, have caused the Professor's death. But it would have taken an appreciable time to make. Moreover, the initial pain would undoubtedly have caused screams and cries which would probably have been heard by someone in the houses in the Square. Whereas if the Professor had been stunned by a heavy blow in the first instance, the person who made the hole would have had time to do his work undisturbed. The passive state of the victim would have allowed him to proceed unhindered and at his leisure. Either the blow on the head or the perforation of the occipital bone to such a depth would have sufficed, in itself, to cause death. I have given my reason for supposing which was in fact the actual cause. I should say that Mr. Toogood had been dead about two and a half hours when I first examined his body."

"You say that the hole was *drilled?* Are you, then," asked the Coroner, "of the opinion that some sort of surgical operation was in fact, performed?"

"I am of that opinion," rejoined Dr. Haywood.

The Coroner summed up to the jury. He dwelt upon the fiendish nature of the act which had removed from the City and from the University one of the most brilliant, and, he might add, the most benevolent of their residents. Hard as it was to conceive that there was anyone within the precints of that ancient City who should desire to compass the death of so harmless a man as the deceased Professor, the fact remained that there seemed no other explanation than that a most foul and brutal murder had been committed in the heart of Oxford. Its victim had been one of its most esteemed and most enlightened inhabitants. The jury must, he thought, without any question, bring in a verdict of "Wilful murder by some person or persons unknown." Hard as it was in this case to assign a motive, unless indeed the culprit were some unhappy madman, whose brain was so deranged that he had come to imagine that Professor Toogood had done him some wrong, there seemed no alternative. The jury would at once he thought, dismiss from their minds the idea that suicide could for one moment be entertained. And, besides, the medical evidence was entirely against it.

Without the formality of retiring for their deliberations, the jury, through their foreman, one of the best known dons in Oxford, returned a verdict in accordance with the Coroner's direction.

The bare little room began to empty. The widow, weeping silently, withdrew upon the arm of a grief-stricken friend.

One of the last to leave the Court was Police Constable Merrilees. He turned to take a last look round before he left. Old Joseph Lee, the caretaker, was just about to pick up his hat from the chair on which he had placed it, and was preparing to close and lock the doors. Touching Foster, the Chief Constable, on the back as he was about to quit the building, the policeman exclaimed excitedly:

"My God! sir! I've seen it!" He pointed in the direction of Lee's hand. "*That's* the hat I found in Wellington Square!"

CHAPTER VII

"Good-bye!"

THE mysterious death of Professor Toogood had left England—and Oxford—perplexed. During the few months which had elapsed between its occurrence and Reggie's final "coming-down" and departure for "The Coast", nothing had transpired to throw any further light on the cold-blooded murder of a man of unquestionably blameless life. It sometimes happens that even men and women of irreproachable character, people whose cupboards have no skeletons to hide, are done to death with robbery as the motive.

There was nothing to show that the man who had struck down the Professor of Latin in Wellington Square that dark November night had done so for greed of gain. Such valuables as the old man had had on his person remained undisturbed in his pockets. Yet it was hard, if not impossible, to suggest a reason for anyone desiring to murder a man so obviously without enemies as the late Professor.

Of course Toogood, like all men who rise to any eminence in the world of scholarship, had fought some fights. But the subjects in dispute had been novel theories on the Ablative Absolute, revolutionary uses of *cum,* with or without the Subjunctive, hotly argued reconstructions of corrupt passages in *Cicero's Letters.* Pretty heated contests they had been, too.

The battle-ground had been the columns of the *Classical Review* or the *Oxford Magazine.* It was scarcely to be supposed that Sir Martin Brasted, the eminent Cambridge scholar, who had been the dead man's doughtiest opponent in a long-fought out question as to whether *nunc* or *jam* were the correct word to interpose in a vexed passage of the *Annals* of Tacitus, would go so far as to assassinate the man who had so ably worsted him in the academic fight. And however attractive the idea might have been to some, Sir Martin had an unshakable alibi. He could have proved, had he been called upon to do so, that at the time of the tragedy by the Isis he was soundly asleep in his bed at his College on the Cam.

The efforts of the Oxford Police under Chief Constable Foster and the diligent inquiries of the Proctors had revealed not the vestige of a clue. Mr. Barnes, the University Lecturer in Criminal Law and Fellow of St. Antony's, was working on lines of his own. He was firmly convinced that the professional police were off on a wrong tack altogether.

"I have not," said he pompously one night of the Summer Term in the Senior Common Room, "studied the theory of Law, which, after all, is in a way, but the complement of the Theory of Crime, without being, I may say, able to see things which are unobserved by the eye of the so-called 'practical' policeman. He is a mere thief-*catcher*—an apprehender of wrong-doers more or less caught in the act. He does not see—one can hardly fairly expect him to see—the finer shades—the *chiarascuro* I might term it—of apparently insoluble mysteries of crime."

"Have you, then, Barnes, any theory of your own to account for this terrible murder?" Mr. Brightwood leaned forward, an eager look in his solemn, unwinking, grey eyes.

"I was about to continue," said the egregious Mr. Barnes, well away on his hobby and resenting the Senior Tutor's interruption, "with a few observations of my own which may have an important bearing on the case. One of the greatest incentives to crime, as human history sadly teaches us, is the desire rapidly to acquire wealth. In a word it is the wish to thieve, to appropriate unlawfully the property of others—to get rich quickly, and with the least possible effort," Mr. Barnes, who had had an eye on the port decanter which was circulating with less rapidity than he could have wished, managed to secure it in its passage. He poured out a generous glassful. Having drunk a good measure of the wine, he felt in better fettle and continued. "This motive, as we are aware, was not the one which prompted the horrible crime which robbed us, only a few short months ago, of one of the ripest Latin scholars of his age. We must seek another hypothesis. Latin is an insidious language. No one respects more than I the noblest gems of Roman literature bequeathed us from the finest classical periods. But unfortunately—ah—a sadly *amatory*—I might even say *erotic* strain pervades much that is, from the purely literary point of view, the finest work that the writers of the era produced. I need but mention the names of two of the poets— Ovid, and—er—Horace—for you to understand my meaning. The late Professor was—it is not necessary for me to remind you— steeped in the study and knowledge of the literature of every known epoch of the Latin era. And *now* you will doubtless see my line of thought. The desire to acquire property is only *one* of the *two* main incentives to crimes of violence. The other, and I may perhaps be permitted to say, the *greater,* is connected with— ah—the feeling or passion of *love.*"

"As a teacher—a humble teacher, I grant . . . of logic in the School of Literae Humaniores, I feel that I fail entirely, sir, to follow the trend of your argument." The Senior Tutor, ascetic and an abstainer, was not too favourably inclined towards the fat, prosy, and rather bibulous Mr. Barnes. He opined, and possibly with truth, that the wine of which the lawyer had partaken with a freedom which he himself deprecated, was confusing his powers of argument.

"I should have thought," said Mr. Barnes a little pettishly, "that my meaning would have been sufficiently clear. You will admit that the motive for this murder is obscure. I have made it clear what, to the legal mind, appear to be the two main incentives to crimes of violence. I have indicated the voluptuous nature of much of the literature of the Romans, of which the late Professor was so profound a student. I——"

"You mean—to put it shortly—that you think there was a *woman* in the case." The Warden was absent from the Common Room and Mr. Ferguson felt that it was unnecessary to mince matters. The trend of the Law Lecturer's train of thought began to dawn upon the pious Brightwood.

Reddening and utterly scandalised he blurted out, "You do not mean, sir, to insinuate that the late Professor Toogood met his death as the consequence of a mere, vulgar, illicit intrigue?"

Quite a hush fell upon the little gathering. Before the awkward silence could be broken, the door of the Common Room swung open and in stalked the formidable old Warden. It was rarely that his entry was as welcome to the little company as it was that night.

.   .   .   .   .

That same evening Reggie Crofts was passing the last few precious hours of his remaining day in England with Barbara Playford. The kindly Master of St. Thomas', her uncle, had asked the couple to dinner at his house. After the meal the old man had pleaded, whether truthfully or not, urgent work which would keep him occupied till midnight or even later. With a gleam made up partly of tenderness (for he loved his pretty niece), and partly of amusement in his eyes which looked out under shaggy, whitened brows, he had left his guests to their own devices.

It was a fine summer evening, and Reggie had suggested a walk before he saw the girl back, for the last time for more than a year, to the gates of Somerville. As they stepped out from the Provost's Lodgings into the "Broad" Reggie felt that he had never, till that evening, sensed to the full the fascination of Oxford. As the pair strolled down towards Holywell the setting sun threw into relief the massive outlines of the Old Clarendon Building. The finely balanced proportions of the Sheldonian Theatre assumed an almost ethereal aspect. Never had the quaint mutilated stone heads which had for so many decades gazed down stolidly upon the generations which had trodden the paths beneath them, looked more ghoulish, more mocking, than they did to Reggie Crofts on that, his last evening before leaving for West Africa.

They reached the corner of the "Broad" and Holywell before they spoke.

"I feel so miserable," the girl at last first broke the silence. "And I feel, Reggie dear" (she squeezed his arm), "that it's unfair of me as it may make you unhappy, too."

"Barbara! Barbara! I wish we could be married *now,* and that I could take you out with me. But of course I *can't.* I must see first what sort of a place it is myself. One hears so many different stories."

"Of course—I know that, Reggie. Don't think that I want to make you wretched. And why should you be?" She struggled bravely against her tears. "You're going out to a new life, and why shouldn't you be all right? And, after all, a year and a half is not so *very* long." She was biting her lips in a vain effort to keep back the tears that would, in spite of her, keep welling up into her eyes. Her lover heard the break in her voice—knew from her downcast head what he should see if he looked into her face.

They turned into Mansfield Road and up past Manchester College. There was no one in sight. Putting his arm around her, Reggie Crofts drew Barbara towards him and kissed her passionately, full upon the lips.

"Darling,"—he released her from his embrace. "You love me and I love you. You have promised me that you will marry me when I come back. And it won't seem very long. You have your work and I shall have mine, and I expect my leave will come round before we know where we are. I'll write—every mail. And think of all the things—new and interesting things—I'll have to tell you. And you—you'll write every week to me, won't you?"

"Of course I will, my dear. But oh—" her voice began to break again and falter—"you'll be so, *so* far from me. And it will be so strange, so hard to think of you out there in that beastly country amongst all those strange black people."

The young man tried to reply banteringly—leading the conversation back into more cheerful channels. "Well, you'll be able to follow the career of our friend Konti—(he's failed in French this time, by the way, as well as in all the things he bossed before)—and, of course, his *wives!* Then if you multiply it all about a million times and think of the hottest summer day you've ever known, with a Turkish bath thrown in, you'll get some sort of an idea of what I'm putting up with!"

The girl laughed in spite of herself. But her heart was heavy within her. An atmosphere of gloom had pervaded her uncle's home ever since the tragic death of Toogood, the amiable old Professor who had been the Master's greatest friend. And now that she and Reggie had plumbed the depths of their own love and felt its growth within them day by day, her lover was to be torn from her to go out for many months to a strange and ill-omened country of which she had heard little that was reassuring.

Their last walk together in England for many months to come was nearing its end. As they turned from South Parks Road to cross by Keble into Museum Road where the lamps were now lighted, something occurred to distract their thoughts.

Down the road were running two undergraduates, in flannel trousers and gaudy pull-overs. In hot pursuit followed two burly bowler-hatted figures—the Proctor's bull-dogs. Far behind, at the best pace he could manage, followed the flying figure of the Junior Proctor himself. His bands were all awry—his mortar-board in his hand. His gown flew out behind him like the wings of some not very alarming Angel of Terror. He mopped his perspiring brow as he ran, a fat little man with short legs which refused to carry him at the pace at which he wished to go. When the procession was safely past, the girl and her companion burst out laughing.

"Good old Billy Gould! About as much chance of *his* being in at the kill as of a coster's donkey winning the Derby!"

Though the incident had been amusing for the time being, it reminded Reggie very forcibly of the very definite break he was making from the old life and all that it had meant for him. For Reggie loved Oxford and its easy, care-free life with a love which was eclipsed only by that which he felt for the lovely young girl beside him.

Almost before they realised it they were before the gates of Somerville. No place, that, for tender long-drawn out partings.

A hasty kiss—the girl's face wet with the tears which *would* come—a few short protestations of love—of promises to write—the paraphernalia which have accompanied lovers' partings since the world began. Reggie was off again to his digs for the last time, to prepare for the long journey which awaited him on the morrow.

He had a note to leave at a house in Wellington Square. As he passed out into St. John Street the sounds of an altercation floated through the quiet air of the summer night through a first-floor window.

"You na foolish, foolish woman! You done spoil my 'chop'! I go flog you *good* fashion!" The civilised Mr. Konti was reverting to type. In the rage of the moment against one of his erring spouses his customary faultless English degenerated once more into the customary jargon of "the Coast."

There was a scream, followed by another scream in a different female voice. A blow was struck.

"Lord a *mussy*! Lord a *mussy*! My friend—you de *kill* me!"

There was a crash of breaking glass. Something hurtled out into the darkness. At Reggie's feet there lay the twisted remains of a ruined frying-pan. Mr. Konti might exchange the loin-cloth of his native "bush" for the plus-four suit and Fair Isle jumper. But the leopard cannot change his spots.

CHAPTER VIII

The Notice-Board

"CAN'T say *I* think much of the place. I spent a good many years there too. But give me Nigeria every time."

The old *Appam,* her sensational capture by the Germans in 1916 long since forgotten, was slipping steadily through a Bay of Biscay which was not living up to its evil reputation. Reggie Crofts, in grey flannels and a blazer, lay lazily out on deck in a steamer chair chatting to the pert little West African trader who was his cabin mate.

They were discussing the Colony for which Reggie was bound.

"But what's the difference? Aren't all these places very much the same?"

"Not on your life," said Charlie Williams—"not on your life. Why, in Edwardsville if you kick a African or knock his hat off in the street, you're run in before the 'beak'—and a white 'beak,' too—and get five of the best taken off you before you can say ' knife'!"

"And why should one *want* to kick a 'African' or knock his hat off if it comes to that? And if you do, why shouldn't you be punished for it?"

Charlie Williams, with a look of pity and disgust, bit the cherry from the stick in his third Martini. He summoned to his insignificant features the best substitute he could raise for a scorn and contempt which were meant to be withering.

"Ah, you're one of these first-timers—you don't *know.* When you've been on the Coast as long as I have perhaps you'll know better."

It may be that Mr. Williams' powers of argument were not as great as he assumed them to be. It may be that Reggie Crofts, who had only taken a second in Greats, was more obtuse than he thought he was. As far as he could gather from the little man's rather disjointed remarks, it was at least a breach of gentlemanly etiquette, if not something worse, for a "African" to wear European raiment, and for him to neglect to salute a member of the white races, whatever his position might be. As Reggie's knowledge of the African was so far restricted to his acquaintance with Septimus Konti, of his own College, he could not easily grasp the point of view of the half-educated and rather contemptible little trader who was holding forth with such confidence and assertion beside him. There had, it was true, been occasional lapses reported in the conduct of the last year's "fresher" at St. Antony's, but there were lots of allowances to be made. The word "gentleman" presents a good many difficulties in its proper application as an epithet. But the unorthodox Reggie felt that it would on the whole far better become the quiet, simple African chief's son than the egregious Mr. Charles Williams who was laying down the law so confidently to him that morning.

But it scarcely seemed worth while to waste further powder and shot on so insignificant an adversary. Conversation had, however, to be made until lunch time, and there were still ten minutes or so to go before the gong summoned them to the saloon. So Reggie, not wishing to snub his companion, who was well-meaning if not exactly welcome, tried another tack.

"You know that fellow Garston—the fellow who sits next to the Captain at his table?"

"Yes, the chap from the Colonial Office. One of the assistant secretaries I think they call them."

"That's the one," said Reggie. "I believe he's going out to make some sort of report or other on the conditions of living amongst Europeans in the different Colonies on the Coast. That's a jolly good thing I should think."

The little trader gave a wink of prodigious proportions. Whether this was due to the portentous nature of the remark he was about to make, or whether it had some connection with the distinctly large quantity of alcohol which he had absorbed in small doses between breakfast and lunch, Reggie did not hazard a guess. Probably, he thought, a combination of the two.

"Not a bit," said "Charlie" as he was known, *tout court*, to his acquaintances. "Only makes things a bit worse than they were before. I've seen a lot of the same game in my time, you believe *me*."

"But if he sees, as he's bound to see, some of the disadvantages that white men have to suffer in their bush huts and so on, surely it helps the people at home to see how to improve them?"

"Old son," said Mr. Williams, becoming familiarly parental under the influence of a mixed liquid diet, "you don't know the Coast and its ways, and that's a *fact*. That fellow *will* do a tour round the bush—*will* live in mud huts during a part of the rains; and all the Government fellers, before he comes, will say they've a chance of a lifetime. Let the rain pour in through a leaky roof on a fellow straight from the 'C.O.' Give 'im a taste of what they 'as themselves! But just as 'e's due to arrive, they think better of it. And the old Chief will be hauled in 'one-time' to put on an extra thick thatch of grass, the stores we fellers keep will be ransacked for champagne and 'patty der for gror' and all, and he'll go back and say that life on the b——old Coast is a perfect picnic, and a damned sight more comfortable than what it is at 'ome. Charlie Williams knows what 'e's talking about—believe *me*!"

The wink which brought down the curtain on this outburst was of such prodigious proportions that the eclipsed eye seemed in danger of never opening again.

Reggie was quite relieved when the gong at last sounded. For a little of the undiluted company of Mr. Charles Williams went a very long way. Conversation with him *had* a value of its own, for his point of view was by no means that of the stereotyped Government officers whom he had met before. And it served as a useful corrective of other opinions he had heard expressed on similar subjects.

The occupants of the other seats at Reggie's table were a very mixed lot. There were seven of them in all. At one end sat a majestic matron, Mrs. Attwood, the wife of the agent for one of the big European firms at one of the largest Coast ports. She was well past fifty, but was handsome and had worn well, despite the many trips she had done to Africa to join her husband, a little man who seemed always very meek in her presence. She was extremely jealous of any younger woman who chanced to cross her path in her attempts to attract the males, attached and unattached, around her. And the prettier her rival the more envenomed were the darts of slander she would hurl around her victim. It was reported that no less than three divorces, a dozen or so estrangements of wives from their husbands, and at least one suicide had been due to the work of her foul and poisonous tongue. To Reggie, so far—they were only three days out—she had only shown her more pleasing side. And she was clever and could be quite attractive when she so desired. She could be very charming and seemingly innocuous when she thought that it suited her game.

The table was headed at its other end by "Daddy" Dawson. No one knew his Christian name. He had spent many years in solitude in the bush in the Colony for which Reggie was bound. He had been a beachcomber in the old days—a type of the genuine "old Coaster" that is rapidly dying out. He was returning from one of his rare periods of "leave" as he called it. In his thirty odd years in West Africa he had only been home to England three times before. But as he grew older and felt more the need of the company of men of his own colour, he was beginning to curtail the length of his lonely sojourns in the bush. With his keen brown eyes, hooked nose, wrinkled face and greying short brown beard and floppy wideawake hat, he was spotted by Reggie as a "character" the moment he set foot aboard.

On his right sat Reggie's stable companion, Charlie Williams, and on his left, Reggie himself. The chair on Reggie's own left was at present unoccupied, and he learned that its tenant was a Mrs. Driver, wife of a lieutenant in some West African corps, going out to join her husband. She seemed to be one of those women who feel sick if they even see a steamer and had, despite the wonderful weather they were having, taken to her bunk on the day of sailing and kept to it ever since.

On Mrs. Attwood's left sat Jasper Crowsmith, the pompous Solicitor-General of one of the smaller Colonies. Mr. Crowsmith was, in reality, not more than forty-five. But he looked a good fifty, and the impressive and dignified manner in which he spoke of trivial matters made his hearers almost believe that they were listening to the propounding of views which really were momentous. He was in his best vein when he was expatiating upon the duties of his own high office. The drafting of a by-law to compel a motor-cycle to carry a rear lamp in the lanes of a village in the back-of-beyond in West Africa, assumed, in his grave and stately diction, the weight and importance of a new clause to Magna Charta. If self-advertisement be one of the high-roads to success, Mr. Jasper Crowsmith was not to be accounted one of the laggards by the way.

The great man's *vis-à-vis* was a short stoutish man of forty, neatly dressed almost to the extent of foppishness, a gold-rimmed monocle for ever in an eye for which it could serve no possible useful purpose. He was Eric Kurwen, a Secretariat official from somewhere down the Coast, and his main ambition, judging from his conversation's trend, was to figure as the dashing co-respondent in some *cause célèbre*. Rumour indeed had it, a rumour, started by the majestic Mrs. Attwood, that he would yet be the cause of Lieutenant Driver's donning a pair of horns.

The remaining member of the party, who occupied the place between Kurwen and "Charlie" Williams, was a Miss Daniel, an European nursing sister bound for Edwardsville. Not her best friend could have called her anything but plain. She was short, plump, dumpy, and a more than incipient moustache spread uninvitingly across her upper lip. But her dark brown eyes danced with fun, and her good-natured *bonhomie* had an attraction all their own. She could flirt with her right-hand neighbour in the most outrageous manner without their hearers ever having the slightest fear that the strictest canons of morality would ever be in danger of being broken: though some of the epithets which she was not loth to use would have graced, with more fitness, the smoking-room than the boudoir.

When Reggie went down to the saloon Mrs. Attwood was already in her place. If her ample proportions needed the maximum amount of nourishment permitted by the ship's menu, Mrs. Attwood was not the woman to neglect the matter. She really did look rather handsome Reggie thought as he approached the table. She always made the very most of her waning charms, and there could have been no more skilful *coiffeur* living than the man who had so cleverly changed her mousy, greying crop to a rich dark chestnut hue.

"Good morning, Mr. Crofts," said she. "Won anything in the sweep?"

Reggie had not even bothered to take tickets, and said so.

Such neglect to share one of the few excitements—legitimate excitements—which shipboard life permitted seemed unaccountable to Mrs. Attwood, who must herself have a hand in everything afoot, whether her presence were desired or not. They were still the only two who had yet reached the table.

"Seen anything of Mr. Kurwen this morning?" She spoke in a low tone and made an inclination towards the vacant chair on her left.

"No," said Reggie, "I've not seen him at all this morning." He did not care, for that matter, whether he ever saw him again. He disliked the professional philanderer's type. But he did not say so.

"I've heard," went on the mischief-making Mrs. Attwood, "that *she's* up this morning." Her eyes were deflected towards the chair on Reggie's left, which had not been occupied since the ship left Liverpool. She gave a salacious wink and lay back in her chair with the air of a little boy who had lighted the fuse of a cracker and eagerly awaits the expected explosion. But Reggie proved a damp squib. He did not go off. The lady was disgusted at having failed to produce the effect she had desired. She made a mental note that, before the voyage was over, she *would* succeed somehow in arousing the young man who was much too apathetic and reserved for her tastes.

Mr. Jasper Crowsmith now took his place on her right with as much dignity as the Lord Chancellor taking his seat on the Woolsack. He had absorbed not a few "Gin Coasters" in the smoking-room before going down, and was feeling in great form for argument and laying down the law. He was in the middle of a long and pompous criticism of a judgment of the Lord Chief Justice which had been recorded in the wireless news that morning, when Daddy Dawson and Miss Daniel joined the company. Mrs. Attwood ceased even to pretend to continue to listen to the learned legal argument on her right.

"Good-morning Daddy," said she to Dawson, for he had been down to breakfast before her. "Been having a cocktail with Cissie."

Miss Daniel was known to all Coasters by her Christian name. She did not resent the fact: it showed that she was popular—in with the crowd—and popularity to her was as the very breath of her nostrils.

"Daddy's a real sport," said Miss Daniel. "Bet me a Martini I wouldn't put down a 'Coaster' in one go—and lost!"

The lengthy peal of laughter with which Cissie followed up her remark indicated that the drink had not been without its effect. "Here's Charlie," she said, as Reggie's stable companion came in rather more unsteadily than the motion of the ship seemed to warrant. As he stepped into his place, Eric Kurwen, dapper and immaculate in white flannel trousers, came to the chair on Reggie's left, drew it back and paused. Down the steps into the saloon came a very striking figure. Kurwen was looking in that direction. Mrs. Attwood delivered herself of a colossal wink to Daddy Dawson and continued it to the rest of the occupants of the table. The woman who now took her place in the chair which Kurwen had prepared for her was extremely good-looking. She was taller than the average Englishwoman. Her bobbed hair was of an arresting golden hue and very soft and silky. Her dark blue eyes were liquid and expressive. Her nose was small, but beautifully shaped. Her ears, from which hung tiny platinum ear-rings, peeped out enticingly from under the tendrils of her hair. Her mouth was small but the lips looked voluptuous. Her short-sleeved blue silk dress showed a slender white neck and arms, the skin of which had the sheen of satin. Her figure was perfect.

"Good afternoon, Mrs. Driver. Glad to see you down at last. I hope you feel all right now?"

It was Mrs. Attwood—the self-appointed leader of the table—who voiced the general sentiment. Eric Kurwen had taken his own place.

"Quite, thank you," said the girl in a soft, musical, rather drawling voice. "I was dreadfully upset when I first came on board. I've never been on a long voyage before, and I think it was more nervousness than anything else."

Reggie was favourably impressed. This girl was certainly the most attractive person he had yet met aboard.

"It's the finest passage to the 'Coast' that *I've* ever done," said Cissie Daniel, "and I've done a good many."

"*And* I," put in Mrs. Attwood. "But then I'm *never* sick, however rough the weather."

The meal passed uneventfully enough, though Mrs. Attwood studied Kurwen and Mrs. Driver minutely Whenever they were looking another way, and conveyed her findings to any others of the assembled company whose eye she happened to catch by a series of contractions of one part of her face or another.

Reggie Crofts, who had not, up to now, been particularly interested in any of the people he had met in the *Appam,* felt, in spite of himself, an interest in his new table companion which he found it a little difficult to explain. He countered the feeling by drawing mental pictures of Barbara Playford and found himself thinking that if *she* were the most desirable girl in the world, then Mrs. Driver was quite a good runner-up. No thought of any disloyalty to his fiancée entered his head. But he *did* think that if Barbara Playford had not already come into his life, then Mrs. Driver would have had a very deep attraction for him.

Lunch was over. It was, he thought, the pleasantest meal they had had since they had sailed, marred only by the suggestive conduct of the vulgar Mrs. Attwood and the heavy pomposity of the small-minded Crowsmith.

He climbed the stairs to pass through the lounge out on deck, for he meant to take a turn round in the open air before having the customary afternoon siesta. He glanced idly at the notice-board. A supplementary page had been added during lunch to the wireless messages.

The latest cricket scores did not interest him. He was not in the least thrilled by the news that "Oils" were "active" and "Gramophones" had "hardened a shade."

But in the General News he saw the word "Oxford." He looked again and read the following paragraph:

"OXFORD, Friday. Sensation caused early this morning by discovery body of Boissard, lecturer in French to University, in Turl Street. Police suspect case of murder."

CHAPTER IX

The Reader in French

THERE were few more popular men in Oxford than M. Gaston Boissard, the Reader in French. M. Boissard was a bachelor and not much over fifty. He held an official fellowship at Norfolk College, and had occupied a set of rooms in the front quad of the little college in the Turl for more than twenty years, with a break for the period of the war. For M. Boissard had not sheltered himself behind his academic position in a foreign land when danger had threatened his native country. M. Boissard was a little man. His keen dark eyes, rather sallow face, and his quiet, nervous, rather excitable manner would have made him the typical Frenchman of Victorian farce had he adopted the legendary stovepipe hat, waxed black moustache and clipped Imperial of his stage prototype. As it was his chin was beardless. His moustache, if small, was brown, its tips were innocent of wax.

Despite his long association with Englishmen and England M. Boissard's accent was still markedly French, and there were certain idioms of his native tongue which he still translated, especially when roused, into the medium of a foreign language. The little man who still seemed nervous and apprehensive before a class of peaceful English undergraduates in the lecture-room had performed prodigies of valour as a *poilu* in the trenches before Verdun. It was almost amusing—had his earnestness not been so obviously genuine—to hear him, struggling fiercely with the intricacies of the English idiom, fight his battles over again.

"I take ze bomb—like this," he would say, grasping his well-worn *Petit Larousse*. "I swing it—so!" He suited his action to the word. "You see the Englishman bowl at cricket? Is it not so?" He went through a fair imitation of the bowler's action. "I let ze bomb go—so!" *Larousse* would hurtle through the air with no little force, and there had been times when the glass of some of the little Frenchman's pictures had suffered as the deadly missile crashed against the wall. "The heads of two—two, my friends, at one *coup*—of these *sales Boches* they go off! Two more enemies of *La Patrie* will trouble her no more!"

Exhausted by his efforts he would sink back into the well-worn armchair which almost swallowed up his small proportions. After a few moments he was his calm scholastic self again. The fortunate visitor would be offered a cup of coffee such as only a Frenchman can make, for the excellent Reader never permitted his scout to perform the quasi-sacred rite. M. Boissard was permanently installed in his adopted country. Only twice a year would he permit himself a few weeks' sojourn in his beloved Paris. A single man, he gave out that his visits were to his aged mother.

One of M. Boissard's associates was Barnes of St. Antony's, the Lecturer in Criminal Law. Mr. Barnes too was a bachelor. But he made up for his lack of practical experience of the ways of the fair sex by an intensive study of literature of all ages bearing upon the subject. He was prone to adopt the view that feminine influence was the basis of almost every questionable action in the world. The thing had got on his brain and had become almost an obsession. He would never travel alone in a railway carriage with a female passenger, unless the train had corridor compartments, and he was haunted by the idea, whenever he chanced to be alone anywhere, that some siren might be at hand seeking to destroy him. Those who knew the little man's failing were not as apprehensive for him on that score as he was himself. Short of stature, bald, red-faced, in the early sixties, with ill-fitting dental plates, prominent eyes and a negligent way of dressing, he had not, to the normal eye, much sex appeal. To turn to the more mercenary side of the business, men of Mr. Barnes' profession were not sufficiently well paid for their academic attainments to attract the attention of harpies who had an eye to a commercial deal.

Mr. Barnes, to a select circle of his private cronies, would expatiate upon the manner in which *he* supposed that M. Boissard passed his holidays in France. Being a traditional Englishman he would heave sighs of sadness at the passionate temperament of his Continental brethren which was always so apt to lead them into temptation and finally to achieve their destruction. He had hinted, not once but many times, that the proclivities which he imaginatively constructed in the French Reader would one day lead him to disaster.

The genial Boissard, however, pursued the tenor of his way without being aware of his friend's misgivings about him.

One fine evening in June the little Frenchman sallied forth to dine at St. Antony's high table. He had been invited by his friend Mr. Barnes. There was a full gathering of dons and members of the Senior Common Room, for it was a Sunday in Term. No lamps were lighted—there was no need of them. The mellow rays of the waning sun passed through the windows filled with rich-tinted stained glass bearing the arms of past distinguished members of the College. Reggie Crofts, of course, had gone. Brightwood, the Senior Tutor, had had a card from him, posted by the pilot after he had left the steamer when she had been safely guided down the Mersey and was well started on her way down the Irish Channel on her voyage to West Africa. He had promised to write from Edwardsville when he landed, giving his impressions of the voyage and of his introduction to "the Coast."

Konti was still there—now in his third term. But still no notification had appeared on the board at the Examination Schools to the effect that KONTI, SEPTIMUS E., E. COLLEGIO SANCTI ANTONII had satisfied the hard-hearted Moderators who, Cerberus-like, barred the way through the Pass Schools. And that royal father of his, in far away Batkanu, had threatened finally to cut off supplies and order his son home to Africa if he failed again in the next examination which was to be held at the end of the month. He had arranged, with the help of his private tutor in Norham Road, Mr. Day, to take English, French, Latin and Logic. Like many of his race, Konti had a very good memory, and could acquire a good deal of superficial knowledge parrot fashion. At the March examination he had managed, by dint of learning by heart *King Lear* and another Shakespearean play, together with Dryden's *Absalom and Achitophel,* Part One, and Part One of *The Pilgrim's Progress* to reach the necessary standard in English. He had mastered in the same way the notes in the editions he had used. He had added, to make up the rest of the subject, the committal to memory of the entire text of somebody's *English History for Children.* He had, in a similar manner, mastered the first and second *Philippics* of Cicero, together with the annotations and a rendering in a "crib." He had managed thus to get through in this subject also with more or less flying colours.

But his brain refused to absorb, in addition, and by the same method, a play of Molière, and another by Corneille, together with de Tocqueville's *L'Ancien Régime et la Révolution,* and the necessary notes and commentaries. So he had failed in this part. And Logic, too—even Elementary Logic, did not seem to lend itself to the mnemonic methods he adopted. A little natural freedom of thought and originality, qualities which the excellent African did not possess, seemed to be required in the mastery of such a subject. So in this paper also he had failed to reach the standard required by his hard taskmasters. And the inexorable rule in Pass Moderations is that he who fails in more than one subject out of the chosen four must fail in *all.* No number of princely titles could affect the stern, incorruptible examiners.

The heart of the worthy Mr. Diplock of Queen's, who set the Logic papers at the Hilary Examination, had failed to be softened by the gift of a sheep, with an inscribed label attached around its neck, which the despairing African had tied one morning to the railings of his house in Charlbury Road. All that had happened was that the eminent logician had been summoned by an officious policeman for causing an obstruction in that part of the city, and the irate don had reported the undergraduate of St. Antony's to the Proctors for playing upon him an unseemly practical joke. Truly these white men were a strange and incomprehensible race! Septimus had known a sheep less in size than that to be accepted in his own country as fair barter for a comely wife, surely a much weightier transaction than the mere effecting of a Pass in one subject in Moderations!

But Konti, dismayed by the prospect of returning to his home without the coveted degree, was getting desperate in his exertions to extend still further his plastic memory to cover the remaining subjects. He did not look unduly concerned to-night as he sat at the Freshmen's table in the College hall, making a substantial meal off cold meat, apple tart and bread and cheese.

The Warden himself presided at the high table. He was a man of indomitable energy and determination. But the appalling way in which, only six months before, the distinguished Professor of Latin had met his death at the hands of an unknown assassin seemed to have left its mark upon him. He never seemed quite to have recovered his former buoyant youthfulness and sanguine manner. In the many years that he had known the University— first as Scholar, then as Fellow, and finally as Head of one of its most famous Houses, no tragic event had ever cast a greater shadow of gloom over the quiet academic body than the cowardly blow which had brought about the death of Professor Toogood that fatal night in Wellington Square.

Mr. Barnes, the plump, busy little lecturer in Law seemed, on the other hand, to have gained renewed energy as the result of the tragedy. He was, this term, serving for the first time the office of Senior Proctor. It was not often given to men in his position to play the role of detective. He had always hankered after trying his hand in such a part. And at last the opportunity had come his way. What King Charles' head was to Mr. Dick the incident of the Professor's tragic end had become to Mr. Barnes. He was impatient of the methods of the trained professional detective and his stock-in-trade: the finger-print, the time-table, the measurements, the laborious piecing together of small but relevant facts. Crime, he thought, was best approached from the broader standpoint of the psychologist. Find the obscure motive, plumb the publicly unknown depths of the victim's inner mind, and the solution will appear. Mr. Barnes' handling of the Toogood case was not a very good testimonial to the practicability of the methods he advocated. His own psychology, rather than that of the deceased, had led him to the belief that feminine issues were involved. Knowing as he did, and as everyone in Oxford did, the purity and rigid morality, the practical ethics of the dead man, he was forced to some new conclusions on which to rear a theory which would fit the facts as he wished to see them. He had enlarged upon the view that frequent reading of erotic passages, which could not be escaped, in the works of the Latin authors he had studied so deeply, must, without the student's knowledge, have stamped their imprint on the victim's brain. Even assuming that there was anything in the theory at all, a more than doubtful point, there remained the fact that there was nothing at all to show that the influence which he supposed might have been exerted had had any effect whatever upon the Professor's actual life. *Cherchez la femme* might be a sound line to pursue in nine out of every ten of the crimes of violence reported in the columns of the daily press. But to minds saner and more balanced than that of Mr. Barnes the tragedy in Wellington Square was the tenth, and must be investigated from a different angle. The view of the Senior Tutor, Mr. Brightwood, was that the crime was the work of a maniac. This was the opinion of the majority of the people of Oxford and in fact of England, who had given any time or thought to the study of the outrage. It was thought, too, to be the belief of the police, though they had been very reticent in their statements on the matter, and gave out that unremitting enquiries were still proceeding.

Mr. Ferguson was understood to be incorporating the incident in a novel, which he hinted was to be in the nature of a satire on the psychological methods of the Lecturer in Law.

The life and soul of the high table party was M. Boissard. He, no more than Ovid's soldier with his wine-stained finger, could be restrained from fighting his battles anew.

"You would appear," said the solemn Mr. Brightwood, "to assume that it is only the actual combatant in the ranks, in the trenches, who is entitled to the soldier's meed of praise. Let me assure you, however, that it was only my age that forced me to handle munitions at Didcot. I am not sure, either, that ours was not the harder lot to bear. The excitement of battle, they tell me, is in itself a kind of anodyne. You do not have time to brood much over your troubles in the hurry and bustle of a front line trench. The thoughts of the unwilling stay-at-home packer of munitions may well be ten times more painful and galling than wounds, or the prospect of wounds and even death itself, in the heat of armed conflict."

"It is true! It is true!" cried M. Boissard. "But for me—no—whatever my age, whatever my health, it is the fight, the bayonet, the throwing of bombs that is the soldier's life. Look—I will show you how—at Verdun—at noble Verdun—I blew off the heads of——" The excitable Reader's hand was already clutched around his tumbler, which appeared in serious danger of emulating the usual experience of the well-worn *Petit Larousse.*

"I am sure," boomed the voice of the Warden, roused to speech at the prospect of imminent damage to the College property, "that we all quite understand M. Boissard, the heroic nature of your action on that great day. But I would point out that the College glass is of at least as great an intrinsic value as the graphic illustration of your prowess you were about to give us."

M. Boissard came to earth. In his martial ardour he had almost become guilty of a breach of peace-time propriety. The apologies, profusely rendered were graciously accepted, and Ferguson, in ironical banter of the fussy Mr. Barnes, led the conversation into still dangerous, but less highly explosive channels.

It was late that evening before the general company in the Common Room broke up. Midnight was not far off when the volatile Reader in French bade his adieux to the last survivor of the debate, who escorted the visitor to the lodge of St. Antony's as he set out for bed in the little college in the Turl.

.   .   .   .   .

Sergeant Bertrand of the Oxford City Police lifted the receiver of the Charge Room telephone.

"Yes? P.-C. Blake? Speaking from the cab rank in front of St. Martin's Church?—Where?—in the Turl?—Yes—No one else with you?—Wait till I come. I'll 'phone the Police Surgeon and be with you in a few minutes."

He called the constable on duty in the Charge Room.

"Blake reports he's found a dead body in the Turl. Says it looks like a case of murder. I've told him I'll be along at once. Ring Dr. Haywood and tell him he'll find me by the gate into St. Martin's churchyard—opposite the book shop by the Mitre."

.   .   .   .   .

"As I passed along here at twenty past twelve I saw a man lying over this iron bar." P.-C. Blake indicated the iron bar locked across before the gate of St. Martin's churchyard when it is closed. "I thought he was drunk. I touched him on the shoulder. He did not move. I examined him further and found that he was dead."

The limp body of a man—a short man in evening dress and a short black overcoat was lying, face downwards, across the iron bar. Sergeant Bertrand flashed a torch upwards on the dead man's features. He at once recognised them as those of M. Boissard, the Reader in French. A thin stream of blood ran down across the lower part of the left cheek and dripped sluggishly, in oozing drops, to the pavement below.

CHAPTER X

The Mystery of the Felt Hat

NEARLY six months had elapsed between the inquest on the body of Professor Toogood and the discovery of the body of M. Boissard by Police-Constable Blake in the Turl. Very little of any value to the police had transpired at the University Coroner's enquiry. The medical evidence was to the effect that death was due, as in the previous case, to severe shock and concussion of the brain, to the wielding of some heavy, blunt instrument. A scratch—a fairly deep one—and one which seemed to have been made by some sharp pointed instrument had been discovered at the left base of the skull. And it was from this scratch or cut that the blood had still been oozing when Sergeant Bertrand reached the body. But there was no actual penetration of the skull in this instance, and no sign that any drilling had been attempted. The nearest approach to an eye-witness had been an undergraduate named Carton, of Lincoln College, who had been hurrying down the Turl from the direction of "The Broad" after a bridge party in Beaumont Street, in a vain attempt to reach his College before midnight, which he had heard strike in Exeter College as he ran past. He remembered seeing, as he waited for the porter to open the gate, two figures in the shadow of the corner of St. Martin's churchyard. As far as he could make out they were those of two men. One man appeared to be hanging across the iron bar outside the gate. The other was bending over him. The porter had let him in very soon after he had kicked on the door in the traditional Oxford way of gaining admission to a college at night. He had really not given the incident much thought. It crossed his mind that a couple of fellows were coming back a bit tight from some dinner or other, and that the more sober one was trying to help the more drunken one along.

As far as he could remember the man standing up had an overcoat on. He could not say what was the colour. It was a warm night, but a fellow in evening dress would be quite likely to wear an overcoat even if it were. He had no idea of the age of either of the men. He could say nothing whatever with regard to the clothes of the man whom he had supposed to be helplessly drunk. He thought that the upright man had on a cloth cap. It was only an impression. It was quite possible that he had been bareheaded. No change had taken place in the attitudes of the two by the time he had gained admission to Lincoln.

The evidence of several of the St. Antony's dons, as well as that of the College porter, was to the effect that M. Boissard had been quite normal when he left after dinner on the night of his death. And the testimony of his own scout and the porter of his own College had shown that there was nothing unusual in his demeanour, when he left his rooms to keep the appointment. A careful search of the letters and papers in his room had re-vealed nothing of a threatening or sinister nature, and no one whose statement had been taken by the Police could give any information tending to show that there was anyone at all who had had a grudge against the popular Frenchman. The verdict returned by the jury had been similar to that in the earlier case of Professor Toogood—"Wilful murder by some person or persons unknown."

The death of the Professor of Latin had been the greatest crime sensation of the preceding year. Not only was the brutal murder of a distinguished Oxford *savant*—a man of absolutely irreproachable character and blameless life—a novelty in the history of crime. But the success with which the murderer had covered his tracks, had focussed on it the interest even of persons whose preoccupation with the advance of learning was not their most prominent feature. The absolute—or apparently absolute—lack of any adequate motive whatever was the most puzzling feature of the mystery. It was certainly not with the intention to rob that the crime had been committed. Nor did the most meticulous researches into the past life of the unfortunate Professor reveal the existence of a single soul who could reasonably have been supposed to be interested in his decease. No one but a lunatic would have given even a moment's consideration to the worthy Mr. Barnes's preposterous theory of a brain unhinged by the reading of erotic passages in the Latin poets, goading the man into some vulgar amorous intrigue and raising passions of jealously which had proved his undoing. There was not a vestige of material evidence to support the far-fetched hypothesis. Not since the far-off days of the Whitechapel murders and the exploits of "Jack the Ripper," had a crime aroused so profound a sensation in the British Isles. The European fame of Toogood's scholarship, had stimulated interest far beyond the confines of his native land. Ever since the actual event the columns of journals devoted to the discussion of crime in many countries, no less than those of periodicals which existed for the fostering of fine scholarship and high academic ideals, had been filled, and filled often, with articles dealing with the murder in its every aspect.

As a crime pure and simple it evoked the attention of detectives, professional and amateur, the world over. As a disaster in the history of classical scholarship and erudition it monopolised the attention of many of the most distinguished literary men the world had known. And the interest in the subject had by no means waned when the second, and equally inexplicable, tragedy once more robbed the University of Oxford of one of its most prominent educational figures.

Here again was the case of a brilliant and much-respected scholar struck down, in the heyday of his fame and popularity, by the hand of some mysterious, unknown assassin. An added feature of interest in the second tragedy was the fact that the murderer had actually been seen, either in the actual execution, or only just after the commission of his horrible deed. For that the man whom the undergraduate of Lincoln had seen bending over the inert body of the luckless M. Boissard, had been the murderer himself, no one had any doubt. The shortness of the lapse of time between Carton's impression and the discovery by Police-Constable Blake—the mysterious disappearance of the unknown man immediately before the policeman's appearance on the scene, left no doubt of that. And popular opinion, which in this case coincided with the theories of the professional police, identified the murderer of the Reader in French with the untraced individual who had struck down Professor Toogood, only six months before, in the garden in Wellington Square.

After the December tragedy, Chief Constable Foster had conducted a very careful enquiry on the very few lines which seemed open to him. One of his moves had been personally, or by means of a competent deputy, to try to take statements from all the householders in the Square, and also on both sides of St. John Street as far as its junction with Pusey Street. The receptions of the Chief Constable or his representative had been a little mixed. Both took the precaution of paying their calls in plain clothes.

The general demeanour of the occupiers was courteous. They were willing to do anything within their power to assist the forces of Law and Order, in their difficult task of bringing to justice the cold-blooded murderer of the kind-hearted Professor. But there were exceptions.

Mr. Bruford, for instance, a retired College servant who kept a University lodging-house was a tough proposition. He had once served as scout to an undergraduate who in later years attained legal fame as Solicitor-General. And Mr. Bruford liked to bask in his reflected glory. He played the *rôle* of a kind of unofficial magistrate, solicitor and barrister rolled into one, to such of his cronies as, in their troubles, cared to turn to him for legal advice. And in Mr. Bruford's eyes the shadow of the Law loomed always big behind the pettiest of life's little worries. Mr. Bruford was not to be put out of countenance by even the Chief Constable of the Oxford City Police.

Answering a ring at his bell one morning, Mr. Bruford, in his shirt-sleeves, recognised his visitor in the plain clothes which for the nonce replaced his smart uniform.

"Good morning, Mr. Bruford," said Foster.

"Good morning to *you*," said the ex-scout, eyeing the Police officer in a suspicious and half-defiant manner.

"I just wanted to ask you a few questions," said the Chief Constable politely, as he put his hand in his pocket to reach his note-book.

"I suppose you know," said Mr. Bruford firmly, and with the air of a man who will stand no nonsense from anyone, "that you 'as to *caution* me before I makes a statement?"

Mr. Bruford's ideas on the powers of the Police and kindred matters were a little hazy. But the reading of articles on this subject in his favourite Sunday journal, together with his own previous convictions on the question, made him feel strong in the line he was now taking.

"I was not aware, Mr. Bruford," said the Chief Constable, a little irritated, but unable to repress the glimmer of a smile, "that I had made any charge against you. And I don't think that a question or two in connection with the murder of Professor Toogood can possibly bring your liberty or your character into any jeopardy."

The proceedings were interrupted by a loud feminine shriek from the direction of the door of the first-floor front, whence Mrs. Bruford, a plump and florid lady of mature years, had been listening with open ears to the conversation going on below her. The chivalrous Foster made a step forward over the threshold, his intention being of the best. This was an outrage in the eyes of the legally-minded Mr. Bruford—an outrage not to be brooked. Indignantly he placed a restraining hand on his visitor's shoulder.

"Not so much, Mr. Foster, *please*. An English-man's 'ome is 'is castle—and don't you forget it—policeman or no policeman! And none of your Third Degree methods '*ere!*"

As Foster took a step back the door was banged loudly in his face by the outraged Briton, whose heavy footsteps were heard ascending the staircase as he went gallantly to the rescue of Beauty in distress.

The good-humoured Chief Constable laughed, turned on his heel, and descended the steps.

Inspector Teesdale had no better luck with Lady Browne, the impoverished relict of an ex-Colonial Civil Servant, who lived on the ground floor of a house in St. John Street, letting off the two top floors as flats to pay the rent. There was some pathos in the manner in which the dignified old lady austerely refused to answer the simplest and most innocuous enquiries of the polite Police officer.

"I have," said she, "attained the age of eighty without having had to suffer the indignity of being questioned by the Police. And," she continued, stamping her foot, the fire flashing from her brave old eyes, "at my age, an entirely innocent person, I refuse to begin. If your superior officer desires to communicate with me, he may do so by letter in the appropriate manner, and I shall send my reply, at my own time and in my own way. Good morning!"

As it was quite obvious from the statements made by such residents as were willing to make them, that no information would be forthcoming from the neighbours on the subject of suspicious movements in the Square on the night of the Professor's murder, neither the Chief Constable nor his officers were at great pains to press for stories from those who were unwilling to give them freely.

There were cases in which the willingness and volubility of the persons approached proved a source of embarrassment to the officers in the execution of their duty.

Mrs. Crabtree, who happened to be the landlady of the house in which lodged Miatta and Regina, the wives of Septimus Konti, was a case in point. She was a tall, stout woman, very clean and tidy in appearance, and of proportions large enough to dwarf the size of her small "hall." She was of the type that loves a gossip— good-natured gossip, be it understood. Mrs. Crabtree, whom facetious under-graduates were wont to dub "The Merry Widow," was none of your tight-lipped, soured, backbiting type of woman. She ushered the Chief Constable into her ground-floor front as she would have done any other distinguished visitor.

"I remember that night, Mr. Foster, as well as any night I ever remember in my life. *That* cold it was, even for December in Oxford. And *that's* saying a lot. I expect you're too young, begging your pardon, to call to mind the time when they roasted an ox on the river before the College barges? That would be—let me think now—in——"

Patient and good-humoured as the Police officer was, he had a long and busy day before him. He was obliged to curtail the garrulity of the talkative dame,

"I have two young black ladies staying with me. you know. I'm a Christian—as all who know me can tell you, Mr. Foster. Yes, and a strict one at that—none stricter." She heaved a sigh of conscious piety. "Well, these here young ladies are the wives, you must know, of a Mr. Konti who comes from St. Antony's College. And a nicer, quieter-spoken young man and two nicer young ladies you could not wish to meet, Mr. Foster. Though, mind you, I'm not saying they haven't had words at times."

A disquisition on the differing ethics of European and African on the question of the marriage laws was checked at birth by the long-suffering Foster.

"I remember that night," repeated Mrs. Crabtree, "as well as I remember any night in my life—and that has been a long one, I *do* assure you."

After nearly an hour—or what seemed to him to be nearly an hour—the Chief Constable elicited the fact that all the estimable woman really knew about the fatal night was *(a)* that the African undergraduate had dined that night with his wives instead of in College, on stewed meat and vegetables, rice and mashed potatoes, and had left alone at about 9 p.m., and *(b)* that, looking out of one of her front windows just before retiring to bed at 10 p.m., she had noticed that it was raining, and that there were occasional strong gusts of wind. Chief Constable Foster had never realised fully till that day the real significance of the operation known as "ploughing the sand." He felt, at the end of the day's work, that he sympathised very fully with the desert farmer!

The Police had not been slow to follow up the clue of the felt hat of the caretaker of the Settling Room in Gloucester Green. The tragedy had occurred on a Monday night. The inquest had taken place on the following Wednesday morning. When Merrilees, as he left the Settling Room, had recognised the hat claimed by Lee as the one he had seen on the night of the murder, Foster had asked the old man to show it to him. The poor old man, as honest and law-abiding a soul as had ever breathed, had hastily surrendered it, and Merrilees had inspected it at close quarters.

"Yes, sir. I'd be prepared to take my oath that this is the very hat that attracted my notice on the railings that night. Here's the tailor's name—the name I told the Coroner in court—and here's just a faint trace of the stain I mentioned. The colour and shape of the hat are the same."

"Of course," said the Chief Constable, "it's not much to go by. There'd be hundreds of the same colour and shape in Oxford alone. But there's more to it than that, I'm afraid," said he, turning to the old man who was shaking with nervousness, "that I'll have to ask you to lend me your hat. Where did you buy it? Had it long?"

"No, sir," said Lee, "I've not." His accents were cracked and quavering, and his timidity was pitiable.

"To tell the truth, sir" (there could be no doubt of Lee's veracity), "I bought it at a second-hand clothes shop—Smith's, in St. Ebbe's—only last night." Foster and Merrilees exchanged a glance. "My wife said to me—on Sunday evening t'were—' Joseph,' she says, 'if you don't get a new 'at soon I'll be ashamed to be seen in chapel with you.' Well—seemed to me my old 'at was good enough for me. But a woman don't see things—not in the matter of clothes she don't—the same way as a man. 'My dear,' says I, 'what you says goes as much this day as the day we was married. I'll have a look round to-morrow.' Well, next day—t'were Monday—I didn't get the chance. I'm not a rich man—I knew I couldn't afford a new 'at—not a *really* new 'at—of the kind my missis would like. And with Christmas presents to buy for all the kids and so on I hadn't too much to spend—not on myself, you see." The old man's narrative was becoming unnecessarily long and circumstantial. Foster was a kindly man, and did not want to hurt old Lee's feelings. Also, from the professional point of view, it was as well to let him ramble on so as to give him a chance of giving all the details he remembered, some of which might prove of importance later. But the time had come when some sort of abridgment was necessary.

"Yes," said the Chief Constable soothingly. "We all know that Christmas is a very expensive time and all that. But what I want to know is how you came to buy this particular hat, and who sold it to you?"

Lee then told him that he'd noticed it in a box outside the clothes shop in St. Ebbe's—a box marked "All one price, 1/6," that it had seemed to him a bargain at the price, and that, finding it fitted, he had bought it then and there. His wife had "had a go at it" only the night before with some petrol she'd borrowed from her employer's chauffeur—(Mrs. Lee worked five days a week as a charwoman). He had been served by Rosie Smith, the fifteen-year-old daughter of old Alf Smith who kept the shop.

Foster's next move—retaining the old man's hat—was to visit Alf Smith. The upshot of his encounter was the discovery that the hat in question had been brought to his shop on Tuesday afternoon by Joe Pearce, a dustman in the employ of the Corporation, who had sold it to him, together with one or two other trifles he had discovered on his morning round, for the sum of one shilling. Later in the day, Joe Pearce, a fine figure of a man, but trembling like an aspen leaf as he stood before Foster's desk in the Chief Constable's cosy little office, told the story of his find.

"We ought, by rights," said he, "to have cleared the St. John Street stuff Monday morning. But I weren't too well—not Monday morning. So me and my mate went the round Tuesday morning that week. We were a'clearing out the bins and the boxes in Pusey Lane, back of St. John Street, when I sees this 'ere old 'at—a'lying alongside the dustbin outside of 24 or 25 it would be. Both the bins were chock full, seein' as we were a day late. I thinks as 'ow the 'at came out of one of these two—t'weren't much to look at, anyway, all wet and dusty. So I takes it as my perks and sells it that very afternoon when I goes off duty, to Mr. Smith down there in St. Ebbe's."

So far the trail had not led to any very hopeful conclusions. A further enquiry of all the house-holders on the side of St. John Street elicited no claimant for the hat, and the scent seemed, at any rate for the time being, to have been lost. But Chief Constable Foster was not despondent—he was not that kind of man. He cheerfully dismissed the relieved dustman, and, whistling softly to himself, locked up the object in a roomy official safe. Foster was not the man to admit himself beaten so early in the chase. He was sure that, between the time that Merrilees left the Professor's body and the time when he had returned with Dr. Raymond, the hat had been deliberately removed and, again, as deliberately disposed of. What the remover's intentions were the Chief Constable would not permit himself to guess. But he felt, with the certainty of conviction, that once he could lay hands upon that person, the mystery of Professor Toogood's death would be more than half solved.

CHAPTER XI

Barbara's Aunt

"THIRTY love!" Barbara felt she *must* beat the young man. She didn't, however, quite see how she was going to do it. He had won four games already this set—two of them "love" games.

It was July—a hot July—and the girl had had her first letters from Reggie since he had sailed. She was staying for a week with her aunt, Lady Shortways, her father's sister, at her country home amid the Surrey hills. The day had been oppressively hot—but as the evening drew on tennis was a pleasant relaxation.

The tennis lawn was set in the midst of a lovely flower garden, the pride of Lady Shortways. She lavished upon it all the love and attention which she would have poured out upon the children who had been denied her. Sir William Shortways was a Judge of the King's Bench Division. He was delayed in town at present as Vacation Judge and had not been able to come down, except for the week-ends to his country home. Lady Shortways had invited her niece, of whom she was very fond, to keep her company in her grass widowhood. There were also certain schemes in her mind. Having no daughter of her own to marry off, she had caught at the idea of making a successful match for her pretty niece. Not that she had disliked Reggie Crofts—she had even taken rather a fancy to him. But lack of means—lack of any reasonable future prospects in a candidate for Barbara's hand amounted in her aunt's eyes almost to a vice. In fact some vices, in her opinion, were not of any very great account, provided of course that they were not too obtrusive and were palliated by both cash and social position. And absence of vice was, in Lady Shortways' eyes, tantamount to positive virtue.

It had been a great stroke, thought Barbara's aunt, to conceive the idea of inviting the girl to stay with her at a time when young Lord Ruislip was her only other guest. The heir of the wealthy Lord Petersfield—sufficiently lacking in vice to attain Lady Shortways' standard of positive virtue—he would be a much more satisfactory match for Barbara than the good-looking clever young man who had gone out to seek fortune or the other thing in the bush and swamp of the West African Coast. Lady Shortways had never taken kindly to the idea of her niece's engagement to Reggie Crofts, and her invitation to her to spend the week with her was, in reality, the opening manœuvre in what was going to be a stern and hard-fought campaign. Whether its duration were long or short Lady Shortways did not care, so long as it ended, as she fully intended that it should, in the marriage of Barbara Playford and young Lord Ruislip.

Her gardening labours of the day completed she sat in a basket chair on the lawn and watched the young couple at their game. Lord Ruislip, she reflected, might not be as clever as Reggie Crofts—quite obviously, to be sure, he wasn't. But the prospect of stepping eventually straight into an exceedingly properous business made up for a good deal. Lady Short ways could not bear the thought of her niece's risking, even for one trip, a visit to that horrid West coast of Africa. Why—she might die of one of those horrible fevers after a month or two. And, even if she didn't actually die then and there, she might impair her health for ever. And supposing that all these gloomy prognostications *didn't* materialise. What was the most that Reggie could ever expect to be? A Colonial Governor! She took the most optimistic view possible. Well, she had known not a few of these dignitaries. They were, for the most part, charming men, it was true. Clever—and on their own subjects—interesting! But then their outlook was rather a narrow one—was bound to be. They were only home for a few months every now and again, and then went back, out of the limelight, to their respective jobs, important entities in the Colonies they governed, but of less account in the general world than the newest elected M.P. or the lesser known stars of the stage and the film. Nor were they even well paid. And of course it was quite possible, highly probable in fact, that Reggie might never attain such dizzy heights of promotion as even these. She sighed to herself. His fate and her niece's, in such a case, did not bear contemplation. Lady Shortways determined to open the direct offensive at the earliest possible opportunity.

"I'm *frightfully* sorry"—the young man, wrapping a white flannel scarf about his neck, was escorting his late opponent to one of the seats beside his hostess for a breather after a pretty strenuous set in which he had proved the victor.

"And why *should* you be? What have you done to be sorry about? I'd have been *really* annoyed with you if you'd played down to me." The girl laughed at her companion's disturbed composure.

Barbara Playford looked delightful in anything. But she had never, thought her aunt as she approached her, looked more completely bewitching than she did after her vigorous set against Lord Ruislip. Her cheeks glowed with radiant health. Her pretty short brown curls, a little disordered in the movement of the game, had an attractiveness now which even the best efforts of a Bond Street coiffeur would scarce have succeeded in giving them. Her white silk jumper showed off her figure to better advantage than the most divine creation of a Paquin or a Worth. The girl could even wear plain white stockings to advantage, a quality which by no means every woman possesses. Her legs were very shapely, and even rivals of her own sex were compelled to admire the slimness of her trim ankles.

"I'm afraid I played up a bit harder than I really meant to. But then, you know, I *really* thought you were going to beat me when we started—really *did* you know."

Lord Ruislip was hardly a dashing figure. Of middle height, he was fairly broadly built. His arms were plainly muscular, and the grip which he gave you in a handshake told you that he was no physical weakling. His face was amiable enough, and his eyes were of an attractive shade of blue. His hair was fair and wavy and he had a pleasant frank face. His worst feature was a receding chin, which, together with his rather colourless mode of speech, gave him the air of being a little less intelligent than, in point of fact, he was.

"You needn't have thought so," laughed the girl. "Why you've given me more exercise in one afternoon than I've had in the whole fortnight since term ended."

"Really?" said the young man, with a smile which looked rather foolish.

"Yes, I *do* mean it. You saw the game didn't you, Aunt Kate?"

"I only saw the last few minutes," said Lady Shortways. "I've only just finished the round of the garden."

"I say—but—you know! I'm most *frightfully* sorry if I've tired you out."

"Are you really and truly?" asked Barbara with mock seriousness.

"Yes, *awfully,*" replied Lord Ruislip.

A large part of his conversation was made up of adverbs and adjectives expressive of the varying degrees of fear and terror. But as they were all uttered in the same tone of voice and with similar expression—or the lack of it—they did not give as much light and shade to his talk as one might have expected.

"Well," said Barbara, "I'll forgive you. It'll put me in better training for to-morrow. You'd like to play again?"

"*Fearfully,* Miss Playford," said the young man.

"I suppose you're very keen on tennis?" ventured Barbara.

"Rather! Most *terrifically,*" said Lord Ruislip, with as much animation as he ever put into his speech.

The evening was getting rather chilly, as evenings can in England, even in mid July.

"Well, my friends," said Lady Shortways, rising from her chair and drawing a scarf around her shoulders, "I think it's time we went in and got ready for dinner. I suppose you're pretty hungry, both of you?"

"*I* am," said Barbara.

"Oh rather. So'm I—*appallingly,*" said Lord Ruislip, sounding a fresh chord in the gamut of terror.

.   .   .   .   .

Amongst the letters which had arrived by the evening post was one in the handwriting of Reggie, and bearing a West African stamp. Barbara felt quite excited, but decided to go to bed early and not read it until after dinner. As her thoughts were far away at the meal, the monosyllabic conversation of Lord Ruislip interested her rather less than usual. She replied more or less mechanically to her aunt's questions, hardly addressing her unless she were spoken to first. The young man on the opposite side of the table might almost have been in another world. It was not that she wished to snub him. That was the last form of rudeness of which she would have cared to be accused under her aunt's roof. But her thoughts were so taken up with mental pictures of Reggie, working and waiting for her three thousand odd miles away in some fœtid tropical swamp that Lord Ruislip's neutral personality found less response in her even than usual. Her aunt, who was quite clever enough to divine the cause of her niece's preoccupation, only addressed to her a few remarks, and those more as a sort of sop to social convention than as a serious attempt to engage her in conversation. She kept up a flow of talk with Lord Ruislip. This was an easy enough task for any one with a fair amount of volubility, though not particularly so for a hesitating talker. For the young man's method when the dictates of polite society made some sort of an answer imperative, was to let off a few of his timorous adverbs and recommence the cycle when the supply began to run short. Barbara was quite relieved when the meal was over at last, and, pleading a fatigue which was at least partly genuine, went up to bed.

.   .   .   .   .

Reggie's first letter had been comparatively short. It was written in bits from day to day as the *Appam* ploughed on towards

Africa, and posted at the first port at which he had called, the Gambia. An account of the general characteristics of his fellow passengers had been intended to serve as a preface to a fuller and more detailed review as the voyage progressed. But the news received by wireless, only three days after the ship had sailed, of the second murder in Oxford within six months of a prominent member of the University had rather eclipsed the more trivial side of the letter. Disturbing news from home is never made less disquieting when the recipient is many hundreds of miles away. Ashore one realises that, with competition as keen as it has become in the newsmongering world, the startling headlines in scare type and lurid descriptions which daily flood the breakfast table may be considerably diluted in the cold light of commonsense. A piece of news, baldly conveyed in a few startling words on a radiogram at sea, acquires a prominence which it would hardly achieve amidst the mass of other news which crowds the columns of the daily papers on land. But, taken in conjunction with the sensational murder of Professor Toogood at the end of Reggie's last October term, the crime which had laid low the genial Reader in French acquired in the young man's mind a sinister significance. There seemed little doubt to all who read the news that some criminal lunatic, possessed of diabolical cunning, was abroad at his nefarious work in the ancient city. And Reggie, who did not know that Barbara was not still staying with her uncle in Oxford, was tortured with fears which might have seemed to others a little unreasoning. But it was not her lover's fears and theories concerning M. Boissard's murder that, to the girl, was the most disturbing feature of his letters. She knew, well enough, that the risk to herself was negligible—not worth contemplating seriously. Though, indeed, she had had qualms for the safety of her uncle, the Head of one of the University's oldest foundations. It did not seem a mere coincidence that the mysterious murderer, obscure as his motives might be, had singled out, with no kind of method or purpose, two men whose only claims to public notice had hitherto been their academic distinctions. But the fear which was later in Oxford to develop almost to the proportions of a universal panic had not yet laid its grip upon the city. The greater part of its academic population had already left it for the Continent or other parts of their own country for the Long Vacation, and two unsolved murder mysteries were not sufficient to inspire any real dread in a community of sixty thousand souls.

Barbara's real fears were connected with other parts of the letters. Amongst the passengers whom he had singled out for notice was a Mrs. Driver—the wife of a West Coast military man, going out to join her husband. She sat at Reggie's table—occupied, in fact, a place next to his own. The others at the table were described also, it was true. But whereas the accounts of the behaviour and attributes of Mrs. Attwood, Jasper Crowsmith, Cissie Daniel, Daddy Dawson and the other two men grew longer and more frequent, the notices of the military grass widow decreased in number and in length. Yet it was clear enough, from his first allusions to Mrs. Driver, that Reggie had been not a little impressed with her good looks. And he *must,* from the fact that he sat actually next to her at table, have conversed as much with her as with his other table companions. Yet references to these conversations hardly ever occurred. And when they did they were extremely scanty and sketchy.

"*She didn't come down till to-day. But, by Jove—she's a jolly good-looking girl. Knocks spots off the rest of the ship's beauty chorus!"* And then, "*This fellow Kurwen's a regular lounge lizard, quite one of the worst. A nasty piece of work through and through. Never seems happy unless he's pawing some female or other about. And the way he goes on with Mrs. Driver is pretty sickening. Wonder she can't see it and tick him off good and hearty! But I suppose some kind of women don't mind that sort of man! Personally I should say that any fellow who pushed him over the ship's rail on a dark night would be doing the rest of the world a service!"*

Pretty strong language that for the usually impassive Reggie. Looked almost as if he were himself jealous of Kurwen's success with this Mrs. Driver. And why should he be unless he felt some attraction in that direction himself? Then—towards the end of the voyage, no reference to the woman was made at all. And the second letter, which Barbara had received to-night, maintained what she began to believe must be a real conspiracy of silence. Womanlike she was not slow to detect the fact that Reggie's omission to say very much about this other woman was due to his feeling a little more drawn towards her than he cared to admit.

Barbara was by no means an abnormally jealous girl. But she was human. She had not been engaged to Reggie for so very long: and now he was going to be away from her for, oh, such an age. And men *did* change their minds so. Barbara had never been for a long voyage herself. But she had heard much gossip about such trips from friends of hers. And all kinds of little romances, begun on shipboard, had ended in broken engagements, or, in other circumstances, in the Divorce Court. And India and Africa and all those sort of places had none too good a reputation in the realm of married or affianced fidelity.

The more she read his letters the more she became convinced that Reggie was on better terms with this hateful Mrs. Driver than he cared to own. Of course, as she told herself, she was more upset over the Oxford murders and their possible sequels than she had at first realised. But that alone was not sufficient to account for her disquieting suspicions. She would have to write and have it out with Reggie. But then, now that he had actually reached "The Coast," from five to six weeks at least must elapse between the writing of a letter and the receipt of an answer. And all those weeks between would be filled with ever-growing suspicions and misgivings.

She pulled herself together and went to sleep. But it was much later than usual when slumber overtook her, and the dreams which followed one after another that night were as vivid and sharp as they were disturbing.

.   .   .   .   .

The morning brought saner thoughts to the girl's mind. She told herself she was worrying over nothing. Over trifles, anyway. She was a jealous little fool, and this last murder in Oxford and the fears which it had engendered were getting on her nerves. It was just as foolish for her to suppose that her lover was forgetting her in another woman's society as to imagine that any real danger could be threatening her uncle. At breakfast in the big sunny morning-room, with its long French windows opening on to the smooth green lawn, she forgot most of her worries of the night before. Lady Shortways had been out in her beloved garden before breakfast. There she was, bending down at a flowerbed by the old sundial, digging away with a fork at the parched earth round the roots of a variegated herbaceous border, a basket of blooms cut freshly for the table reposing on a quaintly carved stone bird-table by her side.

"Good morning, Barbara," called her aunt, cheerfully. "Don't wait for me. You can begin at once. You'll be hungry I expect—or ought to be I'll be in myself in a minute or two. But I must give these poor darling roses a little water before the sun gets too hot. The earth's as dry as a bone."

Truth to tell, Barbara was not feeling the least bit hungry. But as the door opened and her fellow guest came in, she had to take her place at the table and put him at his ease.

"Good morning, Miss Playford," said the youth, whose features had at least the saving graces of amiability and good humour. "I'm most *frightfully* hungry!" The emotion of fear was getting into action early this morning!

"Glad to hear it. It's all that tennis you had yesterday I suppose?"

The girl helped herself to a sparse plateful of some light cereal from the sideboard and took her place again at the table.

"I suppose you're very fond of tennis?"

"Yes—awfully," replied Lord Ruislip cheerfully.

"It does seem to tire one a lot if one hasn't played for some time," went on Barbara.

"Yes—fearfully," was the economical reply.

Barbara was a very attractive girl—and she knew it. She was not greatly drawn towards this young man. But she could not help being just a little piqued by his rather offhand manner with her. It was not that he was actually rude: far from it. No one could have found the slightest fault with Lord Ruislip's irreproachable manners. But there were lots of young men she knew who would not even have attempted to disguise the pleasure which they took in her undivided society. And this young man either felt no particular thrill at his good fortune, or else was concealing it with great success. The girl determined to discover which was the true explanation. If Reggie was consoling himself in the society of a member of the other sex, there was no reason why she should not follow his example.

Lord Ruislip would have felt a little more concern than he showed at Lady Shortways' breakfast table that morning if he could have known that he was going to be used as a sharpener for Cupid's darts.

CHAPTER XII

A Steamer Siren

THE effect of the wireless notice on the *Appam's* news-board was very different on the several persons who sat at Reggie's table. Reggie himself was profoundly moved. He had known the mercurial little Frenchman well. He had met him more than once at social gatherings in North Oxford. He had had the pleasure, on more than one occasion, of tasting his impeccable coffee in his rooms in College. And to be invited to such a sanctum for the hallowed rite was to ensure one's getting to know one's host at his best.

And the spell of Boissard's fascination had not failed in its effect on the young Englishman. The war was long since over, and it was hard to conceive an enemy of the little don of such malevolent disposition as to wish to murder him. And to murder him in cold blood in a public street of the old University town. Reggie had never heard of old hostilities of the war revived and carried into private life in so violent a manner. M. Boissard was not the only Frenchman (Reggie knew of his little weakness and of the use to which he frequently put his *Petit Larousse),* who fought over again in his imagination his battles with the common foe. And even the phlegmatic English had been known to indulge in similar practices.

Reggie felt that the murder, whoever had committed it, had not found its motive in the more or less forgotten rancours of a war that was passed and finished these many years. And he felt, too, that there must be some connection between the tragic death of Professor Toogood in Wellington Square and the end of the Reader in French in the Turl. Though what that connection could possibly be he was at a loss to conceive.

Both men had been prominent in the University world in their varying spheres. Were the crimes the work of some diabolically ingenious maniac whose deranged and distorted mind had concocted some imaginary grievance against the collective body of the University's teaching staff? It was indeed difficult to suggest any other hypothesis which would go any way towards fitting the facts. And yet it seemed so grossly far-fetched and fantastic that a well-ordered mind felt considerable difficulty in entertaining it.

Charlie Williams, one evening, in the smoking room, his mental processes artificially quickened by a course of double whiskies, found less difficulty than Reggie in evolving a solution.

"I can't see anything so very mysterious about this murder, Crofts." He became familiar under the soothing influence of the spirit. "Except, of course, as far as they don't know exactly 'oo did it. Come to think—this feller 'oo was done in must 'ave been one of the big noises in this motor business."

Mr. Williams was fully convinced that Oxford's importance in the world was as a centre for the production of motor-cars. He *had* heard of the University of course. But he visualised it—if he ever bothered his head about the subject at all—as a sort of State elementary school—rather larger in size than usual—occupying a definite site in a definite building lost somewhere in the maze of car factories which surrounded it.

"You bet these motor people have got 'old of some new idea. They're a working it out." He shook the end of his pipe impressively at Reggie. "And this Frenchman—these 'parleyvoos' are pretty smart engineers, for all their fal-lals and funny language— was probably working it out for them. And this comes to the ears of some big Yankee or German car firm. There's plenty of these 'ere foreign machines been driven off the roads at 'ome along of these new cars from Oxford. Well," continued Williams, placing a restraining hand on the arm of the steward who was diluting his whisky with rather more soda than he liked, "these here Americans—or Germans if you like, for argument's sake—gets to hear of this new stunt. if it goes through—bang!—wallop!—" he struck his right fist noisily into the palm of his left hand, "*more of their cars go off the roads in England.* So they puts their 'eads together and decides to do in this 'ere interfering feller!"

It was not worth quarrelling with the half-tipsy little trader, so Reggie made some excuse and tactfully withdrew before any further imbecilities from "Charlie" prompted him to make a cutting comment. This, in Mr. Williams' present condition, might have caused a scene.

Mrs. Attwood dismissed the matter of the murder in a few ill-chosen words.

"The more of these bloody kill-joys get wiped out the better for the country! We want a few more hundred per cent *he*-men instead of a lot of old women in trousers!"

Mrs. Attwood's acquaintance with University circles was not considerable. The mention of Oxford dons conjured up in her far from Puritanical mind visions of the Revd. Mr. Stiggins and his kind.

Mr. Kurwen's theory would have rejoiced the heart of the worthy Mr. Barnes.

"Ah—you know these Frenchmen! *What* lads! Even if they have got as far as being Oxford dons!"

Mr. Kurwen's mind always ran along certain well-defined lines in dealing with the startling events of life, and the mention of murder in connection with a man who claimed Paris as his native city admitted of only one possible explanation.

Mr. Jasper Crowsmith, in whose manner the judicial and pontifical were almost inseparably blended was led into a disquisition on legal theories of right and wrong, and an exhaustive recital of the facts of unsolved murder mysteries from the time of "Jack the Ripper" to the present day. Anything was grist to the pompous lawyer's mill, and the central point of the murder of M. Boissard was completely obscured in the swirl of verbiage, most of it quite off the point, which surged around it in the Solicitor General's impressive tones. Anything which gave him the chance of listening for a prolonged period to the sound of his own voice was as balm to Mr. Crowsmith's soul. And it was easy to work a mass of ill-digested legal verbosity into the discussion of a case of murder. It was indeed sad that his table campanions did not appreciate to the full their good fortune at forming his audience.

It was Cissie Daniel, who was nothing if not direct in speech, who cut him short at the dinner table, in the middle of one of his finest flights of windy eloquence.

"I've a good idea," said she stridently, "that if there were less lawyers in the world there'd be less murders too—and that's a fact! If some guy would get busy in the slaughtering line, with one or two of the *law* professors instead of going for harmless old mutts who spend their lives bringing dead languages to life and making wretched kids plough through fusty old French plays, there'd be something to be glad about instead of sorry!"

The wind was taken completely out of Mr. Crowsmith's sails by this energetic broadside, the conclusion of which was marked by a devastating wink at old Daddy Dawson who was looking on admiringly from his end of the table. Daddy Dawson's opinion of lawyer's coincided with Miss Daniel's. He had seen something of litigation in "Coast" courts in his lifetime, and always swore that the next time anyone saw him go to law, however strong his case might appear to be, he'd there and then eat his hat. And as Daddy Dawson's hat was a pretty tough proposition, the asseveration was taken as being a decidedly strong one.

Reggie Crofts did not feel like taking any part in the conversation which had wandered far away from the real crux of the matter. To him, as perhaps to no other of the two hundred souls aboard the ship, the Oxford murders were a real and vital matter of interest. How was it all affecting Barbara? And might not the fate which had overtaken Professor Toogood and the Reader in French eventually encompass the Master of St. Thomas's, her uncle? The Professor had been his *fiancée*'s friend: M. Boissard had been his own. Their horrible fate was to him no mere impersonal problem in crime. It was a very real and very terrifying fact.

And who was to say airily that the Master himself was not in danger?

There was one person, and one person only at the table who seemed to grasp and to sympathise with the young man's point of view. And that person was Mrs. Driver. She really looked most fetching on this particular evening at dinner. There was to be a concert afterwards in aid of the Seamen's Orphanage. And the ladies on board had all done justice to the great occasion by putting on their best frocks. Mrs. Driver looked very well in hers. So much so that she had quite clearly aroused the displeasure of the vindictive Mrs. Attwood, whose opulent charms, lavishly displayed by a dress which did not err in being any too high in the neck, looked decidedly vulgar and ostentatious. She was clearly feeling more than usually catty, for it became increasingly plain as the meal proceeded that the flirtatious Mr. Kurwen was taking more notice than ever of the prettier and younger woman and becoming a less and less efficient chorus to his companion's always spiteful, and usually vulgar, remarks.

"Mr. Driver would be pleased if he could see you to-night," said she to the grass widow. The words in themselves were harmless enough. But the tone and the manner in which the jealous harridan made them conveyed all kinds of acid innuendoes.

"So'd a good many *other* people's husbands I should think!"

This from Cissie Daniel—not in any unkind spirit, nor with any suggestive undercurrent of unspoken meaning. The last fault of which anyone who knew her could accuse the coarse but kindly little woman was spitefulness or ill-nature. In honour of the evening's festivities she too had arrayed herself to kill. A lack of artistic sense had caused her to overlook the fact that a bright pink dress is not the best setting for a sallow complexion, and that scarlet and magenta as the respective colours of stockings and shoes are scarcely a happy harmony. But the hirsute burgeoning of her upper lip was mercifully, if temporarily, eclipsed by a lavish spread of powder, and her eyes danced with jolly good humour.

"Thank you for those kind words!" said Mrs. Driver across the table. She caught old Daddy Dawson's eye. The old trader threw her a gallant kiss which she returned with alacrity.

The evening was hot and the broad blades of the electric fan were revolving swiftly above the table. Charlie Williams, who was to make his appearance at the concert as a comic vocalist, and who had been fortifying himself for the ordeal with a few well mixed stimulants, threw up a roll of variegated paper ribbons. It caught in the vanes of the fan and the bright streamers whirled rapidly around the diners' heads. Before they realised quite what had happened, Reggie and Mrs. Driver were entangled in a swirling mass of red, blue, yellow and green ribbons. As the fan revolved the knotted rope of tinted paper drew their heads closely together.

"Steady on, Crofts!" cried Kurwen. "No kissing in the snow-storm!"

"What price the Babes in the Wood?" gurgled Charlie Williams as the steward hastened to stop the fan, and Reggie and the girl strove to disentangle themselves from the paper toils about them. Amidst a fusillade of jocose remarks from all but Mrs. Attwood, whose shafts of coarse wit were so tinged with jealous spite as to lose any of the humour she may have intended them to possess, the couple at last disengaged themselves. The party settled down again to their food and conversation, which flowed into normal channels.

But Reggie felt, unwillingly, that his heart was beating a little faster at his forced encounter at close quarters with his fair table companion. He had divined, as their faces came closer and closer together in the whirl of the paper streamers, a dangerous and provocative look in Mrs. Driver's eyes. It was clear that the young woman had not entirely regretted the circumstance which had brought her own, whether she would or no, into such dangerous proximity with Reggie Crofts' lips. And Reggie himself had a hazy idea that in the confusion of the moment their lips *had* met. And he was not altogether sure that the incident had, on one side, been entirely the result of an accident.

The concert was in full swing and the comfortable lounge was crowded. On the low dais which formed the stage sat an assertive

looking young woman in tortoiseshell spectacles who had volun-
teered her services as accompanist. She was pounding, with a
vigour which made up for her lack of feeling and expression, the
music of "The Bandolero." The vocalist, who termed himself a
tenor, but whom Mrs. Attwood had summed up in terms more
graphic than polite, had only a foggy impression of the words. It
was, however, slightly less imperfect than his notion of the music.
His high notes were always a shade flat—his low notes invariably
a *little* sharp, and it was not at all easy to imagine him, in real life,
performing the splendid deeds of which he sang. He was short,
plump, a little bald, and wore a sandy moustache. The more he
gesticulated and stamped, the less he remembered the words.
But a crowd of ocean passengers, after a festive dinner, does
not make too critical an audience, and the little man, whose sin-
cerity was as manifest as his lack of art and talent, received a
rousing encore. He responded by bursting, less in tune than ever
after his previous efforts, into the martial strains of "The
Trumpeter."

Reggie Crofts, a little disturbed by the incident which had
occurred at the dining-table, had sought the obscurity of the corner
of a small settee in the lounge. At the conclusion of "The
Trumpeter's" thrilling story, he saw the head of Mrs. Driver appear
above the balusters of the stairway leading from below. She
glanced about her as if she were at the same time looking for
and seeking to avoid some one. Her eyes caught Reggie's, and
she at once made for his corner.

"I'm afraid I *can't* get up the right sort of spirit to enjoy a show
like this," said she in her languid, measured tones. She settled
herself comfortably on the settee in the corner opposite to
Reggie's with her back to the platform. She made a pretence of
rummaging in the little silk bag she carried. The young man could
not help admiring the small white slender fingers on which were a
few simple but exquisitely tasteful rings.

"What a bore!" She made a petulant little *moue* of annoyance.

"What is it?" asked Reggie, thinking she looked as alluring as
any girl he had ever met. "Can *I* help?"

"You could be an absolute *angel*," she said, smiling again, turning a little to show her profile and then looking again straight into his eyes. "I've left my cigarettes in my cabin and it's getting much too hot to go racing around the ship unnecessarily."

Reggie thought it was not only the weather which was getting warmer. And he felt a sensation steal over him which was not the least bit unpleasant. His fingers trembled a little—he could not have said exactly why—as he lighted the cigarette which she accepted. Her lips were of a delicious red. He thought he had never seen a softer, more peach-like bloom on any woman's cheek. And as his mind ran on in this way his thoughts went back to Barbara, and he flushed slightly.

Mrs. Driver was not slow to notice the change in the young man's colour. But the reason she gave herself was not exactly the true one. She could see that she had begun to make an impression. She was beginning to take a real interest in Reggie. He was so much more attractive than the professional steamer flirt, Kurwen, whom she could see, across the lounge, in the toils of the blatant Mrs. Attwood. They seemed to be discussing herself and Reggie, and she was determined that there should be a substratum of truth for the story they were undoubtedly spinning about her and her present cavalier.

"I should think you'd enjoy your trip to "the Coast"? It'll be all so new and so unconventional."

"Oh, I don't know," said the girl in a bored voice, drooping her long lashes over her large blue eyes. "I never wanted to go at all, you know. Only Tom said he was beginning to feel so lonely and all that. I don't suppose he really is, you know. He likes shooting, and an open-air life. I expect he'll find me a bit of a nuisance when I really *do* get out there."

"He'll be a strange chap if he *does*—that's all I can say!" Reggie was unable to keep a slightly indignant strain out of his voice.

"Tom's dreadfully conventional, you know. Lots of Army officers *do* get like that—once they're safely married!"

Her expressive eyes gave a world of meaning to Mrs. Driver's unspoken suggestions. She succeeded, as the conversation trickled desultorily on between the alternating humour of Mr. Williams on the dais and the saccharine tragedy of the amateur female serio-comic, in insinuating that she was not entirely happy. And all that was chivalrous in Reggie Croft's nature pitied and sympathised with the pathetically beautiful woman who lay so close to him on the sofa as the steamer ploughed gently and soothingly on through the semi-tropical night on the bosom of the broad Atlantic.

.   .   .   .   .

The concert was over. It was late. The lounge had become unpleasantly stuffy.

"Would you mind if we took a few turns round the deck before I go down? If I go myself, that awful bore Mr. Kurwen is sure to waylay me."

It would have taken a harder heart than Reggie's to resist the appealing tone of the siren's voice.

"Of course," said he. "I've never seen a finer night in my life. It's a pity to miss it."

.   .   .   .   .

There was no one to be seen on the deck half an hour later. Reggie and Mrs. Driver were taking a last look at the lovely moonlit sea before turning in.

"You've made me happier to-night—so *much* happier!"

Reggie looked down into the girl's face. Her beautiful features looked pale—almost ethereal, he thought, in the moonlight. If she had seemed unearthly, spiritual, she broke the illusion. Before he realised what she was doing, her arms were about his neck.

"Good night, my dear," she said, her lips scarcely moving in the soft whisper.

Instinctively, for the man was but flesh and blood, Reggie's hands rested for a moment on her shoulders. The couple turned to go back to the lounge entrance on their way down to the cabins. From a chair, still spread out behind a pile stacked ready for next morning's scrubbing of the deck, there slowly arose the sneering malevolent face of the mischief-making Mrs. Attwood.

CHAPTER XIII

A Suspicious Character

IT was certainly a sultry evening.

"I expect you're not too pleased about all this extra work, Foster?" said a tall, broad-shouldered, florid-faced man with a heavy brown moustache and merry blue eyes. He was dressed in thin, rough tweeds and might have been a farmer in Oxford for the day on agricultural business. But deception was part of his stock-in-trade; for he was, in fact, Chief Inspector Bramley of Scotland Yard. The local police, after the sensational murder of M. Boissard had felt that they were getting a little out of their depth. Two unsolved mysteries within six months in the usually tranquil University town were enough to cramp the style of the most efficient of provincial Chief Constables. So Foster had wisely decided that the time had come to consult with the biggest experts in crime that the country could boast.

The efforts of the Proctors, those annual amateurs of the Police world, if they had achieved anything at all, had acted as a drag on the exertions of the professional Police. The thought that next term would see that keen *dilettante* in detection, Mr. Barnes, performing more zealously than ever, the office of Senior Proctor, was sufficient to strike dismay into the heart of even the self-reliant Foster.

After the discovery of the murder in Wellington Square and the tracing of the hat to its finding in Pusey Lane, Foster's enquiries seemed to have come to a dead end. With the concurrence of the municipal authorities the Chief Constable had determined to seek the assistance of 'the Yard.' And it was whilst the hat was still with the London Police authorities for examination that the second tragedy had occurred in the Turl.

Chief Inspector Bramley stretched out his legs and tilted back his chair, brought the palms of his hands slowly together, and bent his head forward. The pose was characteristic of the man when he was concentrating on the solution of some puzzling problem.

"No, Foster. You're up against a bigger thing even than we— up at 'the Yard'—usually have to face. In London, as a rule, we have some sort of an inkling of the class amongst which a particular criminal is to be found. And we work, afterwards, more or less by a process of elimination. In a country town like Oxford the thing is not so easy. And these two crimes are about as difficult a proposition as I ever had to tackle. Your enquiries haven't shown that anyone, either here or anywhere else that we know of, is likely to have profited by these murders. And there doesn't seem to be a ghost of a reason for suspecting revenge as a possible motive. Of all the classes that go to make up society in this country I should have said that the teaching body of an old University like this was the most immune from violent crime of this sort. And here within six months too, two perfectly harmless old fellows are murdered in cold blood in the very streets of the city, without the slightest vestige of a motive that I can even *guess* at."

"And what about the hat I sent you? Any sort of hope in that direction?" It was clear from the tone in which the Chief Constable asked the question that he did not expect a very hopeful reply. And his expectations were soon realised.

"I've done all I can for you, Foster," said the Inspector, in slow, measured tones, "and I'm glad to say that the experts (I don't happen to be one of them myself you know) in finger-print work have been able to bring out a pretty clear thumb mark on the lower side of the brim. And that, mark you, in spite of the rain that night and in spite of the petrol, and I've brought it back—for what it's worth—and that's not a great deal, I should say, at the present.

"He tapped a neatly wrapped brown paper parcel on the table beside him. "What good it's going to do you now we *have* done it I'm blest if I can see. Of course you can run through your local collection of finger-prints with it—I suppose you keep 'em—and if the feller has been convicted before, you'll begin to know which way the wind's blowing."

"I don't think, myself, that we're likely to get on the track as easily as all that," said Foster, shaking his head moodily. "And if we're driven—as I suppose we're *going* to be—to the theory that the murderer was some lunatic, or some bird with at least a temporary bee in his bonnet—this thumb-print's not going to be the slightest use to me or you. For it's hardly likely that the man will have committed a crime before. And where's the special class of crime merchant we're going to fix on in which we're going to start operations?"

"Yes—*where?*" said Bramley, with a blank look of resignation.

There was a knock on the door.

"Come in," said the Chief Constable. A sergeant stepped smartly in.

"Well, what is it, Jones?" asked Foster.

"There's a man here who's heard that an Inspector is down from the Yard. He says he'd like to see you with him. Thinks he can tell you something which may have a bearing on these two murders."

Foster looked across at Bramley enquiringly. The Inspector laughed mechanically.

"Ah," said he. "The same old game! We of the Yard attract these detective cranks like a magnet. If all the hours I've spent in interviewing amateur Sherlock Holmes's on wild goose chases were an inch long and we're put end to end in a straight line, they'd reach from here to the moon and back, and then from Marble Arch to Carfax, going via Henley, not High Wycombe! Vide *Answers*, replies to readers!"

"Shall we see him?" said Foster, a little wearily. "He's the first voluntary informant that's washed up, to *my* knowledge. What's he like, Jones? Give any name?"

"Looks like a respectable workman—navvy or bricklayer. Name of Nutkins."

"Well—I think we'd best see the worthy Nutkins, if it's all the same to you." This from Bramley. And Jones was sent out to bring in the visitor.

He was a man of middle height, sallow-complexioned and with a thin, sharp nose and little dark eyes, set rather too closely together to give him a pleasant expression. His hair was of a nondescript colour and scanty. In place of a collar he wore an old blue cashmere scarf. His well-worn grey suit was threadbare and much patched, and his boots, polished though they were, showed signs of much rough usage. He had not shaved for a day or two. He was obviously nervous and ill at ease.

The Chief Constable motioned him to a chair.

"Sit down, Mr. Nutkins," he said affably. "I understand you want to tell us something."

The visitor sat down in his chair as if he thought the seat were going to blow up. He coughed and looked apprehensively from the Chief Constable to the London Inspector.

This process demanded another cough from Mr. Nutkins. Inspector Bramley looked across at Foster as if seeking his consent to interrogate the man. The Chief Constable nodded.

"Don't be afraid of us, Mr. Nutkins," said he, genially. "We shan't give you away, if that's what you're afraid of. And nobody's going to write anything down either: anyway, not yet."

Nutkins coughed again and cleared his throat.

"I'm a law-abiding man—although I'm only a working man," said he, as if implying that, normally, the working-man were a revolutionary outlaw. "I don't 'old with these 'ere foreigners 'oo comes over 'ere a trying to make trouble. I says, says I, *always*,—that we Britishers can settle our own grievances without the help o' the likes of them. Now take Russia——"

He took a deep breath, and, losing his nervousness in the excitement of his speech, was about, it seemed, to launch out into a general tirade against aliens.

"Look here, my man," said Bramley, kindly but firmly. "You must tell your story in your own way of course. But we are busy men, we policemen, you know; and you seem to be getting just a little bit off the track. I thought you were going to tell us something you thought might help us about these murders here in Oxford?"

"Ah, so I was, to be sure," said Nutkins. "That were just what I were a' coming to. I——"

"Well," went on the Inspector, "I don't want to have to interrupt you, but the sooner you can come to the point the better, you know."

After a few more false starts, the man got under weigh. He was a member of a Labour Club. But he was no extremist in politics, and had been considerably annoyed, on the first of May, by a speech which had been delivered at the premises of the Club in East Oxford by a Russian out-of-work agitator who had been persuaded to 'say a few words' by some of the more revolutionary members.

"Fair savage 'e were. Down with this and down with that—the Royal Family and the 'Ouse of Lords, o' course. 'Is sort *always* 'as a knock at *them*. I've 'eard 'em many a time before. But this fellow ain't content with that—not 'arf 'e ain't! You bet yer life, no!" A string of adjectives which would not look nice in print were applied to the obnoxious Slav. "Keep on 'arpin' back to Russia 'e does. Says as 'ow the Professors and school teachers and the likes of them—parsons too, according to 'im—'grinds the face of the poor' (them's 'is very words, those is) and only teaches the kids and all what *they want* 'em to know. And then 'e turns round like to Oxford 'ere, and talks about these University Professors and the likes of them. Of course 'e don't threaten nobody in particlar—too cute by a long chalk I should say for *that*." He uttered a raucous and mirthless laugh at the thought, and, clearing his throat with more vigour than politeness, continued his story. "'E goes on to tell us 'ow some of these fellers 'ave been done in in 'is own country. Doesn't *advise*—*as* you might say—anybody 'ere to do the same—o' course not. Ho no, I *don't* think! But it seems to me, thinking it over now, and after what's 'appened and all that, as 'e warn't so much tellin' us all about Russia and what 'ad 'appened there, as giving *us* the tip as to what *we* might do *'ere*—see?" He paused dramatically and sat back to watch the effect of his story in the faces of his listeners, who might have been wooden images for all the emotion they evinced. "Then—" he paused as if to emphasise a particularly dramatic point,—"only a few days arterwards, I reads in the *Oxford Times* about the murder—in the Turl too—of this 'ere Mister Boissard." He pronounced the Reader's name phonetically. "I remembered the death of this other Professor chap—can't call *'is* name to mind just now—in Wellington Square at the end of last year. Cold shivers I gets down the spine—I can tell you. We puts two and two together—me and my wife—and she tells me to come along and see you two gents and see as if you wouldn't like to cop this 'ere Mr. Tomboysky, or whatever it is 'e calls 'isself."

.   .   .   .   .

A few hours later Chief Inspector Bramley was sitting in a small ground floor room in a poorly furnished tenement house in Paradise Square. Chief Constable Foster awaited him in Queen Street, close to the gates of the Prison. On the walls of the mean apartment, from which a once gay, tawdry paper hung in tattered strips—glistening with damp and mildew, were placed enlarged photographs in cheap, ill-made frames of Lenin, Trotsky and other leading lights of Russia under the Bolshevist régime. A half-opened package of scarlet-bound copies of "The Red Flag," in pamphlet form, stood on a rickety bamboo table by the side of the empty, rusted fire-place.

Mr. Vladimir Tambovski, ex-droshky driver, Bolshevist and political agitator, eyed his visitor across the dirty table with a ferocious glare. He was thin and wan—dressed in clothes worn but well-cut. His features were well marked and handsome, and he lacked the traditional beard and moustaches of the Nihilist of the boys' magazines.

"You have no power to make me answer your questions," said he in a high-pitched, excited voice, in admirable English, with scarcely the trace of a foreign accent. "We are in England—not in Russia now. And I know your laws. You cannot compel me to make a statement. And why should I of my own accord? You charge me with nothing: *can* charge me with nothing! I don't know who has put you on my track. Some interfering, meddling fool who cannot mind his own business! If I denounce your Government—cry shame upon your upper classes—your snobbish little clique of teachers—who is to prevent me? Your own law allows it." He laughed boisterously. "Ho—I know what's in your mind! You think because I say that the teaching classes—your Professors—your snobbish bookworms—should be exterminated, that it is I—Vladimir Tambovski—the representative of a free people, who should soil his hands with the task!" Again he laughed—an almost demoniacal peal. "But no—" he became calmer. "That is not the way of Vladimir Tambovski!"

Again he laughed, loudly, as if in contempt for his visitor's powerlessness.

Taking advantage of the momentary pause, Inspector Bramley began:

"I know, Mr. Tambovski, as well as you do, that I have no power to force you to make a statement—to answer any questions you do not wish to answer. Of course I've heard of your threats—if they were meant to be threats—against the Professors and dons of the University. And it was because of those threats—because of what has—to your knowledge—twice happened during the past six months, that I am giving you the chance of making a statement which may help to clear you of any suspicion."

At this remark the agitator broke into a derisive chuckle. But Bramley, who had dealt with many specimens of humanity, even more weird than this one, continued imperturbably.

"Of course you'll see, Mr. Tambovski, that if it can be proved—as it *can*—that you have made speeches of the sort you admit, and if no one else seems to have had any kind of grudge against the Professors of the University—you are bound, in the eyes of the Government, of the Police, to incur at least a certain amount of suspicion. I make no allegations—it is not my duty to do so. But I can offer you one way of setting aside for ever, any suspicion which may have been directed towards you."

Chief Inspector Bramley leaned heavily forward—his elbows on the table, looking straight into the eyes of his unwilling host.

"And why," shouted the Russian, banging the table with his fist—his eyes blazing with his pent-up fury, "should I meet your wishes in any way whatever? Whatever you may suspect—and I deny that there's any ground for suspicion at all—you've got no *sort* of *proof*—no—nor ever will have because—because—" his voice rose to a shriller pitch in his excitement, and Bramley saw through the grimy windows more than one head peer from the doors and casements of the surrounding houses—"your suspicions are all *false*—founded on nothing—wrong—ridiculous!"

He sank back, exhausted by the fever of his utterance. Bramley remained as calm as ever, and waited until the mercurial foreigner's frenzy had somewhat abated.

"I'm going to make a report, that's all. You needn't grant what I ask. I shan't press it, and I have no power to compel you to agree. But *if* you agree—and *if* what you say is true—and I have no real reason to disbelieve it—*unless* you refuse," his voice hardened a shade and the inner sternness of the Inspector's nature came for the moment to the surface, "I can *promise* you that there will be no need for me—for the Police—to interfere with you again."

"And what, might I ask, is this request that you wish to make?"

Bramley leant back in his chair. He put his hand into an inner pocket and brought out a notebook from which he took a folded sheet or two of plain white paper which he placed upon the table. The Russian eyed him in a furtive, suspicious manner. Diving into a side pocket the policeman next pro-produced a small flat tin box. He opened it and disclosed an ordinary inked stamp pad. The foreigner appeared to tremble slightly.

"All that I want you to do," said Bramley in measured tones," is to let me take the impressions of your finger tips."

Vladimir Tambovski's face went a shade paler than was its wont. He drew a sharp short breath—appeared to be about to speak.

Then—his hands dropping limply on his knees—he fell heavily forwards on the floor in a dead faint.

CHAPTER XIV

A New Anxiety

THE voyage was over. The *Appam* lay at anchor, early in the morning, in a West African harbour. Reggie Crofts dressed and went up on deck before breakfast, though the ship was not due to sail till the afternoon. He was glad, in many ways, that the voyage was ended at last. The sooner he began his tour of service the sooner he would be back home—home to marry Barbara. But there was a tinge of regret in his gladness. The days had passed, for the most part, pleasantly enough. It was all so delightfully new to him. Not only had he never before been on a long steamer trip; but, as he now reflected, walking round the empty deck of the ship which had brought him to "the Coast," never before in his life had he encountered such a quaint collection of types and people. He had always thought that University life produced the most comprehensive collection of queer characters obtainable in one place at one and the same time. But he confessed to himself that, if his fellow passengers were a true epitome of "the Coast," West Africa had Oxford beaten hollow.

Till he had come aboard he had supposed that men like Daddy Dawson only existed on the films, or in the pages of imaginative—highly imaginative fiction. And yet here was a man, in the flesh, who had spent more than thirty years in the Bush in the "White Man's Grave," and attained almost the age of sixty—for the most part entirely alone, or without any other white man within thirty or forty miles of him. And, as Daddy Dawson truly said, forty miles were as good as four hundred, or even four thousand, when one's only means of locomotion was one's own feet or a carrier-borne hammock; where the roads, in any other country, would have been called field tracks—muddy as swamps in the rainy season and not more than two feet wide in their widest part, and fringed on either side by thick elephant grass twelve feet high, well-nigh impenetrable, or thickets of closely growing untidy trees. Daddy Dawson's knowledge of the native language of the people of the part he inhabited, and of their ways and customs, was as thorough as it was possible for a white man's to be. He did not share the average missionary's belief that all one had to do to make a black man a Christian was to baptise him, give him a coat and a pair of trousers, and teach him to snuffle the Lord's Prayer in his own particular dialect. His acquaintance with the Human Leopard Society was intimate, and he cited cases where even ordained native pastors had, without openly discarding their Christian principles and ethics, lapsed into their indigenous cannibal rites, and finished their holily begun careers at the bottom of a ten-foot drop. As the queer old trader hailed from the very Colony to which Reggie was himself going, and as Reggie's political post would certainly eventually land him somewhere in the hinterland, it was pretty sure that some time or other the two would cross each other's paths again. The Colony was not a large one.

Reggie had been at first rather impressed when he had heard that a real live Solicitor General was to be on board. And he had felt, insignificant newly appointed officer that he was, somewhat honoured by being actually placed at the same table at which this high dignitary was to sit. Mr. Crowsmith's manner, on their first meeting, was not such as to weaken Reggie's conviction. For the legal luminary took himself *au grand sérieux,* and not a real live King's Bench Division Judge could have comported himself with more becoming gravity than the worthy Solicitor General. As he became a little more familiar with the facts of Colonial life in West Africa, Reggie began to lose a little of his first respect for the great man. Mr. Crowsmith's Colony was a small one, not much bigger in size than Scotland, and the total population did not exceed two million souls. And even so the pompous officer was only of minor importance after all; for it transpired that an Attorney General too graced the little country's legal staff. Reggie found it hard to conceive what airs that high mandarin might give himself, if his subordinate could throw his weight about with such magnificent effect as Mr. Jasper Crowsmith. He always spoke as if his Colony's affairs were the daily concern of all good Britons, the decisions of its Courts the cynosure of all legal eyes at home. When, in a moment of rash honesty, Reggie confessed to him one day, in the course of a constitutional round the decks, that he could not remember even having heard of the particular Colony till a month or two before, and had even then jumped to the conclusion that it was some minor French possession near Cochin China, Crowsmith had expressed the blankest incredulity. Later, when his informant still protested the truth of his assertions, he had intimated that this must be some form of jest—and a highly indecorous one at that.

Reggie had met people like Kurwen before, in shops of third-class standing, performing the office known in the States as "floor-walking," leering at the prettier girls on his staff when he supposed that the attention of customers was directed elsewhere.

Mrs. Attwood seemed to be in a class by herself—Reggie hoped so, anyway. Her many spiteful remarks about Colonial Governors, their wives and entourage generally, encouraged the idea that there were strata of Coast society where women of seeming respectability, but whose language was freely interspersed with the phrases and epithets of the tap-room, were not received with open arms. Since the night of the charity concert the lady had been quite openly hostile towards him and Mrs. Driver, and he suspected, and not without good ground, that she was circulating all kinds of unsavoury rumours about him and the grass widow all round the ship.

He had discovered by now that Charlie Williams was of a type very common on "the Coast." He served behind the counter of a store belonging to a large company which had made its fortune by selling cheap Manchester cotton goods, soap and American leaf tobacco to the negroes of West Africa; buying in return the produce of the districts, in which its stores were situated, palm oil, palm kernels, ginger, ivory as the case might be. He and his class invariably referred to themselves as "merchants," and were given first-class passages to the Coast by their company boards to keep up the prestige of the firms they represented, when they would have been much more comfortable in the second-class portion of the steamer, where there was no need to don boiled shirts for dinner, and generally to ape the manners of a class of society to which they did not belong; and for which, indeed, they, in private, expressed a withering contempt which might be born of envy. Considering their status and education, these men were well paid, and the camaraderie of colour on "the Coast," where such a tiny sprinkling of whites is swamped in an over-whelming mass of blacks, caused them to speak of Governors, Judges, Residents and military officers lightly by their surnames, with no prefix attached; except, as a rule, in the presence of the owners of the names.

There were also a few missionaries among the passengers. Some of them hailed from the United States. They had apparently decided that their own country was sufficiently advanced to be able to dispense with any further evangelical propaganda. Unkind passengers, however, suggested that, as they appeared to be drawn from the humbler grades of American society, they acquired in Africa, among a people of a more primitive race a prestige which their colour alone would have failed to ensure them in their own home circles. This artificial raising of status, coupled with a comfortable flow of cash from the open-handed faithful of the States, ensured them a far pleasanter walk in life than they can ever have hoped, for in Pennsylvania, Kansas, or Dayton, Ohio.

Two gaunt, horn-rimmed bespectacled couples, were accompanied by pallid, ill-mannered, noisy children, whose parents proudly proclaimed that they had been born in West Africa. The honest Cissie Daniel more than once openly declared that she thought their parents would have been better employed in teaching their children to be civilised beings in their own country, than in dressing up a lot of cannibals in petticoats and trousers, and handing out cheap Bibles to civilised Africans who used them as lucky dips for texts to be mouthed in revolutionary political sermons aimed at the expulsion of the white races from Africa.

Reggie felt an odd pang of sorrow at the thought that to-day he must say good-bye to the dainty Mrs. Driver. Had Mrs. Attwood refrained from catty remarks about her: had she not made capital out of the innocent little scene she had witnessed on deck on the night of the concert, and had there been no silly nudgings and winks amongst certain of the ship's passengers when they had been seen in each other's company, it is probable that he would have given less thought to the coming parting with his pretty table companion. But a sense of opposition in the crowd against two individuals jointly begets a bond of union more rapidly almost than any other feeling. And in no case is the bond more strongly forged than when the pair are of opposite sexes, and not personally unattractive to each other. Reggie, wearing his solar topee for the first time since he had brought it, looked over the rail of the steamer into the deep blue waters of the landlocked harbour. Although it was only seven in the morning, there were clusters of small boats and launches round the ship's side. A large flat barge in charge of a couple of negroes, whose coaldust-blackened clothes matched in tone their swarthy, broad-nosed, good-natured faces, was discharging fresh water into the *Appam's* tanks. The chugging of its steam pump made a deafening din as Reggie stood above it. A smartly dressed native policeman stood at the gangway, preventing, in theory, the entry of any but authorised persons, In fact, as no white officer was in sight, the promise of a large present, or the actual offer of a small, procured admission for swarthy visitors in every form of garb, from the long-gowned, red-fezzed, aboriginal dealer in native curios—(bottles covered in bright red leather—cigarette tins in leopard skin—quaintly-shaped and brightly coloured baskets)—to the immaculate black "civilised" gentlemen, in faultless European brown boots, white spats, spongebag trousers, tail coat, stiff collar and straw "boater", who had come on the chance of a cool, iced, white man's drink when the bar opened.

The mails were being lowered into a lighter flying the Government flag under the direction of an African postal official, whose crown-badged cap proclaimed his rank, and whose language varied between the most unintelligible brand of "pidgin" English as he bawled orders to the labourers handling the sacks, to polysyllabic "civilised" periods when he communed with men of his own class serving the shipping company or other Government departments. It seemed a very far cry from Oxford. And the thought brought back to him the memory of Barbara's tearful parting from him at the gates of Somerville that night in June.

He had lots of things still to do before going ashore, so turned to go below. He glanced idly at the wireless notice-board. A fresh sheet had been pinned up that morning. He looked down it, more from habit than because he expected to see anything that might be of interest to him. Among the names of places whence news had been collected, he saw, once again, that of Oxford.

"It is reported, on good authority, that an unexpected development has occurred in the case of the murder in Wellington Square, and an arrest is shortly expected."

He was excited at the news. He had never ceased, since he left England, to worry about the possible danger to Barbara Playford or her uncle. The victims of the criminal, who was still at large in the City, were all of the class to which her uncle belonged. Who was to say that he might not, for his own strange reasons, decide to continue his successful campaign against yet more helpless victims? It was pleasant news to Reggie that the Police seemed able to make a move at last in tracking the assassin whose two horrible crimes had gone, till now, unpunished. The Police in England were a wary body, more especially cautious and circumspect in dealing with cases of murder. It was very rarely that they went so far as to make an arrest in such a matter unless they were pretty sure of their ground, and pretty certain that the evidence they had collected was sufficient to secure a conviction. An arrest on inadequate evidence had, in times past, proved an irrevocable blunder. For once a man, tried for his life, is acquitted, he cannot again be arraigned for the same offence, however strong any new testimony which may later come to light. Reggie was as convinced as anyone who knew anything of the cases of Professor Toogood and M. Boissard, that the hand which had struck down the unfortunate Professor in Latin was the same as that which had taken the life of the distinguished Reader in French. And once the assassin was safely under lock and key, or even in imminent danger of arrest, Reggie's apprehension on behalf of his fiancée's uncle would be relieved.

He was just turning away when the wireless officer came down the stairs with a fresh sheet in his hand.

"Excuse me, sir," he said, "just got a few more items in. May as well get them up before the passengers for this port go ashore. You won't be having news quite so often, I'm afraid, once you're away up in the back of beyond!"

He winked, and, unlocking the case, pulled out the tacks and arranged the old sheet afresh and the new one in its place. Nodding a cheery good-bye to Reggie, he went back to his cabin.

Reggie went forward again and read the fresh piece of news. There were only two lines new:—

OXFORD. Late news. Mysterious attempt was made last night by unknown person, who has escaped, to murder Dr. Playford, the Master of St. Thomas's College.

.   .   .   .   .

"It is *so* sad to have to say good-bye! I *have* so enjoyed my talks with you. It's not of many of the people on board that I can say the same."

Mrs. Driver, in her simple one-piece frock with a bright red belt round her slender waist, looked as fresh as a new-blown rose as she gazed wistfully into Reggie's eyes as he stood by the opening before the Jacob's ladder. He decided at once that the most becoming headgear for woman was just such a sort of soft plaited straw hat as Mrs. Driver wore. Worried as he was by the shock

he had received only an hour or two before on reading the terrifying wireless telegram, the girl's sympathetic words had a greater
effect upon him than they would have had at any other time. He
bent over her and pressed her little hand with warmth.

"Good-bye, Mrs. Driver. It's very kind of you to say such nice
things to me, and I've enjoyed it all much more than you can
have and I'll write and tell you how I get on. I hope you'll keep well
and have a jolly good time and enjoy yourself. I think your
husband's a jolly lucky man!"

Before he released his hold of her hand, and as he still bent
over her, he heard a sharp metallic click behind him. He turned
just in time to see the cynical-looking Kurwen slip a small folding
camera into his pocket.

CHAPTER XV

The Master of St. Thomas's

DOCTOR PLAYFORD was always a little relieved when the Long Vacation settled down upon Oxford. Not that it meant much real holiday for him. Not in the accepted sense of the word, anyway. For it was during the months in which the undergraduates were "down" that he got through what was, to his own mind, his most serious work. He liked the young—none better. But he was irritated by the routine duties which he was compelled to perform as the head of a large and busy College. Not a great disciplinarian himself, and intolerant, even as a boy, of the petty and trifling restrictions which conservatism compelled schoolmasters to incorporate in their curricula, it irked him not a little to have to enforce regulations a good many of which he did not himself really approve.

The atmosphere, too, which prevailed at so many College meetings worried and annoyed him. He could remember, even yet, the belief which he, as an undergraduate, had entertained, that the life of a don was a placid and unruffled existence, untouched by the petty bickerings and quarrels which chequer the life of the great world which surges around outside the confines of an age-old University. It was an unpleasant shock for him to find, when, in his turn, he became himself a fellow of a College, that not a little acrimony and spite were vented behind the venerable walls of the old Common Room, where the benevolent faces of dons long since gathered to their fathers, looked down serenely from their heavy, gilded, dusty frames upon the long table with its green baize, its quill pens, and its massive old-fashioned leaden ink-wells.

Mr. A. would oppose the election to a scholarship of Smith of Winchester solely on the grounds that his papers showed a scientific frame of mind. For he was well aware that it was this factor which had weighed with Mr. B. in so stoutly championing his cause. For Mr. B.'s own subject was Natural Science, and he hoped, if Smith were finally elected, eventually to lead him to a degree by way of the Science Schools. Mr. C. who was a well-known exponent of advanced Assyriology, and had no interest whatever in the respective subjects of Mr. A. or Mr. B., but who found Mr. B. less repellent to him personally than Mr. A., would support the election of Smith merely to annoy Mr. A. He would not, of course, admit this motive, even to himself. But it was the truth for all that, and his colleagues were not so blind as to be deceived by the Assyriologist's pretences.

All these petty bickerings and jealousies, and a hundred others, were very disturbing to Dr. Playford, who believed that the Fellows should put the cause of good scholarship and the fair repute of the College before their own private animosities and prejudices.

It was painful too, to the kindly Master, to have to send a young man down, unless the offence consisted in some very grave breach of any of the established canons of morality. For although his own religious beliefs were somewhat nebulous, and were really only formally expressed at all because the University had not yet reached a stage of development or degeneracy in which an avowed agnostic could hold the headship of a House, his ethics were of an austerity with which the most conventional of Christians could find no fault. In his heart of hearts he thought it both cruel and unjust to send down a youth, who might be a most brilliant scholar, merely because, on one occasion, in a bout of drunken revelry, he had been detected by the stern unbending Proctors and reported to his College for condign punishment. Boys would be boys, and, remembering his own undergraduate days, he could count up, on his fingers, a list of distinguished men—including two bishops and the head of a great public school—who had only escaped the dire disgrace owing to the sympathetic conspiracy of friends—a conspiracy in which he himself had played no minor part.

Well the Long Vacation was well begun—the routine work of the previous term had been satisfactorily cleared up, and the Master was once more free to apply himself to the research work he really loved.

He was at the present time employed upon an elaborate task. He was trying to write a full history and description of all the houses which Dr. Johnson had occupied, or even visited, in his life, as recorded by the devoted Boswell. The Master's degree had been a classical one, but he had taken a very deep interest latterly in the great English masters, and was an enthusiastic admirer of the Great Lexicographer. In fact, some Johnsonian theme or other had been the subject of the thesis for which he had been granted his Doctorship of Literature.

Barbara, the Doctor's niece, had returned from her visit to her aunt. Dr. Playford had always been deeply attached to his brother, her father, who had been killed by a bomb dropped from a German aeroplane when he had been serving as a colonel with the army in France. The widow had never recovered from the shock, and had died within a few months of the Armistice. Barbara's normal home was in the Master's lodgings at St. Thomas's, and so firmly had she established herself in her uncle's household, and in his affections, that the old man thought almost with dread of the time when love and marriage would divide her ways from his.

Dinner had been cleared away in the old oak-panelled dining-room in the Master's house. Playford, and his only guest, Lord Ruislip, sat on with Barbara, who was the only woman present. Lord Ruislip had brought her up home in his car, and the Master had repaid his kindness by inviting the young man to dinner.

"Are you at all interested," asked Dr. Playford, "in English prose and literature generally?"

The young man's face, had his host troubled to study it with any intent, would have shown him pretty plainly that its owner had no particular interest in *anything* intellectual. He reddened a little as if somewhat confused. He did not, however, wish to be rude to the Master—and this for more reasons than one. At the same time, he had no desire, by giving too encouraging a reply, to be drawn into some discussion which was beyond his depth. His depths were a little shallow.

"Well—er—" he coughed, "not *frightfully* you know, sir, I mean—that is to say—I like some of Scott you know, most *awfully*. But then, I'm afraid it's a *fearfully* long time since I really read any."

This admission of Lord Ruislip's had at least established a common ground for discussion, which, without being too profound for the young man would at least be not uncongenial to the learned Doctor himself.

"Ah—it's some time, too, since *I* read any of Sir Walter's works. But I enjoyed them very much when I did. And some of the prose is very fine indeed. Which, might I ask, of his novels do *you* like the best?"

This was rather a poser for the unfortunate Lord Ruislip. But Barbara was listening to the conversation. And he had begun, during the last day or two of his stay at Lady Shortways' to realise what a very desirable girl Barbara was. For Barbara had not been slow to open the campaign on which she had determined on the night of the receipt of the letter from Reggie which she had thought a little less warm about than it might have been. And she had succeeded, even more quickly than she had expected, in piercing the armour of the young man's indifference. Lord Ruislip decided that a bold stroke must be played. It sounded so very weak, after the assertion that he had made, to say that he'd forgotten even the names of the whole "outfit," as he would have called it. And worse still would it be to admit that he had never even read *one* of them right through from start to finish.

"I think," he managed to get out at last, "that *Vanity Fair* takes a lot of beating."

The girl looked as if she were about to explode.

The Doctor, for his part, found no difficulty in agreeing with this statement as an isolated expression of opinion, though the context in which it happened to be made was just a little confusing. But he did not wish to make his guest uncomfortable, and sought a way of helping him out.

"Perhaps," said he, with all the gravity he could assume, "you prefer the *poetic* works. Do you like *Marmion?*"

"Ye-es—and n-o-o—" said Lord Ruislip, feeling that somehow something had gone wrong somewhere, without at all realising what it could be, "but I think—" he rashly plunged again, "that I really prefer *The Ancient Mariner.*"

The pretty girl in the long Minty chair could hide her emotions in silence no longer. She dared not catch the eye of her uncle who sat opposite her, and she felt that to look Lord Ruislip in the face would be to court utter disaster. Controlling herself by a great effort she said:

"And *I* think, myself, that *The Jabberwock* beats them *both* hollow!"

This remark had the effect of a safety valve. In the general laughter which followed, Barbara's, expressing the relief to her pent-up feelings was by far the loudest.

"Have you heard yet from Reggie?" said her uncle, now that the time had come when the subject could legitimately be dropped.

"Yes," said the girl. "But the letter was posted from the first port of call, the Gambia. He hadn't reached his own colony when he wrote."

The Master thought that the tone in which his niece spoke was a little cool. But he never pretended to understand the present generation, which was an enigma to him. These post-war girls and boys seemed of a race different from his own. He never thought that there might be some other cause underlying the rather obvious frigidity. The conversation trickled on in a desultory sort of way for another half-hour or so. Lord Ruislip looked at the clock.

"I'm sorry, sir," said he to his host, "but it's nearly ten o'clock. I'm afraid I shall have to ask you to excuse me. I've got to get home to Banbury to-night. I've left my car at the Randolph, and I've got to be up early to-morrow to drive my mother up to town."

.   .   .   .   .

Lord Ruislip stood in the hall putting on his coat, for the July evening was inclined to be chilly, and he had a thirty-mile drive, in an open car, before him.

"Good-bye, Barbara," said he a little nervously to the girl who was deputising for her uncle in seeing his guest off. The Master had accepted the service, as he was anxious to get to his study and his work. And he grudged, as a rule, every minute after dinner in Vacation time which was not given up to his Johnsonian researches.

"Good-bye,"said Barbara, "and many thanks for running me up. It was a topping drive."

The young man seemed to hesitate about something. The lamps in the Broad were lighted. The door opened on to the famous old street, and but few people seemed to be about. When term is "down," even now that Oxford is becoming so rapidly a commercial and industrial town, as well as being an ancient seat of learning, there is not much life in its streets after nine o'clock.

Lord Ruislip turned again, like Whittington before him.

"I'm sure," said he, a little diffidently, "my mother would most awfully like to put you up if you cared to come and stay a week-end with us."

"Thank you very much. I'd love to."

The girl's immediate object, rousing the lethargic young man's interest in her, had been achieved. She liked him well enough. But not in the way in which she liked Reggie. And it was only as a kind of stalking-horse that she might need his services in case her *fiancé* became recalcitrant and difficult. Lord Ruislip felt that he had gained a point, and came right back into the hall.

"I suppose," said he, his breath coming rather more quickly than before, "that you wouldn't mind a lot if—if—if I gave you a kiss—Barbara?"

The girl took a pace back. Things were moving a little more swiftly than she had expected or intended. Smiling she said:

"I don't know that *that's* quite necessary, is it?"

The hall was dark. There was an alcove, on the right as one looked towards the street, under the stairs which led to the upper storeys. The girl had her back to it. Lord Ruislip had stood eagerly awaiting her reply. As she gave it, she took a step backwards and was in the alcove. The young man moved quickly towards her. He put his arms behind her back. He bent down, obviously meaning to kiss her in spite of her reply. He had not expected resistance, and seemed surprised when she pushed him back. For the way in which she had encouraged, and then received favourably such advances as he had made during the last few days of their visit to Lady Shortways, had given him reason to think that his suit, if he made it, would not be rejected.

Barbara, who now realised that the fault lay at least partly with her, pushed him at first roughly. Then, as he receded and loosened his clasp about her, her movement was more tender.

"You *mustn't*," she said, under her breath, "Lord Ruislip, *please!*" Then, "What was that?" She looked over his shoulder into the hall passage behind.

"What was what?" said Lord Ruislip.

"I thought I saw somebody slip past in the passage behind you."

"Where's the light?" said the youth.

Barbara went rather timidly forward and pulled down the switch. There was no one in the passage. The door of the dining-room opposite was open. It was on their right as they looked down the hall with their backs to the front door. At the end of the hallway was a long, narrow French window opening on to one of the quadrangles of the College. It was unlocked as it always was in the summer until the servants shut up the house on going to bed.

"Let's go and have a look round the dining-room."

It was Barbara who spoke, rather breathlessly. "I'm certain something passed behind you just now. I think it was a man."

The pair turned on the dining-room lights and made a thorough search, even looking behind the heavy velvet curtains which, summer or winter, covered the windows which looked out on the quadrangle. There were broad, old-fashioned, cushioned window-seats. There was no sign of any living occupant.

"We'd better lock the hall window," said Barbara. "If anyone went through that way he can only get out through the Porter's Lodge. The gate's locked, and he'd have to ask the porter to let him out, and we'll know who he is."

The final adieux were at last said by Lord Ruislip in a more chastened manner, and the front door was locked and bolted.

Barbara, mentioning nothing of the incident, which had rather upset her usual equanimity for the time being, wished her uncle good-night in his study on the first floor, and went to bed, her thoughts fully occupied in tackling the new position which had arisen.

.   .   .   .   .

Dr. Playford was so immersed in his work that, before he thought he had been settled at his desk for more than an hour, he glanced at the little clock on the mantelpiece and saw, to his astonishment, that it was just after midnight. The green-shaded reading-lamp on his desk, which threw only a small circle of light in the large, comfortable, book-lined study, was the only illumination.

The Master of St. Thomas's felt distinctly tired now that at last his attention was distracted from his task. Behind the big leather arm-chair into which he now threw himself for a few minutes before going to bed, the door of the room was ajar. On his right was a large revolving book-case on the top of which, untidily and precariously stacked, was a big pile of books to which he had been constantly referring as his work progressed. He became suddenly aware of his own fatigue and drowsiness, and closed his eyes for a few moments before going upstairs.

.   .   .   .   .

The Master suddenly came to his senses with a feeling of alarm. There was something over his face—something black—rough—

cloth—with, he was sure, human hands behind it. He felt the pressure of a man's knee painfully against his stomach. He was aware of a sickly odour creeping into his nostrils. He tried to rise—to cry out. He failed in both attempts. A hand was groping at his throat. In wild terror and alarm he thrust out his arms. His right hand came into contact with the pile of heavy books on the revolving stand. They gave. He was aware of a terrific crash—of the releasing of the pressure against his stomach, face and hands. Then he swooned into oblivion. . . .

CHAPTER XVI

Was it a Clue?

DR. PLAYFORD was a little shaken on the morning following the outrage. He was a man hale and hearty enough, but he was nearing seventy years of age, and it was his first experience of an attempted assassination. Barbara did her best to make him stay in bed that morning, for she felt that the interview with the Police, which was bound to follow, would be rather distressing to him in the circumstances. But he was obdurate, and had his way.

At nine o'clock, when Inspector Bramley and the Chief Constable were announced, the Master of St. Thomas's was awaiting them in his study. The room still showed signs of a disorder which was not usual in it. Dr. Playford, though he had not before had any intimate dealings with the Force, knew well enough that, when a crime was being investigated, they preferred to have objects near the scene of the occurrence left untouched, until they had conducted their examination and drawn their deductions.

When the two officers had been conducted into the room, the Master motioned them to be seated. He presented to them a box of cigars which he had asked Barbara to place close at hand.

"No, thank you, sir," said Bramley. "I think that at present I'd rather not smoke. We have a pretty busy morning before us."

Foster, too, politely declined the offer.

"Of course," said the Master, "I know why you have come to see me. There's one thing, however, I should like to ask you before you begin. Have you any objection to my niece being present?

I have an idea that she will be much more helpful to you than I can be myself. For, as you may have heard, the thing happened so quickly and so suddenly, that I became unconscious before I was able to realise exactly what was occurring."

"There is no objection at all, sir," said the Chief Constable, smiling. "We have taken the liberty of asking Miss Playford a question or two already, and her presence here would be most useful."

Barbara, who had followed the two men into the room, murmured a word of thanks and sat down in a chair beside her uncle. She was grateful for the permission accorded her, for she had doubts as to what extent the Master had suffered as a result of the terrible shock, which he had had the night before.

"If you don't mind," said she, turning to Bramley, who seemed to be in charge of the proceedings, "I think that I had better tell my story first. You see it was I who noticed some rather queer things before my uncle was attacked, and it was I who found him after the thing had happened." She gave an involuntary little shudder.

She looked tenderly towards the dignified old scholar, who seemed so out of place as the central figure at a police enquiry. Bramley acquiesced, and the officers nodded in common consent. The girl began her story.

"I was in the hall—seeing off a friend who had been dining with us——"

"Excuse me, Miss Playford," said Bramley, "for interrupting you, and please don't think me impertinent. But I think you had better tell us at once the name of your friend. You must not think that every question a policeman asks involves someone in any suspicion—far from it." He smiled broadly, and his companion joined him. "But it is useful for us to have the names of *everyone* who may possibly be called upon as a witness in investigating a case like this. And it's not going to be an easy one. It saves one, too, from asking a whole string of questions at the end of a statement."

"Of course—I quite understand, Inspector. It was Lord Ruislip"—

the shadow of a blush spread over her pretty face as she uttered the name. It recalled the incident which had preceded the departure of her uncle's guest. The Master, looking across at his niece, noticed her change of colour, but was in ignorance of what had prompted it.

"The hall door was open—the French window at the end of the passage was unlocked. The dining-room door was open—the Master is always particular about having it so after a meal to air the room. The man, whoever he was, ran through the hall and disappeared. Lord Ruislip and I were not in time to see where he went. But it must have been either into the dining-room or else through the French window."

"I suppose, Miss Playford, that you can't give me any idea at all as to whether the man was short or tall—dark or fair—what clothes he had—and so on?" suggested the Inspector.

"I'm afraid," said the girl, "I can't give you any help at all in that way. You see the hall lamp was not lighted then. Some light comes through the fanlight over the front door which opens on "the Broad," and I very often don't bother to switch it on."

"Then—so far as you can say—the person might have been a woman—not a man at all?"

"Yes—that's quite possible," replied Barbara. She told the police officer of her examination, with Lord Ruislip, of the dining-room. The windows which looked out on the quadrangle were closed. Those facing "the Broad" were open. But no one could have got either in or out that way, for there were iron bars fixed perpendicularly in the stone frames. Many years before, in the time of a former Master, there had been a burglary—the thief gaining admittance from the street. The College authorities had taken steps to prevent a recurrence of the incident.

"And the French window in the hall passage?"—it was Foster who asked the question.

"It was open—wide open," answered Barbara. "I don't quite know if it was open before. But it was at any rate unlocked. It is always left so in the summer until the servants lock up and go to bed. And they had not gone then—it was only just after ten. The kitchen is in a sort of half-basement downstairs. The person cannot have gone down there or the servants would have seen who it was. And they didn't."

"So the intruder *must* have got out either by the French window in the hall or by the front door?" It was Bramley's turn to take up the interrogation.

"He can't have gone out by the front door. I slammed it to on the catch before we went to search the dining-room. We weren't in there long, and the door was open all the time."

"But he might have slipped back and gone upstairs?" continued Bramley.

"I don't think so," said the Master's niece. "You see, the hall light was on by then—I'd switched it on. And I think that one of us would have been bound to notice anyone passing again outside the dining-room door. Though we didn't, as a matter of fact, I think, take any particular notice."

"Did you examine the dining-room window fastenings?" said Bramley.

"Yes," replied the girl. "The windows are in metal frames with leaded glass panes. By pulling a handle you fit a small iron tongue into a slot in the side of the frame. And there's also a sliding bar with a screw so that you can fix the window open as little or as much as you like. The windows—there are two of them—were both shut and fastened on the inside."

"Have you seen them this morning?" said Foster.

"No. Dr. Playford had breakfast in bed this morning And I went up and had mine in his room. Everything was rather upset after this terrible thing, and I don't think the servants have touched the room yet this morning."

Barbara Playford was a girl of spirit—not easily upset. But her pretty face began to show disturbing signs. Tears were not very far off. Excitement had strung her to a pitch which she was only now beginning to realise. She had had quite enough to upset her within the past few days. Her lover's letter—she thought—had not been very satisfactory. Then there was the scene with Lord Ruislip the night before. And then this alarming attack on her uncle had happened to strain her nerves even more. She had had time, in the sleepless hours of the early morning which had followed the attack, to worry over the sinister incident. She could not help connecting this outrage in some way with the cruel murders of her friend Professor Toogood, and of the Reader in French, M. Boissard. Was there some dark, malignant fate hanging over her uncle too? The accumulation of worry and anxiety of the past few months were enough to have dismayed a girl even braver and more resolute than the niece of the Master of St. Thomas's. Bramley and Foster were not slow to notice the changes in the girl's demeanour.

"I think, Foster," said Bramley to the Chief Constable, "that the best thing we can do for the present is to go and ask the porter a few questions. He ought to know if any one went out of College after midnight last night. And we can have a look round the dining-room and the hall at the same time. I'm afraid sir" (he turned to the Master) "that we'll have to come back a little later to get any information you're able to give us."

Dr. Playford acquiesced, and the two men left the room. In other circumstances they would have continued then and there the examination they had begun. But feelings of chivalry for this plucky, high-spirited, attractive girl, and for the rather badly shaken Master, suggested a change in the order of their immediate plans.

.   .   .   .   .

The welcome they received a few moments later from the porter of St. Thomas's did not err on the side of cordiality. Old Sawyer was far more of an autocrat in the college than its Master. Seeing, through the little glass window in the Lodge, the approach of the two men, he did not attempt to rise from the old wooden-armed Windsor chair which was his throne of office, though he guessed that their business must be with him. He had an inborn suspicion of the police and all their works. Brought up as a boy in a country village, where poaching was viewed in the light of a heroic venture rather than of a crime, his early encounters with members of the Force had done nothing to minimise his dislike. Moreover, like many of his kind, he was a staunch and conservative supporter of the University's government and customs. If wrong were done within the academic limits, it was the province of the Proctors to deal with it rather than that of the common City Police.

"Good-morning, Sawyer," said Foster pleasantly, mounting the short flight of little stone steps which led to the Holy of Holies, in front of the London policeman. The omission of the prefix, by which the Chief Constable intended no offence, was immediately noted as one by the Cerberus of St. Thomas's.

"Good-morning to you," he observed, in tones the reverse of friendly. He looked very unapproachable—with a Sphinx-like expression on his rubicund plump face, adorned by an iron-grey moustache which had resisted the efforts of the worthy Mrs. Sawyer, with a bottle of cheap black hair dye, to restore its pristine black glossiness. Even his pipe was held at an aggressive angle. He made no attempt to rise, nor did he emulate the Master's courtesy in praying his guests to be seated. He sat with his hands folded on his capacious stomach looking straight at his interlocutors, saying nothing as he puffed stolidly at his tobacco and waited for the Chief Constable to proceed.

"I'm sorry to trouble you, Mr. Sawyer" (the title was favourably noted by the porter, whose eyelids made an involuntary movement), "but I've come on business and my friend and I would like to ask you a few questions."

The momentary calm induced by the prefix became again unsettled. It looked, in fact, as if things were blowing up for a storm.

Bramley was a better tactician than his local colleague. His experience of types and classes was more varied—was bound— from the very nature of his position, to be.

"The fact is," said he, ingratiatingly, winking at Foster whilst Sawyer turned for a moment to clear his throat preparatory to an explosive tirade, "we've come really to ask you a *favour*. The Master is, as we all know, a very famous scholar and the Head of the College. We naturally had to go to him first when we had business involving St. Thomas's. It would have been most impolite and irregular to have done otherwise."

Mr. Sawyer turned, a kindlier light in his eye. After all, this policeman had the decency to respect the etiquette of the University, and the porter felt certain, somehow, that a compliment of some sort was to be paid to himself. But it would not do to show signs of mollification too soon. The process must be gradual. He merely grunted. But even grunts can be graded, and this one was not of the gruffest type—even from an Oxford college porter's point of view.

"With all respect, Mr. Sawyer, to the Master—he is, after all, a scholar, first and foremost. Whilst you are—must be, to hold the position you do—a man of the world."

The porter was gratified. Feeling quite sure that the description was fully deserved, he yet felt drawn towards a man who was not only acute enough to see it, but was also polite enough to put the results of his observation into words. And to put it, moreover, into words in the presence of a third party—and that third party the Chief Constable of the City Police. He removed his pipe—emblematically almost, it seemed; a sign that friendly relations were to be established. Or anyway an armistice in hostilities which his hitherto frigid demeanour might be fairly said to have begun.

"Wouldn't you two gentlemen like to sit down? Talking's a bit easier—if talking's to be done—if a chap's comfortable." The police officers availed themselves of the offer, and, thanking their host for his hospitality, sat down in a couple of Windsor chairs—without arms, to signify that they were for the common herd.

"We're very sorry to have to bother you at all," said Bramley, "but——"

"That's nothing—nothing," said the porter, with what passed for geniality in his inflection. "Not so busy—now Term's over—though you might say, a college porter's *never* off duty—not *really*, I mean."

Mr. Sawyer's rotund outline rather belied the gist of his words, which was intended to suggest a harassing, anxious calling. But captious critisicm would not assist the course of justice at the moment.

"You know, of course," said Bramley, who in spite of his refusal to the Master not so many minutes before, even accepted a cigarette from the porter to preserve the harmony which was being so happily established, "that an attempt was made upon Dr. Playford in his study last night." Sawyer nodded in assent—a nod which was portentous—a nod in which respect, fear, suspicion and alarm seemed inextricably mingled. "There is only really one matter on which we wanted—at the moment, to question you. Were you on duty last night in the Lodge, shortly before and after midnight?"

It was, from the policeman's point of view, an unfortunate opening. Mr. Sawyer—after an indignant prelude—got well into his stride. Of course he was the *head* porter—they must understand *that*. Ordinarily he shared night duty in alternate weeks with the under porter. But now was vacation time. As the under porter was taking his holiday, Mr. Sawyer had consented—as duties were not naturally, as arduous as in Term, to doing a double spell of duty.

Inspector Bramley was in a predicament. He had lots more to do that day, and his and Foster's time was limited. He did not want to offend the porter, but he really could not let his precious time be wasted by all this irrelevant matter. Gently he headed him off and managed to get him and keep him to the point. There were few undergraduates in College at the time—only such as had permission to stay up to do a little reading for special examinations in the Vacation. These all had to be in College by nine o'clock. They could however, in special circumstances, get permission to remain out till ten. No such permission had been granted by the Dean or the Master the preceding night, and all had been in by nine, or soon after. Mr. Sawyer had sat up reading a novel till close on midnight. No one had either come in or gone out between nine-thirty, when the last of the few College servants still working had left, and the time when the porter had gone to bed. The key of the gate was in his bedroom, and he always locked his bedroom door at night. He had been aroused by a commotion in the Master's Lodgings and had run there to find out what it was about. He had heard the news from the scared

servants, but of course had not seen what had actually happened
He had stuffed the gate key into the pocket of the overcoat which
he had put on over his pyjamas. It was an ingrained habit of his
to carry the key with him wherever he went when he happened to
be on duty. There *was* another gateway into the College, leading, he said, into St. Giles's. But there was no permanent lodge
there, and it was scarcely ever opened in vacation. The key was
in a locked cupboard in his own bedroom.

When the interview was over, the three were on the friendliest
of terms. And when Foster and Bramley left the Lodge to return
to Dr. Playford's quarters, the porter effusively begged them to
come and visit him some other day, on purely convivial grounds.

"We've established," said Bramley to Foster, as they covered
the short distance in the Broad between the Porter's Lodge and
the Master's front door, "that the fellow, whoever he was, did *not*
leave the College last night by the ordinary way. The next thing
we must do is to examine the dining-room."

.   .   .   .   .

"There's nothing amiss on three sides of the room, anyway,
Miss Playford?" said Foster after he and Bramley, with the assistance of the girl, had minutely inspected the wall in which were
the windows giving on "the Broad," the wall dividing the room
from the hall passage, and the fireplace side. "Now what about
the windows opening on the quad?"

The three made a move towards the old-fashioned window-
seats.

"I suppose no one has been in here since we went to see the
porter?"

"No," said Barbara, "and no one had been in before then—for
breakfast was not laid here."

The curtains were still drawn. For after the event of the previous night, all household arrangements were upside down.

"When was this pane broken?" Bramley was pointing to the
small square pane, set in lead, near the handle which opened
the left-hand window of the pair nearer the door.

"Broken?" said Barbara in surprise. "None of the panes were broken yesterday—of that I'm quite sure. My uncle would at once notice a thing like that before anyone. He never said anything about it."

"Well," said Foster, "look—it's certainly broken *now.*"

And a close inspection showed that on the jagged splinters left by the small broken pane in the lead which had held it, were several spots of a reddish-brown hue which might have been caused by blood.

.　　.　　.　　.　　.

Foster and Bramley had held a short consultation in the dining-room, whilst the girl went up to prepare her uncle for their final visit. It was clear to them that someone—and the permissible inference was that it was the person who had so violently attacked the Master in his study the night before—had broken either in or out of the house by means of the dining-room window. And the further inference was that he had broken *in.* For, had he been on the inside, there would have been no need to have broken the pane near the handle in order to turn it to let himself out. As he had not gone out through the Porter's Lodge in the ordinary way, his means of egress from the College must be sought elsewhere, and the easier means of tracing the intruder which had presented itself to Barbara, Lord Ruislip and the Police officers themselves was of no avail.

.　　.　　.　　.　　.

"Good-bye, sir, and I am sorry we have had to trouble you."

The Master politely thanked the Police officer for the considerate way in which he had done his duty.

"I suppose it would not be permitted to ask you whether your researches have given you any clue to the identity of my assailant?"

"I am sorry, sir," said Bramley. "I'm afraid we're just as much in the dark as anyone. It's a most mysterious business. But you may rest assured, sir, that we shan't relax our efforts until every possible clue has been followed to its very end, for all the criticisms that are levelled at 'the Yard'."

"And sir," said Foster, "I don't think you need fear any such attempt again. I'm giving orders for a specially sharp watch to be kept at night on the front part of the College. And the porter assures me that he and his own men will do the same, with regard to the part of your house which faces the quadrangle."

The Master smiled and protested. But Barbara, who knew him well, could detect a little relief in his expression as he listened to the Chief Constable's assurances.

For some inexplicable, mysterious reason, the lives of men in Oxford, whose only claims, so far, to notice in the world, had been the depths of their learning, the brilliance of their scholarship, were being threatened by some diabolically ingenious, unseen menace.

Inspector Bramley and his companion turned to go. As the London officer shook hands with the pale, tired-looking Master, his eye caught sight of something at the foot of the arm-chair.

"Excuse me, sir. But can you tell me where *this* came from? May be of no importance, of course, but we can't afford to leave anything to chance."

He picked up a small strip of some black material. It was about three inches long, about an inch wide at its broadest part, and tapered to a point. Its sides were jagged and unravelled.

"Looks like part of a gown, sir," said Foster, who was more used to the trappings of a University than his London colleague.

"Just see if I've torn my gown, my dear," said the Master to his niece.

The girl unhooked her uncle's gown from behind the door where it hung. It was old and worn, but there was no sort of rent or tear in it from top to bottom.

"And yet," said Foster, alert now again with the keen interest of a policeman once more upon the scent, "it looks to me uncommonly like a part of *somebody's* college gown."

CHAPTER XVII

The New Life

REGGIE CROFTS was not sorry, in the end, to get ashore. And the first experience of the new continent had the effect, for the time being, of staving off worrying thoughts. Although he did not go so far as to put his thoughts into words, he was, in fact, distinctly relieved when he stepped ashore from the shipping company's lighter, and began to look at the strange scenes going on around him. After all, it was sufficiently clear, from the short message that had come over the wireless that morning, that the assassin had at least been unsuccessful in his attempt on the uncle of his *fiancée*. And now that it was known in what direction his future efforts might be expected to be exerted, those around the Master of St. Thomas's would be fore-armed. Reggie was quite sure that the final action of the lounge lizard Kurwen, in taking a snapshot of Mrs. Driver and himself just before he left the ship, was done with some malicious intent. Though what that intent was he could not guess, and he decided that the effort was not worth the while.

He looked at the big, untidy West African town sprawling out before him as he walked up to his destination, guided by a negro policeman sent to escort him by the Acting Colonial Secretary, and thought that he had never in his life before seen anything so quaint and unreal. It was a conglomeration of wooden and mud houses, thatched with palm leaves and patched with sheets of old and rusty corrugated iron or pieces of kerosene tins, cheek by jowl with pretentious stores of big European firms in rather shoddy-looking concrete, up-to-date stone bungalows on lofty concrete piers, and big and rather ostentatious Government offices, some of which were yet under construction.

Well-metalled roads in red and dusty laterite, fringed by rows of modern electric light standards, were trod as much by natives from the Protectorate, with bare feet and locally made woven gowns of many colours, as by educated negroes in topees, bowlers, lounge suits and European boots, in which they trod clumsily and with obvious discomfort. The fashions designed for the cooler climate of Europe caused these gentlemen to perspire freely. Their women folk encased their figures, often voluminous, in the incongruous corsets since discarded by their white sisters, and forced their feet into high-heeled shoes of the latest Parisian modes.

Modern cars, recklessly driven by native chauffeurs, passed and re-passed in close proximity to hammocks borne on the heads of native carriers, and primitive bullock carts conveyed the refuse of the town to the latest thing in up-to-date incinerators. It was truly a surprising mixture of the primeval and the ultra new.

Reggie was the guest of Major Martin, C.M.G., the Acting Colonial Secretary, a tired-looking, ashen-faced, lean man of forty-five, whose tropical service made him look quite ten years older. He had an equally washed-out looking wife, who had clearly once been pretty. She was now the typical pallid, apathetic West Coast white woman. Her husband was a disappointed man. He had begun his career in the West Indies (his military title did not derive from the Regular Army), and, having passed through all the grades of the Civil Service in one of the less important islands, had jumped eagerly, when it offered, at the chance of joining the better paid West African post. He had got on so well with a former Governor of the Colony that he had been recommended for a C.M.G. in the Colonial Honours List, and now, when a new man came who did not approve of his methods, found himself shelved and for ever blocked from any further promotion. He was a man to whom red tape was the very breath of life. It *was* so comfortable, when one had no initiative of one's own, to gauge every proposed new measure by its conformity or otherwise with some ancient precedent, raked from the dust-laden archives of the Secretariat. Being an old stager he only served a year at a time in West Africa, leading an easy and unambitious life of unmasterly activity. He had formed his opinions and his actions on what he had hoped would be the lines of which His Excellency himself would approve, only to find, too often, that he had "missed the boat."

Mrs. Martin, a simple soul, who even yet, against all reasonable hope, envisaged herself one day with a handle to her name, occupied herself in keeping well to the fore amongst the female population, official and unofficial, by virtue of the precedence officially accorded her in view of her husband's position.

She gave showy but inexpensive parties, played lukewarm tennis, and spent her evenings at the parties of others for bridge and dancing, of which she would tell you, in languid tones, as she gazed upon you with her lack-lustre eyes, that she was *passionately* fond."

The Martins had no children, and, in expectation of their retirement in a few years' time, on a pension inadequate to support them in any real comfort, carefully laid by every penny they could legitimately scrape together from such salary and pickings of office as came their way.

Reggie was having his first meal ashore, for the *Appam* had been delayed unloading cargo, and had not left until after lunch. The evening was, for him, oppressively hot, with a clammy, steamy heat, and he longed to remove the formal stiff white mess jacket which he had donned, and to turn up his shirt sleeves. His host was attired in the conventional black dinner jacket of Europe, and did not appear to be feeling any discomfort. His hostess was wearing an evening dress which even Reggie, being fresh from home, could see was not a little *démodé*. The meal was an unexciting affair. The table was laid on the polished-floored, barely furnished veranda of his host's three-roomed concrete-built bungalow. The only flowers on the table were the eternal magenta bougainvilleas of the Coast, flanked by candles with scarlet

shades, an indication of his hostess's lack of artistic taste. A mil-
dewed punkah flapped disconsolately to and fro overhead, jerked
with uncomfortable alacrity at a shout from his host, when the
sleepy white-gowned negro who pulled it awoke to a sense of his
responsibility, from his dreams of a full meal of rice and palm oil
awaiting him in his shack.

Conversation was desultory and not enlivening. Mrs. Martin
evinced a languid wish to know if skirts were being worn any
shorter in London—which was the more popular at the moment—
the bob or the shingle. Her guest did his best to satisfy her curi-
osity. Major Martin discoursed at length upon the great future
before the palm-oil industry, when certain patent nut-cracking
machines, recently introduced by the Government, really got going
amongst the natives. He impressed upon Reggie the sublime
importance of his future work as an Assistant District Commissioner in the Baoma District of the North-West Province.

"Of course," said he, "you'll be under a very experienced
Resident—Fielding—who's on leave at present—though he may
be finishing this time. And your immediate head, Prescott, the
District Commissioner, is a very sound fellow."

Mrs. Martin got tired of this "shop," and said:

"Of course, Mr. Crofts, you mustn't forget that you've to call
officially on the Acting Governor to-morrow morning before you
have an interview with him. No leaving cards you know. Just write
your name in his book. Mr. Partridge—we all hope he will soon be
Sir Francis Partridge and a Governor himself—" (Mrs. Martin was
always hoping for the improbable to happen in other people's
cases just as much as in her own husband's) "is a very charming
man. Though," she went on with a sigh, "he's only in his first tour
here and I'm afraid some of his new ideas are just a bit *too* new
and progressive for the Colony at its present stage. His wife is
not yet out. I think, from what I hear, that she spends just a little
too much time staying with her children at home instead of looking
after her husband out here. By the way—are *you* married
Mr. Crofts?"

Reggie blushed involuntarily and rather stammered than said.

"No-o—not yet—Mrs. Martin—but——"

"You're engaged, then?"—his faded hostess smilingly helped him out. "Well, it's the next best thing I suppose!"

After dinner the party retired to the wicker-work chairs at the other end of the veranda, where coffee and liqueurs were served by a barefooted "boy" in a white gown, whilst another set out the bridge table.

"We have asked in one of the young men from the Secretariat," said Mrs. Martin, "for a game of bridge this evening. I hope you play?"

Reggie assented, but felt that he would much rather retire, undress, and spend the rest of the time before bed in a cold bath. The second guest arrived, a man, young in years, but affected with the rather ludicrous pomposity of the young Colonial official who sits at headquarters writing snappy minutes to men in the "bush" old enough to be his father, safely ensconced behind the initials of the Colonial Secretary himself. He was condescendingly gracious to the new arrival and the game began.

Reggie was himself no mean player, but he found that he had a lot to learn. He discovered, amongst other things, that for an Acting Colonial Secretary to revoke was not a matter to be visited with the normal penalty: that for his wife to lead from her own hand when she should have played from 'dummy' was followed by none of the usual consequences. This made things a little difficult at first. But, aided by the deportment of Mr. Assistant Colonial Secretary Noke, Reggie began to feel about as at home with this new bridge as he was beginning to feel in the general strange atmosphere. The average Englishman is an adaptable creature and very soon becomes *au fait* with any part of the globe to which the Fates may send him.

He was not sorry when the party at length broke up. But, though he was tired, he found that sleep did not come to him too easily the first time he lay, in the tropics, beneath a mosquito net. It was not only his own doubts and fears about things at home that made him wakeful. The stuffiness was at first almost insupportable, and the strange concert of noises made by the myriad crickets in the garden, so like the sound of water refilling a partly emptied tank, did not conduce to somnolence.

When he awoke at five, the day had already begun to dawn, and the humidity of the early morning in West Africa had damped his sheets and his mosquito net.

After breakfast he went with his host to the Secretariat, where black clerks in immaculate European clothes were piling the office baskets in the Secretary's room with portentous looking documents.

A closer glance at these showed them to be, to an inexperienced mind, of no world-shaking importance. Major Martin sat down in his revolving-chair and motioned the Assistant to a seat. He toyed with a large sheaf of papers tied up with pink tape. Reggie could not help seeing the heading: *Smith—Mr. J.: Query from the Auditor as to whether he should be charged with one shilling, the cost of sending an unnecessary Telegram.*

"A great deal to do this morning," said the Acting Colonial Secretary, as, having importantly initialled a minute in the paper before him, he turned to another headed: *Proposal to purchase locally two wastepaper baskets for the use of the Assistant Colonial Secretaries.* "If you will excuse me a minute I'll just run through these baskets and see what's ahead of me."

So the time passed, until, looking up suddenly, he said:

"It's ten o'clock. I think you'd better go and write your name in the Governor's book."

Preceded by a negro clerk, and feeling rather top-heavy in his sun-helmet, Reggie left the ram-shackle building which housed the Secretariat, and went in search of Government House. This was a building used as a fort in the old slave-trading days, with recent accretions of stone and cement in more modern styles. It was approached by a red syenite road, bordered by the huge silk cotton trees so common in West Africa, the haunt, at evening, of thousands of flying-foxes. The drive within the outer gates was fringed by bright yellow alamandas, scarlet hibiscus, pink and magenta bougainvilleas, and numerous variegated croton bushes. Before the pretentious concrete entrance stood a red-fezzed African private who presented arms smartly as the new Assistant District Commissioner approached. Having duly signed his name in the Governor's book, Reggie was led by his swarthy guide to another part of the building, where, in a cool, big-windowed room sat the Acting Governor's A.D.C. He was a tall, thin, pale young man, with heavy tortoise-shell rimmed glasses, a pronounced stoop, and wearing a light crash suit.

"Ah," said he, rising as the visitor entered, "you're Crofts, I suppose? My name's Burnham."

Having shaken hands, he offered Reggie a cigarette and a seat.

"Hope you've had a good passage out? I think the Governor's ready to see you now."

After a few conventional remarks, he knocked at a door leading to an adjacent room, and later came out saying:

"His Excellency will see you at once."

The Acting Governor, not rising from his office-chair, shook hands rather pompously and stiffly, and told Reggie to sit down. He was a short, rather plump, florid person of about fifty-six. He wore pince-nez which concealed a pair of shrewd grey eyes, and he had a habit of stroking from time to time with his left hand the few remaining greyish hairs upon the top of his head. Mr. Francis Partridge, C.M.G., was a hardworking Civil Servant, who had acted in almost every conceivable capacity in the Service. He, too, had begun his career in the West Indies; been transferred to Ceylon; back to the West Indies as Administrator of one of the lesser islands, and reached the highest rung on the ladder he was ever likely to reach when, a year ago, he had been appointed to a West African Colonial Secretaryship. Hitherto he had been considered a safe, sound man, not brilliant, but unlikely to cause trouble by initiating new-fangled schemes. But his unexpected promotion had filled him with the desire to make his name known in the official world. He had set to work, during his Acting Governorship, to play with that traditional administrator's toy, the Education Department. New schools had—on paper—sprung up all over the Colony and Protectorate. A few were actually in course of construction: fewer still had had staffs appointed and some equipment bought: and fewer yet had acquired a list of prospective pupils. Anyway, here was matter in abundance for the Annual Report to the Colonial Office. Miles of new motor-roads had been inaugurated, and looked very impressive—in sketch-maps. Of course it was not necessary, in an official report, to dwell too much on the fact that none of them had practicable bridges, or that one real road, twenty miles long, properly and effectively equipped, was worth several fifty or sixty miles in length, unembanked through swamps, and with bridgeless gaps at intervals of every few miles. Mr. Partridge was turning his attention to another official hobby—agriculture. Great schemes were brewing, the end of which was to teach the native how much better an enlightened Government could grow and deal with palm kernels than men who had spent their whole lives in doing it. Reggie had heard an inkling already from the Colonial Secretary, and was not at all surprised when the Acting Governor began to ride his hobby.

"Well, Crofts," said he, "you could not have come to the Colony at a more favourable time. The revenue has been, I must admit, in rather a bad way. You know, of course, that it is principally derived from the products of the oil palm. Well, I hope that, in a very short time, we shall be able to *double* it."

Mr. Partridge did not think it necessary to point out that, actually, at the present time, by persuading the Governor to order out a lot of costly machinery which there were not sufficient skilled mechanics to work, and by appointing a number of highly-paid experts in European agriculture, he had very nearly *halved* it.

"It has not been—will not be—easy work. But I rely, under the Governor, on my political officers, of whom you are one—loyally to help me with the scheme. Our previous work in the Education and Roads Departments (you have no doubt read the last Annual Report?)—has paved the way to progress."

His temporary Excellency expanded at great length on the same lines, becoming not a little prosy—and ending up by wishing the new recruit all success in the career he had chosen.

Reggie felt, as he bade the A.D.C. good-bye, and went out once more into the hot tropical morning, threading his way through the jostling, perspiring crowds of sweating, chaffering, noisy blacks, the badly-driven Fords and Morrises which swarmed along the roads to his host's bungalow, that he would not, had he his own way, barter one yard of Oxford's familiar, ancient grey streets for the whole of Africa's sun-drenched shores.

Three days later he left for Baoma. And not, he thought, a day too soon. He felt that he hated the capital's sticky, artificial gaiety, half-hearted unless inspired by copious libations which left the revellers sick and sorry the next morning. Till now, busy with buying stores and kit for the next eighteen months, he had not had time to feel homesick and to worry too much over the disturbing news from Oxford. And nothing fresh had been reported in the Reuter's telegram which came daily over the cables from home. He was human, and felt interested, for the time being at least, in the new sights, sounds—*and* smells!—around him. Baoma, his destination, was only a hundred odd miles from the capital. It was about forty miles from the nearest station on the line, only sixty miles or so by rail from the capital. But the train which left the Coast at eight in the morning was not scheduled to reach it till past one o'clock in the afternoon. And Reggie gathered that railway time-tables were not too reliable on the West Coast of Africa.

The track itself looked like that of a rather magnified child's toy railway—the gauge was only two feet four inches. But, none the less, there seemed to be a fair amount of space in the bare com-partment with its folding table in which his new servant had al-ready installed his camp chair. The flurry and confusion in the station itself—not unlike a miniature and rather dirtier Victoria—was indescribable. African passengers are divided into two classes: that which arrives for the journey hours before the engine is even taken out of its shed, and that which postpones its arrival till about one minute before the train is about to start. And it is the latter category which predominates. The policemen, dressed in smart khaki uniforms of European cut, detailed to keep the crowd in order, made more confusion and noise than anyone else. The wild rush for the train as the guard at last, ten minutes late, blew his whistle and waved his flag, was almost alarming to any one to whom the experience was new. But the fact that all is ready and the guard waves his flag in West Africa by no means implies that the journey is actually to start. Many compliments passed between native officials, many creditors uttered threats against departing debtors, many doubtful jests had time to pass between males on the platform and smiling females in the carriages and vice versa, before a violent jolting of his compartment told Reggie that the train was really off.

Before pulling out into the open country, the train passed through many of the tortuous, dirty streets of the lower quarters of the capital. Small black children in impish glee played games of "last across" before the diminutive, panting engine. Craftsmen of the town, jewellers, basket-makers, itinerant Mohammedan teachers, shoemakers—some in worn-out European garb, their feet bare or shod in gaily-hued carpet slippers, some in blue or white native gowns with brightly-coloured fezzes or turbans, sat or stood at the doorsteps of the dingy hovels which bordered the line, waving hysterical farewells to those whom they would see again in at most a day or two, as if they were departing on a perilous voyage of many weeks. The West African negro is a creature of sudden and wild impulses, of mercurial high spirits or complete abasement. He does nothing by halves. Here and there among the tumble-down wooden shacks, roofed with palm-thatch tiles or corrugated iron, or patched with boards stripped from old packing-cases, arose a more majestic structure in concrete blocks or sun-dried mud bricks—the trading-place of some Syrian huckster, who, in dirty shirt, dirtier shoes and ragged trousers, waved his farewells, accompanied by his pallid, plump, Semitic wife, nursing at her breast a pale and pimply Asiatic baby. There were an African or two of the class called, by courtesy only, "tailors," who squatted by sewing-machines at the doors of their alien masters, ready, for an exorbitant charge, to run up into shapeless, ill-fitting garments, the cheap trade shirting and calico bought from their Syrian employers by their customers. British West Africa attracts yearly a greater number than before of these keen traders. Arriving in the country with little more than the clothes in which they stand, they borrow money from compatriots or the big European firms (for they are honest borrowers), to buy a small stock for a tiny store. Living in a fashion more squalid than that of the poorest native, on a set sum a day, they amass in a few years, if they are lucky, sufficient money to take them back to their own country and keep them in comparative comfort till the end of their days. If the Fates are hard, they wander around in search of fresh loans or petty trade until their own countrymen will do no more for them, and the Colonial Government packs them off home at its own expense.

Two other features noticed by Reggie were those outposts of the rival faiths of East and West—the mosques and the churches. The former were circular in form, of mud, and thatched with grass. The latter were of laterite bricks or concrete blocks, in the familiar form of the poorer dissenting chapels of England, with staring windows of crudely-coloured glass and dilapidated independent bell-towers. Their facades were smothered with "Foundation Stones,"—slabs of ill-dressed concerte inset with the names, in badly-formed black letters, of pious donors, who, Pharisee like, wished to proclaim their questionable virtues in the market-place.

The West African Mohammedan—who can rarely read the Koran, and is not at all averse to having an alcoholic drink with his Christian or pagan friend—has frequently never heard of Mecca.

His Christian brother shows, by his palliation of the system of plurality of wives, that the Old Testament rather than the New is the bedrock of his creed.

As the town was left behind, the little train, with its motley load, drew out at last into open country—wide plains of what seemed to be fine pasture land, but which were in fact patches of hard, laterite rock with tufts of coarse grass of no value even for grazing cattle, sprouting from little nooks and crannies more fertile than the inhospitable whole. In some more favoured spots, a few lean cows, in charge of yellowish-skinned, half-naked Fula boys, were doing their best to make a meal. But, for the most part, there was no sign of life. So the train meandered endlessly on, halting at innumerable small stations which reproduced in miniature the futile clamour of the terminus. To Reggie, newly come amongst them, the African officials, in their cheap, ill-kept uniforms, the petty traders with their scanty stocks of worthless goods, their constant wrangles over pence and halfpence, seemed more like a lot of children, playing at being grown-up than real, adult men and women.

As midday approached the heat of the compartment became almost unbearable. He called his "boy" to bring him a drink, and refreshed himself with some lukewarm soda water. By one o'clock, when the train, almost due at his destination, and over an hour behind time, he felt hungry and sent for lunch. It consisted of soup made the night before from a "square" and kept warm in a Thermos flask, a skinny fowl, cold potatoes and a tin of peaches as a sweet, the whole washed down by a bottle of some cheap German synthetic lager beer. The engine, burning soft West African coal, was responsible for a large admixture of soot and grit in every mouthful he ate or drank. The discomfort which he now experienced at every turn caused the more pleasing feeling at the general novelty of everything to wear off a little. He wondered if he had been quite wise to give up his easier life at home for this plunge into the unknown. He began to think that he never would really settle down here. The higher officials he had met had all tried to keep up the pretence that the whole thing mattered so much more than it actually did, that they really were persons of vast importance in the world. But the more he saw of the reality of things out here the less certain he felt that their conviction was right.

His meal finished, he lay back in his deck chair, and, tired of gazing at the monotonous never-changing landscape—mostly hidden by high rank elephant grass and monotonous green rice patches, with irritating little stations here and there, he cast his mind back to that evening when, full of hopes and ambitions at securing the appointment, he had stammered out his feelings in the Oxford tea-shop to Barbara, and told her that he was at last in a position to ask her to marry him. It seemed to him that the people amongst whom his lot was cast were, from the European standpoint, little more than children, but with all the vices of men and women thrown in.

Now that, for a while at any rate, the spell of novelty was broken, the cynical attitude of many of the "Coasters" he had met at home and on the voyage out began to affect him. He had, in his ignorance, thought that it *must* be all exaggeration and nonsense. But he was beginning to wonder whether his opinion had been right.

And there was the great question—the *greatest* question—of Barbara. He might be able to endure this new uncongenial land and people himself. But how could he ask, how could he expect the brilliant girl he was going to marry to come and bury herself— perhaps literally (he shuddered at the thought)—in a place like this? He did not doubt, now, that she was fond of him—that she loved him. But was it, after all, right on his part to demand such a sacrifice of her? How he longed to be back once more in Oxford, dancing with her the night through at one of the old familiar places they knew so well together—longed to press her body to his, to cover her lips with his passionate kisses—to feel her own embraces in return. A pang of jealousy shot through him. How would Barbara fare, now that her aunt, who was inclined, he knew, to look askance at him, had her in her power? Ready and able to give her all the things she liked best in life—and rightly too. Able to introduce her to, and keep her with all the attractive and wealthy young men who abounded in her circle—men whose incomes for one month were more than he himself could hope to earn in a whole year?

Well, it was no use to keep on musing like this. Somewhere between two and three o'clock—a minor breakdown had been added to the usual delays at the stations, *en route*—the train puffed wheezing and bumping into the station for which he was bound.

As he was alighting and beginning to look about him, a great outcry arose. Down the low platform ran a half-naked negro with a black tin trunk on his head. He was followed by a barefooted native police constable, a ragged railway porter, the guard and a whole rabble of people who probably had not the foggiest notion whom they were chasing or why. Up ran his cook, breathless and dishevelled, and cried:

"Massa! Massa! One boy done thief massa's *bokkis* (box)!"

Reggie's longing for Oxford increased in its intensity!

CHAPTER XVIII

Royal Visitors

WHILST Reggie Crofts was being initiated into the mysteries of West African official life, the home Police authorities were investigating as baffling a sequence of crimes as had ever before occurred in the world—civilised or uncivilised. It was two days after the attempt on the life of the Master of St. Thomas's. The scene was the Chief Constable's office in Oxford Police Station. Chief Inspector Bramley and Foster were both looking extremely puzzled.

"And how about this fellow Tambovski? It seems to me that he must be ruled out once and for all in connection with Doctor Playford's narrow escape. I told you I'd had the fellow watched ever since your interview with him in his house. Here's the report of all his subsequent movements, as far as we are able to trace them. Anyway, the main thing that concerns *us* is his whereabouts between, say, ten and midnight on the evening of the show at St. Thomas's." He turned the leaves of a small pocket diary. "This is compiled from information supplied by the men on duty round St. Ebbe's and Paradise Square. The first entry for the day is at ten fifteen a.m., when my man saw his bird leave the house and go for a shave to a barber's close by. I suppose he's got some of this 'Red Gold' we hear about so much on tap if he can afford to revel in twopenny shaves!"

Bramley chuckled at the Chief Constable's little joke. "I should say," said he, "that the barber who took off the growth our friend was sporting the day I interviewed him would charge a double fee!"

"This barber, as it happens," said Foster, "is one of the city's leading Bolshies. I daresay he obliges the bosom friend of Comrades Lenin and Trotsky free, gratis and for nothing! Anyway, what was our friend's next move that day?" Foster turned again to the dossier. "The constable kept the shop under observation as unobtrusively as possible. Tambovski did not come out till close on eleven. Barbers are always talkative fellows, and when two Bolshies get yapping 'Red' politics together I suppose time is no object. In the end the Russian gent went straight back to his house. He doesn't seem to have left again for some time. I myself passed his place, in plain clothes, at half-past two that afternoon. I could easily see into his room—there are no curtains. He was sitting down at his table, writing away like steam. The place was littered with foolscap sheets—looked like a regular snow-storm— the result of his literary labours! The man who was on duty round about five o'clock reports that Tambovski went to a cook-shop nearby at five ten. He doesn't seem to have left until nearly six, so we'll presume he was stoking up on a meat tea. He returned to his digs. At about seven o'clock he was visited by a fellow called Smithers, whom the constable knew to be a prominent Red member of a Labour Club down somewhere East Oxford way. The two left the house almost immediately. I could not, of course, spare a man to shadow him wherever he went—we've none too many men available even for ordinary duty. . . . But Polstead's a smart man. He rang up the Sergeant in charge in here, and we got in touch with the fellow on duty near the Labour Club of which Smithers is a member. Sure enough, two men who answered exactly to the description of the English Bolshy and the chap from Russia went into the place together about half-past seven. Tambovski seems to have stayed there till close on ten. Bardwell, the policeman there, is friendly with a lot of the members of this club, and got into conversation with a man called Johnson—a carpenter—as he was leaving the premises shortly after. He found out that a meeting on some Socialist stunt or other had been held. There were many speakers, and all had been pretty fiery. But none more than our foreign friend from Paradise Square.

"Ah—so we now come to a gap which may be important," interposed Bramley.

"I'm afraid not," said Foster. "There's no news between ten and a quarter to eleven. What Tambovski was doing then I can't say. It takes less than three quarters of an hour to walk from East Oxford to St. Ebbe's. But I can say that our friend was back in his own house by ten forty-five. There's nothing to show that he ever left it again until nine the next morning. So that's that."

"That, I should say, quite clears him of any complicity in the St. Thomas's affair. And the news *I've* got for *you* is no more cheering. I told you how I managed to get an impression of Tambovski's finger-prints on the day of my interview, when he was off in a dead faint on the floor. I sent them down to the Yard for classification. They correspond with those of a Russian wanted by the Police in Paris for a burglary, and do not show the remotest resemblance to the mark on Professor Toogood's hat. So Tambovski seems completely cleared of any suspicion in either Toogood's or Playford's cases. And the reason why he got the jumps, when I suggested his voluntarily giving me his prints, is also explained. So our nice little theory which seemed to be working so well has all gone west. I'm afraid we've got to begin all over again from the beginning."

"Yes"—Foster sighed. "It *did* seem a bit of luck. But I thought at the time, it seemed a little *too* good to be true. It's not easy to think of a class with a murderous feeling against University professors and dons as such, and our Russian friend, with his views on education generally and on Oxford in particular seemed to fill the bill pretty well. However—no good crying over spilt milk, and off we go again."

"I'm not downhearted yet—not by a long chalk," said Bramley. "There's lots of ups and downs in a job like ours—though I *am* beginning to think that the downs outnumber the ups! We'll get the feller yet before we're through. But at the present rate, what I'm afraid of is that it may, from the look of things, cost another life before we do. I don't see how anyone can fail to recognise that these outrages that have happened here, one after another, and in so short a time, in this usually pretty quiet old city, are connected in some way with one another. The victims all belong to the same class. The injuries in the two murders had many points of resemblance. Fortunately in Dr. Playford's case things didn't go far enough to provide us with any more of those similarities. But the *motive*—that's what gets me beat. I can't even *guess* at one. It seems to me that we're forced back on the lunatic theory. And that's about the toughest nut we could possibly have to crack."

"I wrote a circular letter—after the murder in Wellington Square—to all the asylums and mental homes in the district, asking for information as to any irregularities in connection with the custody of any inmates. I drew blank. I sent out another letter yesterday, and have had a few replies already. And none of them throw any light. No escapes and all mild loonies on parole reporting back to time. Can't say I ever had much hope," said Foster wearily. "But of course we can't afford to leave a single stone unturned. We are up against as stiff a proposition as ever I can remember."

"It seems to me," said Bramley, "that the Police problem of the protection of life is involved."

"Do you mean," asked Foster in some surprise, "that you expect me to take measures for the safeguarding of the lives of all the dons in Oxford? In term time their numbers run into hundreds. And our normal duties keep us as fully occupied as we care to be."

"Yes," replied Bramley thoughtfully, "I know it's a regular teaser—a damned difficult show all round. But *if* some such scheme could be devised, we might even catch the beggar in the act and prevent the occurrence of any more of these horrors."

"That's all very well to *say*—but *how*, I ask you, are we to *do* it?"

"Haven't they got some sort of antiquated mediæval system of their own?" suggested the London man. "I'm not so well up in University matters as you."

"The *Proctors,* do you mean?" ejaculated Foster, with undisguised derision in his tones. "Which reminds me"—he pulled open a drawer in his desk and produced a letter written in an untidy, sprawling hand. "I got this only this morning from Mr. Barnes— he's a don at St. Antony's and has something to do with teaching Law in the University. He was elected Senior Proctor last term, but didn't have time to get really into his stride. Bit of an amateur sleuth he is, too. Got Sherlock Holmes and Hercule Poirot and the whole bally lot knocked into a cocked hat to hear him talk. *His* idea is that the detective who has no use for psychology and inhibitions and all that sort of junk isn't worth the money he draws. Says he's got some sort of scheme or other which is nearly certain, if we put it into action, to end in our laying the murderer by the heels. Wants me to give him an interview before next term begins."

"Gosh!" said the Chief Inspector, with wide-opened eyes. "So you've got cranks to deal with here away in the country too!"

Bramley had no wish to hurt the susceptibilities of his friend, but he could not help occasionally betraying his sense of the very large gulf which separated the provincial Police from himself and his colleagues of the Metropolis. "Are you going to waste our time on *him*?" The latter sentence was tinged with frank contempt.

"I don't know," said Foster, a little nettled, "that you aren't a bit unfair. These dons aren't all such fools, quite, as some people like to make out. In fact I've known quite a number of them who've had quite a lot of common sense." His words gave the impression that the majority of the academic body was a collection of harmless lunatics. The old town and gown spirit has happily dwindled so much that it is unlikely that the streets of Oxford will ever again see another bloody St. Scholastica's Day. But there are times when it still does just raise its head above the surface, sometimes in one party and sometimes in the other.

"Well, you know your own job best. If you think it's worth while, I suppose it *is*. It can't do any harm, any way—if you're able to spare the time. But I should say, from my experience of cranks in general, that it's pretty little of any practical use that you'll be able to get out of the learned gentleman."

A knock at the door prevented any further discussion of the point at issue.

"Two ladies to see you, sir," said the Sergeant, holding out a couple of visiting-cards. The Chief Constable examined them. They were printed in florid fancy Roman lettering. The first read, "Mrs. Regina Konti," with the word, "Princess" in brackets beneath it. The second read, "Mrs. Miatta Konti," and the royal qualification was missing. Both bore the same address—in St. John Street.

"Who the deuce are they, and what do they want?"

"Both are as black as the ace of spades, sir. I've seen them about the town now and again the past few months. Came here last October to register as aliens. Couldn't quite understand their lingo. But they're both very excited and said something about 'protection.'"

"But why couldn't you chat with them yourself?" said Foster, somewhat annoyed. "Didn't you know I was busy with the Chief Inspector?"

"Yes, sir," said the Sergeant, "but that wasn't any good. They said they *must* see you, and looked so like crying that I thought I'd best humour them. One of them called you 'the big policeman past all,' and the other called you 'dem big, big Commissioner man.'"

Bramley grinned broadly.

"Don't mind me," said he. "I shouldn't like it to be said of me that I'd tried to prevent the Chief Constable of Oxford from protecting alien females in distress!"

"Ask them to come in," said Foster shortly to the Sergeant. "What are we in for *now*, I wonder?" said he to Bramley when the man had gone out to execute his order.

"It gets curiouser and curiouser," said the Chief Inspector in the words of *Alice in Wonderland*

The door opened again and Foster's visitors were introduced. The figure of the large plump negress who had been turned brusquely from the door of St. Antony's College on the opening night of the previous Michaelmas Term, had not waned during her few months' stay in the lodgings in St. John Street. She was an excellent testimonial to the flesh-producing qualities of good English food. She was colossal. A large white straw hat of the antique 'Merry Widow' shape concealed her woolly hair. The white ostrich plumes with which it was adorned would have done no small honour to the hat of the principal boy of a pantomime in the production of which "no expense had been spared." Her light blue silk dress, billowing like the waves of some caerulean sea over the curves of her voluminous bust dazzled the eyes of the two European policemen. Around her stout, black neck was clasped a row of gigantic pearls which had never known the Ocean bed nor claimed relationship with the lowly oyster. Long gloves of white kid encased her ample arms. From the pendulous lobes of her ears hung golden drops as large in size as Brazil nuts, and she carried a bright red silk sunshade. From the depths of a capacious purple leather vanity bag she produced a variegated silk handkerchief into which she discharged some noisy introductory sniffs, the obvious precursors of a flood of hysterical tears.

Her companion was a less startling and arresting figure—but rather attractive than the reverse. Short and slim, less thick of nose and lip than the average African woman, she wore the customary headkerchief of her country in dark blue silk. Her earrings were of silver filigree and unostentatious. A simple golden, heart-shaped locket hung from a thin gold chain around her slender neck. Her *buba,* a sleeveless blouse, ungathered at the waist, was of dark indigo blue, and a lappa or wrapper of a lighter shade of the same colour, with splashes of white, completed her costume. Both women wore smart European shoes and stockings.

Foster winked at Bramley.

"Please sit down," said he to the ladies. And the Chief Inspector politely pushed two chairs into position.

"And what can I do for you?" said the Chief Constable reassuringly.

"Massa! Massa!" began the adipose "Princess," in tones of the deepest distress. "We fear—we fear *too* much!" She could, in less harrowing moments, speak perfect, or almost perfect English. But, in her distraction, she reverted as her kind will when agitated, to the "pidgin" English of her forbears on "the Coast." "All dem bad, *bad* murders! We no able for sleep at night for fear dis wicked

man go come kill us too!" The handkerchief became the receptacle of floods of copious tears. "Me and my sister—we no savvy
dis country plenty. When persin go die like dis in we own country,
the Chief, he go send plenty plenty persin for guard us so we no
go die. But here—in Oxford—we no get persin for dat—no!" She
turned for corroboration to the younger woman.

"Sah! Sah!" exclaimed the second Mrs. Konti in shriller tones.
"What de missis say be true! All night—all *night* we de go walka
na room. We no able for sleep at *all!* Fear done catch us too
much!"

She joined her companion in a lachrymose duet, and the two
officers looked at each other in a helpless way. They contrived at
last to restore the damsels in distress to a reasonable measure
of equanimity.

"Look here, ladies," said Foster soothingly. "These things are
very terrible—very frightening of course."

"Ah, massa! Na *true* you de talk—na *true* dat," said the stouter
Mrs. Konti, beating her hands together as if in applause, and
nodding her beplumed head sagely.

"Lord a mussy! Lord a mussy!" chimed in the smaller, "na bad
bad ting dis—bad past *all!"*

"But," went on the police officer calmly, when the sniffs and
exclamations of his visitors permitted, "I think you ladies are disturbing yourselves a little unnecessarily. It's not ladies like you
that have been in danger. It's Professors and dons of the University. And I don't suppose there's any more danger, even for them.
And aren't your husbands doing anything to protect you?" He
glanced again at the cards. "I see you're both married."

A long explanation of polygamous principles followed, for the
Chief Constable was unaware that the ladies both looked to one
and the same man as their lawful lord and master. After a long
time, Foster and Bramley between them managed to elicit the
fact that the step the two women had taken in seeking an interview with the Chief Constable had been taken without the knowledge of Mr. Septimus Konti. He longed more than anything for
the proud moment when he should be able to write the magic

letters "B.A." after his name, and to be able to appear before the eyes of his wondering family, at home in the bush, decked in the dazzling white rabbitskin and the imposing black gown associated with the degree. And the Chief Constable gathered that the happy moment was not likely to be reached in the early future. Konti feared that if his father got to hear of the distress his wives were experiencing, far off in an alien land, and got into his head that his son, too, was running any risk to his own life, supplies would be cut off even sooner than had been threatened, and that all three would be compelled to return home to Africa before he had realised the great ambition of his life. In the end the Chief Constable promised that the men on the St. John Street beat should have special instructions to keep a vigilant eye on the house in which they lodged whenever he should pass it.

The African is almost as easily comforted as he is disturbed, and the two ebon ladies, arm in arm, and beaming with the broadest and happiest of smiles, left the Chief Constable's office together, crying;

"God bless you, massa! Thank you, thank you, massa, *too much,*" as they gained the passage which led into the street.

CHAPTER XIX

"The Course of True Love——"

THE interest excited by the attempt on the Master of St. Thomas's began to wane amongst the general public. And with it the discussion of the murders in Wellington Square and the Turl, which, however, continued to be regarded by most people as part of the same sequence of events. The less discriminating of the Sunday papers gave prominence to the usual crop of "confessions" by cranks and half-wits, impostors and others desirous of a little cheap publicity. The customary number of people remembered—long after the event—some peculiar action of some person or other on the nights preceding and following the crimes. Persons who were supposed to have some connection with the murders and the foiled attempt to murder Dr. Playford were, to the satisfaction of the individuals who made the statements to the Police, seen, at more or less the same time, in Oxford, Cambridge, London, Dover, Paris, Bombay, Yokohama and New York.

Bramley (who was definitely seconded to assist the Oxford Police in their investigations), was inclined at first to smile when some of these tales were communicated to him, in number daily larger after the third outrage. But, after a few weeks of wild goose-chasing, the humours to be got from the process began to wear a trifle thin, and mere reference to the crimes themselves, in hours when he was not officially on duty, was not received in a particularly friendly spirit.

The customary attacks on the police and their methods made their appearance in journals of varying grades and opinions. These effusions were, as usual, hardly ever enlightened by any gleams of constructive criticism. It was easy enough to throw mud, to cast aspersions. But one who troubled to go a little more deeply into the subject would have found it just a little difficult to say what exactly should be the starting-point of the enquiries in each of the three cases.

Professor Toogood had been one of the most popular men in Oxford. A brilliant and inspiring lecturer—a man whose lucid exposition of his subject had helped to turn many a doubtful Second in the Examination Schools into a certain First: a man of highly developed charitable instincts, ever ready to plunge his hand into his pocket, even at times when he could the least afford it, in the interest of some deserving case in the City in which he lived and which he loved. The private life of few men could have passed such a ruthless examination as could that of Professor Toogood without bringing to light some little incident or phase of which the subject was not entirely unashamed. Happily married to a devoted wife, a master of his subject, an ever-ready helper of the man who wished to draw upon his store of knowledge, never reluctant to loosen his purse-strings on behalf of any who could tell a moving story of distress and want, it was difficult to conceive a less likely victim of an assassin's hand.

And the murder had been a particularly brutal one. A few hours before the discovery by the policeman of his dead body in the garden in Wellington Square, the Professor, without apparently a care in the world, had been returning home in the happiest frame of mind from a sociable dinner with a friend of long standing. It cannot have been, from the evidence at the Inquest, more than a few minutes at most after his cheerful parting at the corner of Little Clarendon Street from Barbara and Reggie, when he had congratulated the young man on his engagement to the pretty girl, that the fatal blow had been struck. The scene, too, of the murder was unusual. Wellington Square is the last place in Oxford which one would conceive to be the haunt of bandits and assassins. Even in the City's high general level of respectability, the respectability of Wellington Square ranks high. The circumstances attending the crime itself made it no less remarkable. That Professor Toogood should come to be murdered at all was strange. That he should be murdered with exceptional brutality was well-nigh incredible. And the Doctor's evidence had shown that the brutal nature of the crime was more marked than usual in cases of intentional homicide. For Doctor Haywood had been quite certain that death supervened as the result of some violent shock to the brain as the effect of the wielding of some heavy, blunt instrument. If the murderer had achieved his savage end by this means, why was it necessary further to mutilate the skull by attempting, after death had ensued, to penetrate it with some sharper weapon? The only theory which seemed reasonably able to be put forward was that the tragedy was due to the blood lust of some homicidal maniac.

The second murder, that of the popular little Reader in French, M. Boissard, presented difficulties which were precisely similar. No one who heard them looked with anything but derision on the extravagant *cherchez la femme* theories which the egregious Barnes had constructed solely on the strength of M. Boissard's Parisian birth. The most searching enquiries into his antecedents had failed to yield the slightest grounds for such ridiculous suspicions. Few English Dissenting Ministers of the most strait-laced morality and Victorian austerity could have presented a cleaner bill of moral health than the cheerful and brilliant little Reader in French. Yet, for some mysterious reason, he too had incurred the hatred of some bloodthirsty, homicidal criminal and was done to death, in the open street, in the very heart of the City and University, only a few minutes after the breaking up of a convivial but supremely respectable gathering in the Senior Common Room of one of Oxford's most staid and sober Colleges. The brutality which had marked the assassination of M. Boissard was no less remarkable than that which had distinguished the murder of the Professor of Latin. Here again, after the dealing of the blow which had caused his victim's death, the murderer had not hesitated still further to mutilate his wretched, lifeless body.

In the case of the attack on the venerable Master of St. Thomas's in his own study there seemed little room for doubt that the unseen intruder had intended to compass the destruction of the man whom he had assailed in so violent and so cowardly a fashion. Doctor Playford and his niece both felt that the only thing which had prevented the assault from becoming an actual murder was the noise providentially made by the fall to the floor of the books which had been piled untidily and precariously on the top of the revolving bookstand beside him. The crash had been so loud that the attacker had feared the rousing of the Master's household, and his own discovery before his object was fully accomplished. What was his reason for wishing the scholar's death was another problem. That mystery was no less insoluble than in the cases of Professor Toogood and M. Boissard.

The only claim hitherto of these three men to the world's notice had been their acknowledged eminence in scholarship and learning. There are few men who can honestly claim that they have not an enemy in the world. But hostility and private enmities differ considerably in degree. And the three men who had, during these six months in Oxford, suffered violence at the hands of some unknown assassin went nearer to being able to boast the distinction than any one else in the City. And the claims of all three to universal popularity were exceedingly strong.

It was easy for Foster and his new colleague Bramley to understand the escape of the murderer in the cases of Professor Toogood and M. Boissard. Once the crimes had been successfully committed, as they had both had their scene in public places, and the facts had not been immediately discovered, the easy flight of the criminal was not difficult to conceive. The time and the place had, in either case, been carefully chosen, both for the obscurity afforded and for the small likelihood of any persons being about at the time. Once the murderer's object had been achieved, in the absence of any one who could later prove an incriminating witness, swift and unobtrusive escape was assured.

The position was rather different in the matter of the attack on the Master of St. Thomas's. The miscreant was known to have entered by the front door of the house about two hours before the assault. He had clearly run through the French window into the quadrangle to escape identification by Lord Ruislip and Miss Playford, who, he knew, had had at least a glimpse of him. The fact that the window of the dining-room had been certainly forced from the outside seemed to indicate that the Master's assailant had secreted himself in some corner of one of the three of the College's quadrangles until he was sure that the servants had gone to bed. He had then—the French window being locked for the night—effected an entrance without fear of observation, at the most vulnerable point available.

His escape from the College, after his happily frustrated attempt at murder, would not have been a particularly difficult matter. Bramley and Foster took a walk round the three quadrangles of St. Thomas's one morning.

"You see," said the London man to Foster, "in this quad. (as you call it), alone there are no less than six different staircases. And each staircase has three landings, and each landing has at least one set of rooms. Some have two, and some even more. There are cupboards, too, under the stairs—any amount of them."

"Yes," said the Chief Constable, "that's where the 'scouts' as they call the men-servants here, keep their brooms and pans and their master's kettles and saucepans and so on. As the College is practically empty in vacation there'd be little chance of a man being spotted if he hid in them—at night especially."

"Even some of the rooms themselves are unlocked I noticed. Our friend Mr. Sawyer, the Porter, tells me the 'scouts' aren't too careful about locking them up out of term, anyway. For larceny is not a particularly common offence in College at any time. Though I, personally should be a little more careful myself. But then, I'm a policeman!"

"They get pretty slack in these Colleges, I know. Even nowadays Oxford, as far as the University is concerned, is a bit out of date."

The business-like Foster was unable to prevent a suspicion of contempt from showing itself in his voice. And he had reason, too, for being a little censorious about the conservatism of academic Oxford. On the occasion on which he had had to co-operate with the University "police" he had been amazed at the mediæval inefficiency (as he termed it), of the Proctorial system. Yet a carefully-thought-out scheme which he had evolved and had once propounded to the Senior Proctor of the day had not been at all cordially received. His idea of employing a body of trained ex-professional policemen as University detectives—disguising themselves now as dons, now as undergraduates, now even as "scouts"—able to prove their authority when necessary by the production of an official badge—had struck horror into the mind of his hearer. In vain had he pleaded the futility of adhering to the antiquated plan by which a don, whose previous knowledge of police duties was absolutely nil, paraded the streets of Oxford wearing a gown, a mortar-board, and the white bands of a barrister, at odd times and in odd places on different nights, attended by two undrilled plain-clothes police (which was what the "bulldogs" really, were) seeking to catch one or two undergraduates enjoying illicit drinks in public bars. He argued that in the days when Oxford was a small country town, the University a mere handful of scholars within it, such a system might have admirably achieved its ends. It might have been well enough adapted to the little-frequented, narrow, ill-lighted lanes and purlieus of a mediæval town. But under modern conditions, in the broad, well-lighted, busy, traffic-crowded streets of a city with a large commercial and industrial population, and a University which had grown in dimensions beyond all expectations in the past, it was nothing less than ludicrous.

But this was not the time to let the Chief Constable ride his pet hobby.

"Well," said Bramley. "I can't see that we're doing much more than waste our time here. The porter can't give any help. He's quite positive that no one can have got out of the College, in the normal way, between midnight, when he was aroused by the commotion in the Master's lodgings, and half-past six in the morning, when he unlocked the gate to let in the first "scout" coming in for duty. From then onwards, he said, the door is open and people may come in without hindrance. For the buildings are open to anyone who likes to view them. There's just a notice warning them that they're not allowed to go into any private rooms on any stair. All the windows I've examined (and I've done them pretty thoroughly), whose doors were unlocked on the night of the attack, have heavy iron bars, and none of them show the smallest signs of having been tampered with."

"Of course," said Foster, as the pair walked back to the Police Station. "Sawyer—or whoever was taking his place when he didn't happen to be in the Lodge himself—would not bother to notice *every one* who passed in or out. It wouldn't be either necessary or possible in the ordinary run of things."

"Yet it's plain to me," replied Bramley, "as I see things at present, that our elusive friend hid himself somewhere in the College after his failure to do in the poor old Master. Then, at some time in the morning—probably when some other people were going out too; he made his escape unnoticed and quite naturally."

They had arrived back at the station and resumed their seats in the Chief Constable's office.

"And the probablity," said Foster, "is that the fellow's appearance was quite ordinary and attracted no notice at all. The way to appear especially inconspicuous in an Oxford college would be to appear to be a member of the University—whether one actually was one or not."

"What are you driving at?" said Bramley, interested. For Foster showed more animation as he spoke the last words then he had shown for some time.

"I mean," said he, meaningly, "that I begin to see some sort of niche in which to fit that mysterious bit of black gown."

Barbara was a good deal shaken by the incident, of the attack on her uncle. She had not, hitherto, seriously felt any of the fears on the Master's behalf that Reggie had continually expressed in the later letters which she had received from him. But now the feeling that some uncanny, inexplicable menace threatened a class which had up to now enjoyed as great an immunity from crimes of violence as any that any one could conceive, began to take hold of her.

What possible motive *could* there be for a murderous attack on the Master of St. Thomas's College, who was notable, even amongst a class generally easy going and without serious enemies, for his extreme benevolence and kindness? Uprightness of character and a lovable nature had been no less prominent qualities of Professor Toogood and of M. Boissard. And yet, within the short space of six months, those three distinguished men had met with violence at the hands of some mysterious, vindictive criminal. It was all absolutely unfathomable. And the fact that Barbara shared her mystification and fears with the rest of the country's thinking population, did not in any way assist to calm her troubled mind. It was all so terrible.

She had decided, as her uncle refused to leave Oxford, even for a few days, until he had completed an erudite chapter on which he was now at work, that she would stay on with him. She felt, whether he would or no, that he might still be the subject of some hidden, unknown danger, and she preferred to be near him, and to assist in watching over his safety.

Nearly a month had passed since the two police officers had held their enquiry. And she heard that Bramley had returned to London. Reggie's letters, as the length of his separation from her increased, grew longer and more affectionate. And they were full of interesting accounts of his new life in a new country. It seemed to her now clear that she had worried herself unduly about the suspected flirtation with the woman on the boat. And, anyway, Lord Ruislip, by his foolish impetuosity and unexpected warmth had put himself out of court as a suitable subject for a wild flirtation with ulterior ends—impersonal as far as she was herself concerned. As the pangs caused by her jealousy diminished, so did those caused by her fears for her uncle increase.

She was sitting out one lovely evening towards the end of a hot July thinking of the happy days she would have with Reggie when he came back, after his eighteen months abroad, to marry her. Her aunt had been kindly sending her, every week, copies of a paper dealing with "The Coast" called *West Africa*. It would serve, Lady Shortways had said, to remind her of Reggie. The latest issue had arrived by the post that afternoon, and she had promised herself the pleasure of reading it out here, this quiet evening, in the garden after dinner whilst the Master got on with the last pages of his chapter.

She opened it, and turned first of all, as she always did, to the three or four pages of pictures in the middle. There was one snapshot described as, *"Passengers about to disembark from the Appam at Edwardsville."*

As she looked more closely her face went white, and her heart thumped violently. For, in the foreground—for everyone to see—stood the familiar figure of Reggie Crofts, quite obviously bending over as if to kiss a woman who stood looking up into his face above her. And Barbara instinctively knew that the woman's name was Mrs. Driver.

CHAPTER XX

The Port Meadow Crime

THE Long Vacation—it is *very* long—drew at last towards its end. Once more the station platforms at Oxford looked more like carriers' warehouses than anything else in the world. One sought one's train by threading a way through stacks and piles of undergraduates' luggage sent in advance. The plain wooden box or worn canvas trunk of the "Tosher" (or non-collegiate student), jostled, democratically, the brand-new cow-hide portmanteaux of new recruits from Eton, Winchester and Harrow for Magdalen and "The House."

Scores of raggedly-dressed, unkempt men came out of their four months' æstivation, clamouring in raucous and husky voices for the privilege of carting, at exorbitant rates, the "freshers'" boxes from station to college. Taxis, four-wheelers, hansoms were plying once again their busy trade between the railway and the "digs" and colleges of the University.

The freshmen of this term had other names and different faces. Otherwise there was but little real difference from the night when Mr. Septimus Konti had driven up in the ancient horsed cab to the gates of St. Antony's accompanied by his two wives, to be informed by the porter that married undergraduates who were allotted rooms in College, must conform to the way of life of the celibate. Mr. Konti was now a second year man. He had decided, with the permission of the Dean of St. Antony's to go permanently out of college for the remainder of his University career, and to dwell, for the future, with his two ladies in their lodgings in St. John Street. For though Regina and Miatta had been somewhat comforted by the promise of the Chief Constable, they had urged upon their mutual spouse so strongly their need of his extra protection, that he had perforce at last given way. The persuasive powers of the European wife are by no means inconsiderable. But beside the stridently expressed urgings of her African sister they pale into the merest insignificance. The negro student had spent the whole of the vacation in Oxford, making desperate efforts to acquire sufficient knowledge of his subjects to make certain of a pass in Moderations in the coming December examination. He had proved a veritable little gold mine to his private tutor, the worthy Mr. Day of Norham Gardens, who had gladly sacrificed his usual short summer holiday in exchange for the fees which would ensure at last for his wife and himself a taste of the Winter Sports in Switzerland next season.

Septimus himself was much concerned. For it was quite certain from the tone of his father's letters, that unless he now successfully negotiated the first hurdle on the course towards a Pass Degree, he would be obliged to return home to Africa at the end of the term. His father's insistence had been augmented by his fears for the personal safety of his son and his wives. And Septimus knew well that the only way of staving off the final catastrophe was to get the examination safely behind him. It was the only sort of practical argument which would serve to allay the old Chief's anxiety for his son's well-being and console him, too, for the inroads made upon his own Privy Purse. For, though most of the income which he allotted to the support of his son at Oxford was derived from illegal and oppressive exactions from his people, supplementary to and exceeding the amount of tax which the Government allowed him to collect: and though the negro is a patient, long-suffering creature, there is a breaking-point to his tolerance, and serious and well-founded complaints against the Chief's oppression would lead to an enquiry and his probable deposition, if the matter were taken up with the energy which Mr. Commissioner Prescott was wont to display in such matters.

Mr. Barnes had entered with zest upon his Proctorial duties, and he spent a good deal of time in drafting proposed reforms in the University Police system—reforms of so sweeping a nature that there was not the faintest prospect of their even being seriously discussed by the members of the Ancient House of Congregation. More than three months had passed since the attack on the Master of St. Thomas's, and the University authorities and the Chief Constable had every reason to suppose that an end had come to the tale of mystery and horror which had begun with the crime of the preceding December in the garden in Wellington Square. The term got well under weigh before anyone had any reason to doubt the wisdom of those who held this opinion.

.   .   .   .   .

Mr. Horace Mortimer was not one of life's outstanding successes. But as a "coach" for the Pass Schools generally, and for isolated subjects in the Honour Schools, he had made a certain small reputation for himself. He had been an exhibitioner of one of the smaller and less distinguished Colleges, and had, by dint of hard work and the possession of a brain which was tenacious of small and apparently unimportant details, succeeded in obtaining a Third Class in Honour Moderations, and a similar Class in "Greats." His father, an obscure clergyman somewhere in the Midlands, had left his son, at his death soon after Horace had taken his degree, a small competence which brought him in a hundred and fifty pounds in a good year, and one hundred in a bad. Horace was a confirmed bachelor, and was greatly attracted by the easy, comfortable, care-free life of the Oxford student. He decided that he would remain on in his old rooms in Pembroke Street, and build up a practice as an outside coach. For with the classes which had secured him his degree he realised that an official fellowship at one of the colleges of the University was beyond his hopes. But he had been popular with his fellow undergraduates, and pupils were not long in coming his way when he affixed a brass plate to his door and inserted a comprehensive and dignified advertisement in the columns of the *University Gazette.*

As the years had passed, the circle of his pupils had grown, and, when he was well on in middle life, he had saved sufficient to ensure at least a comfortable and leisured old age.

The royalties, too, on some of his works—"cram" books and "cribs" on one or other of the subjects most often studied by students in the schools, and published in little, undistinguished, paper-covered volumes by a local printer, yielded a revenue which was not to be despised. An undergraduate who fully mastered— (it could be done in a week)—the contents of the pages of his little pilot to "Divvers"—*The Student's Guide to Success in the First Public Examination in Holy Scripture"*—could face his questioners across the baize-covered table at the *viva* with no qualms that his guinea entrance fee would be wasted. No less popular proved his potted *Gaius* for the Preliminary Examination in Law. And there were those who had been heard to say that so sound was his *Logic for the Pass Schools Mastered in a Fortnight,* that they would sooner take their oath on it than upon the Bible.

Mr. Mortimer's life may not have been eventful. It was certainly comfortable and free from care. And as the coach was not an ambitious man it was difficult to conceive a way of existence in which he could have been happier.

He had attained the dignity of becoming a "character" at the Union, where one of the big arm-chairs in the smoking-room was sacred to him from three to six in the afternoon on Mondays, Wednesdays and Fridays, in term. So firmly had he established his right to this seat at the accustomed hours that few who knew his habits ever thought it worth their while to contest it. A "fresher" who dared to occupy it during the times when tradition claimed it for Mr. Mortimer would soon repent him of his hardihood. For the old coach's voice was high-pitched and querulous, and the rule of "silence" had no terrors for him when his feelings were harassed and his customs trampled underfoot. A blush—a stammered apology from the youth, and Mortimer would soon be once more firmly entrenched in his stronghold, with five of the evening papers he had snatched from the rack acting as a supplementary cushion beneath him, whilst he hastily absorbed the contents of the sixth.

On Tuesdays, Thursdays and Saturdays, from four till six o'clock, he went for a walk, whatever the time of year, whatever the weather. His route varied—his custom never. He left his rooms in Pembroke Street punctually at four o'clock and always, whether he eventually turned to left or right, looked up for a few seconds in rapt admiration of Wren's wonderful old Tom Tower which dominates St. Aldate's at this point. To one who saw him for the first time he presented a queer, rather ridiculous figure. He wore a bowler hat—green rather than black in hue by reason of the flight of years. Its brim was broad and dusty. His spectacles were of steel, rusted round the lenses. His face was not easy to discover amidst the mass of tangled greying beard and moustache which surrounded it. Around his neck was a woollen scarf, untidily twisted, which had once been nearly white. A short black coat, frayed at the elbows, a pair of very voluminous and amorphous long plus fours of a greyish nondescript tint, stockings of the same elusive colour, and a pair of large heavy old-fashioned black marching boots, much patched and mended, completed his attire.

It was a Tuesday afternoon towards the end of November. Mr. Mortimer left his "digs" punctually to the minute. As he gazed up at Tom Tower in accordance with his usual habit, he stuffed a large, cracked, blackened briar pipe untidily with thick coarse shag tobacco. He lighted it and puffed at it with evident enjoyment as the thick blue pungent fumes billowed out into the air about him, gripped his thick crooked stick, and set off up St. Aldate's at a pace brisker than seemed harmonious with his bulky, clumsy proportions. Straight up the "Corn" he went, and through St. Giles', not turning to right or left until he reached St. John's Road, where it branches off the Woodstock Road on its way towards the reaches of the upper river. It was clear that the afternoon's objective was Godstow, or away across the fields towards Botley.

.   .   .   .   .

It is very comforting, after a long country walk in the keen winter air, up along the towpath towards Bablockhythe, to get into the cosy parlour of the old "Trout" Inn at Godstow, which looks out across the river towards the farm-buildings which once contained the bower of that Fair Rosamond who, however prosaic and sordid her actual career, has come down as a romantic, almost ethereal figure in the history of England. But though they were both reading for the History Schools, it was not towards Fair Rosamond and her unhappy tale that the thoughts of Peter Naylor of Balliol and John Cary of Hertford turned this winter evening.

"I vote we have half a dozen hot buttered crumpets," said Naylor, as he sat down gratefully in an ancient wooden chair.

"Not forgetting, I hope, an equal quantity of the good old hot anchovy toast, old thing," said his companion, rubbing his hands before the cheerful blaze which was roaring up the chimney before him.

They were both typical undergraduates in their second year.

"And *after* the toast and crumpets I think we might manage to find a use for a few cakes and pastries. We're not in training now," said Naylor, as he lighted his pipe.

This proposal being carried *nem. con.*, the meal was ordered, and the tea and the food tasted even better than it really was after the long, chilly tramp along the riverside. So welcome were the meal and the rest in the comfortable old room of the ancient inn that the two hardly noticed the passage of time as they ate, smoked and chatted contentedly on.

"By Jove!" said Cary suddenly, as he glanced at his watch and got up, stretching his legs, "Do you know what the time is? After half-past five, and I've got to go to old Huggins at six to have my wonderful discourse on 'Stubbs' Charters' torn into little pieces."

"It'll be as dark as pitch along the river now," said Cary. "We'd better get a move on,"

The couple settled their account and regretfully left the old inn together. The warmth which they had accumulated served them in good stead for their walk back to Oxford along the muddy towpath. An icy cold wind had sprung up during the afternoon, and with its keen blast in their faces, and the slippery, squashy ground beneath their feet, Cary and Naylor were quite anxious to get back home. Even listening to a tutor's leaden-footed and pedantic criticism of one's highest thoughts on Stubbs and his "Charters," before a blazing fire in a well-warmed room in Balliol, seemed a trifle more desirable than trudging along the clammy slimy towpath of the upper river in the November cold and murk.

"Supposing a fellow were alone one night and slipped down one of these beastly holes into the river and got drowned"—Naylor had only just saved himself, with the aid of his friend's arm, from stumbling into the swollen river down one of the gaps which had been caused in the crumbling earth which formed the bank by the water's erosion, and had not been repaired for years.

"Yes," returned his friend, "suppose he did. There'd be a new face in heaven—or somewhere else—next morning, and it might be the very devil of a time before they found his corpse."

"Talking of death," said Naylor, "I don't suppose it's half as bad as lots of people would like to make out. It doesn't seem to me that there can be so much in it after all. If there's a future life, well and good. If not, it's just like some long dreamless sleep."

"That," said Cary, "is *not* an original thought. You remember that old blighter Socrates in the *Apology,* before he committed the suicide which was his execution?"

"Yes," said Naylor. "As a matter of fact I was thinking of that. Asked his pals to cast their minds back to the nights they'd looked back on as having been the pleasantest they could remember. They weren't the ones on which they'd had dreams—good or bad. They were the ones on which they'd slept so peacefully and soundly that they hadn't had any dreams at all."

"Well," said Cary, "I daresay it's like that. Anyway—*I'm* not afraid of death—for myself or in anyone else. What must be *must.*"

"Aren't we having a cheery little chat?" laughed Naylor. He was post-war. Neither he nor his friend had had any experience yet of death at close quarters. But they both felt very wise and supremely philosophical as young men will. They began to whistle one of the latest dance tunes.

As they came out of the willow-fringed walk which leads from the old boat-hirers' barges to the railway bridge at the end of St. John's Road, Naylor stopped for a second or two as he stepped on to the road in front of the gate leading into Port Meadow and the allotments.

"Hear anything?" he said, quietly.

Cary stopped dead too. Naylor was looking in the direction of the gate. The young men stood silent—listening. Presently there came to their ears a low, faint, moaning sound as of a man in pain. It was quite dark, and neither Cary nor Naylor had an electric torch nor any other efficient means of illumination.

They approached the long, low gate, which was principally intended to keep the cows which grazed on the meadow from straying towards the town. They pushed it open as quietly as possible, and found themselves standing on the soft, spongy turf. Having got inside the field, they paused and waited again. In the silence all they could hear were the noises of the cattle in the meadow moving uneasily, heavily, before lying down for the night. From across the small brook between the upper river and the canal came the sounds of shunting in the Great Western station. A train went screaming past them on its journey to the North under the bridge for which they had been making when Naylor had been first attracted by the sound of moaning. But not again did they catch the low despairing groan for which they were listening.

"We'd better have a look round," said Naylor. His voice trembled a little. Perhaps it was due to the cold. The evening was certainly very damp and chilly, and the wind wailed mournfully in the willows which bordered the path to the river.

"Here's a match," said his companion, striking one and handing it across.

"Come on. Let's see if there's anyone here."

The pair went towards the spot whence the noise had seemed to come. By the flickering light of the match they could see in the corner where the railings joined with the small brook which, after its junction with them marked the confines of the meadow, a dark, bulky object on the ground. It looked like the body of a man. The two undergraduates paused simultaneously. Instinctively they felt that they might be in the presence of death. Despite their easy, lightly spoken words of a few minutes before, each felt a shudder of an unpleasant kind run down the spine.

"Do you think he's——?" it was Naylor who began; Cary finished his sentence for him.

"—dead? I don't know. He wasn't just now, if that was his moaning you heard."

By the light of the fresh match which he had struck each could see the face of the other—white and tense. Their voices had become a little husky. The thought came to them both at the same time.

"I wonder——" said Naylor, shakily, "if we've found another of these Oxford——?"

"—murders?" finished Cary. "That's just what I was thinking."

Keeping closely side by side the two now thoroughly scared young men went nearer to the heap which lay before them on the sodden turf in the corner of the meadow. Still no sound came from the inert mass—not a movement.

It *was* a man—lying face downwards, prone upon the grass. His hat—a bowler—lay brim upwards, about a couple of feet from the body. Cautiously, as if in fear of something, Cary and Naylor, alternately lighting matches, felt the body, and shivered. It was still warm, but there was no movement of any sort. Naylor raised the head, and by the light of the match his friend was holding, managed to get a glimpse of the features. With a cry he let it fall again and stood upright, shuddering.

"My God, Cary," he cried. "He's dead—no doubt of that. I don't know his name—but I've seen him often before. It's that old fellow who's always sitting on the papers in the Union!"

"Mortimer, you mean! Good Lord!"

The last match spluttered out in the rain which had begun to fall, and the young men were left alone in the dark in the meadow with the corpse of the victim of yet another Oxford tragedy.

CHAPTER XXI

Panic!

BARBARA PLAYFORD, after several letters which passed between Reggie and herself since she had seen the disquieting snapshot of him and the woman passenger in the *Appam* in *West Africa,* had been more or less convinced by her lover that things were really as they should be, and not as the photograph had led her to suspect. She too had met people like Kurwen, the lounge lizard, and was quite prepared to believe that it was he who had maliciously sent in the snapshot, which actually portrayed quite an innocent incident in the hope that it might make things unpleasant for the man who had cut short his own little flirtation on board the steamer. The angle at which he had cleverly poised his camera had made it possible for him to suggest the giving of a kiss which (and Barbara now believed Reggie's explanation), had never actually passed between the two. But the girl's fears at home for her uncle's safety had been revived by the news of the fresh tragedy which had been reported in Port Meadow.

Oxford was now thoroughly aroused, and all kinds of developments were being rumoured. All College porters, she knew, had been given the strictest injunctions to be on the alert, and to be very chary of admitting within the gates any persons of whose credentials they were not entirely sure. The prevailing suspicion that it might even be some of the members of the University itself who were at the back of all these mysterious and tragic happenings made the work of the porters and their satellites the harder.

It was understood that the Ancient House of Congregation was debating general measures in the matter. And Bramley, after the discovery of the body of the luckless Horace Mortimer in Port Meadow had returned to Oxford, accompanied by two more detectives from Scotland Yard, to co-operate with the Chief Constable of the City Police.

Barbara, who was now in her fourth year of residence at the University, no longer lived in Somerville, but stayed permanently with her uncle at the Master's Lodgings at St. Thomas's College.

Mortimer's body had been discovered by Naylor and Cary on a Tuesday evening. The inquest was to have been held on the following Thursday. Barbara, on the Friday morning, was feeling much too worked up and excited to go to a lecture which she should normally have attended, until she had discovered all that there was at this stage to be known of the mysterious occurrence. She felt greatly relieved to think that, in her uncle's case, the assassin had been interrupted before he had had time to complete his deadly work. And she, like most of the people of Oxford, believed firmly that if the Police were successful in tracing the perpetrator of the latest outrage, the murderer of Professor Toogood and M. Boissard, and the assailant of the Master of St. Thomas's would stand at the same time revealed. She was very anxious to hear what had transpired at the inquest the day before. She knew at least that it had been held this time by the City Coroner. For, though Horace Mortimer had once been a member of the University, it was many years since he had removed his name from the books of his College. He ranked, therefore, for the purposes of this jurisdiction, as a citizen of Oxford, and not as a member of the University.

She could not keep her mind concentrated upon the essay she was supposed to be writing. The Master was at some conference with Heads of Houses in the Hall of Balliol College, and she had more than a mere suspicion that the business of the meeting was to discuss various proposed means of dealing with the situation, which had at last been brought about by the Oxford murders. Indeed little else was the subject of conversation throughout the City.

At tea-parties in North Oxford undergraduates shouted news of the latest developments in the case, down enormous ear-trumpets held out by elderly ladies. The subject for debate at next Thursday evening's meeting of the Union Society was, "*That this House is of the opinion that the measures taken in the past and at the present for the protection of the lives of senior members of this University, are totally inadequate and a reflection upon the farsightedness of those in authority.*"

A Somerville friend of Barbara's had told her a story which well exemplified the feeling of terror and uncertainty which walked abroad. A lady of mature years, the wife of a well-known don, had been found the evening before at the corner of Holywell and Parks Road, lying in the gutter before the *King's Arms* hotel. The constable who had made the discovery, to whom the identity and the impeccable character of the lady in question were unknown, had formed conclusions which were a little hasty, but not unreasonable, considering the time of night—just about the closing hour fixed for licensed houses, and the proximity of means for obtaining alcoholic refreshment. The man had, with the assistance of a friendly passer-by, got the unfortunate lady as far as the charge-room of the Police Station before she recovered her powers of speech. It then became abundantly clear that this was no common case of "drunk and disorderly." The lady, fortunately for her feelings, did not realise the nature of the mistake which had been made. The glass of water which had been offered her as an alleviation of her supposed condition had revived her, and she told her story.

The Sergeant in charge was aghast when he became aware of the identity of the supposed victim of inebriety. He listened with growing interest to the story which she—between her gasps after her recovery from what was obviously now a fainting fit brought on by fright—poured excitedly from her lips.

She was an amateur violinist—a prominent member of an orchestral society, which met weekly in an endeavour to put new life into the dead works of a number of highly-respectable defunct composers of foreign extraction, whose compositions the general public showed a deplorable lack of anxiety to hear. The practice had been rather protracted, and it was after half-past ten when she had finally got her instrument packed and left the old Music Room in Holywell. When she got to the corner of Holywell and Parks Road, down which she had to go on her way home, she happened to glance behind her. The night was a little misty. To her horror she realised that she was being followed by a tall figure—human in general shape—but of more than human proportions. It had a long thin neck and a most peculiarly shaped head. She tried to cry out, but had felt a choking sensation at the throat. Having cast another awestruck glance in the direction of the menacing apparition, only to note that it had disappeared as quickly as it had come into view, she said she must have gone off into a dead faint, and slipped into the position in which the constable had found her.

She remembered no more until she came to her senses in the charge room at the Police Station. A very moving tale. She was convinced that she had seen the Oxford murderer, and that she had been herself marked out by him as his next victim. She was certain that she owed her escape from a terrible death solely to the fact that Police-Constable Dashwood had been on duty near the scene of the projected outrage, and that, had he not appeared through the fog in the nick of time, her own name would have been added to the sorry roll of victims of the mysterious assassin, whose misdeeds were now the talk of England, the Continent, and the United States of America.

Enquiries had later showed that a more prosaic, if less thrilling explanation of the true facts was possible. One of the members of the orchestra was the Rev. Augustus Applegarth, a short, slight, myopic young curate of a church down Abingdon way, who was an enthusiastic, if somewhat erratic, performer on the double bass. As few amateurs play this useful, if somewhat unexciting, instrument, the keen little musician had won himself a place in the select society, and was determined to stick to his hard-won position for all he was worth. He had left the Music Room only a few minutes after the violinist, his gigantic fiddle slung across his shoulders, its gaunt, narrow head reared high above his own. There was little doubt that it was the meek little curate and his huge bass viol which, compounded together in the misty evening air, had resolved themselves, for the nervous lady, into the dread presentment of the mysterious uncaught murderer who was holding the city in thrall.

Had the lady been able to shriek, as she had wished to do, the gallant and chivalrous Mr. Applegarth would no doubt have divested himself of his grisly looking burden, and reassuringly succoured frail womanhood in distress.

But her dumbness had prevented this. And the mild little man had branched off homewards towards "the High," humming, out of tune and time, the bass part of some long-forgotten oratorio, blissfully ignorant of the terrible commotion for which he had been responsible.

At about eleven o'clock Barbara, who was working, or trying to work, at her uncle's desk in his study overlooking the "Broad," heard the cries of the old hawker who, wheeling a barrow made of a set of old pram wheels surmounted by a sugar box, was selling the latest edition of the *Oxford Times*. It was the moment for which she had been waiting all the long morning. Dropping her pen she rushed down and out into the street, and ran back into the house with a copy of the local paper. It did not take her long to find the pages for which she was looking. There were the big headlines in "scare" type:

THE PORT MEADOW CRIME.

INQUEST ON THE BODY OF MR. HORACE MORTIMER.

VERDICT OF "MURDER BY SOME PERSON OR PERSONS UNKNOWN."

CORONER'S STRONG COMMENTS.

Throwing herself back into her uncle's armchair—the very one in which he had himself gone so near to losing his own life at the hands of the untraced murderer, she eagerly read the news of the latest tragedy which had roused the quiet old University City to such a pitch of excitement and alarm.

Evidence had been given by the undergraduates, Naylor and Cary, who had found the body; by the deceased's own doctor; by the Police Surgeon, who had performed the post-mortem examination; and by Mortimer's landlady, Mrs. Cowley, who had given formal evidence of identification.

The Coroner's summing-up was given as follows:

"Gentlemen of the jury. You have heard the evidence in this case. But before I ask you to retire to consider your verdict, I will shortly recapitulate the facts upon which you will have to base your conclusions. You have heard Mrs. Cowley say that she had known the deceased for upwards of thirty years. She was a school-girl when he first came, as an undergraduate, to lodge in her mother's house. And she became herself his landlady on her mother's death. You have heard her tell you that Mr. Mortimer did not appear to have any financial worries: that his account was regularly and punctually paid as soon as it was presented. The deceased used to coach undergraduates studying for University examinations. The only persons who ever called upon him in his rooms were pupils whom he was preparing for the Schools. And his pupils were all of the male sex. (The reporter noted that a titter in court, which was sternly repressed, arose at this remark. The late lamented had never been suspected of being a Don Juan in disguise. Or else his disguise was so well conceived as to avert any such suspicion.) Mr. Mortimer's own doctor spoke as to the good health which his patient always enjoyed. He had told the deceased, on one occasion—the last—some five years back, when Mr. Mortimer had sought his assistance in the reducing of a slight swelling or stye on his left eye-lid—that if all his patients were as seldom ill as the coach he would have had to apply long ago for parish relief. Mr. Cary and Mr. Naylor have told us of the circumstances in which they found the unhappy tutor lying dead in a corner of Port Meadow. Now Mr. Cary, leaving Mr. Naylor in charge, went to summon the first policeman he met in Walton Street. The Police Surgeon who examined the body has told you that few men of Mr. Mortimer's age were as physically fit as the deceased must have been. The heart and all the vital organs were in splendid condition. The doctor is definitely of opinion that death ensued as the result of a violent blow upon the head from some blunt heavy weapon. The doctor drew your attention, also, to a small incised wound in the middle of the forehead, made, apparently before death, and with a small pointed instrument. I think that there can be no doubt that this unfortunate gentleman, against whom enquiries show that no person living in this city or elsewhere, had any grudge, so far as the Police are able to ascertain, came by his death as the result of a particularly foul and brutal murder, as he was returning from an evening stroll along the banks of the Upper River."

The paper went on to record that the jury, without leaving the court, returned the verdict indicated in the headline.

Barbara, her nerves strung to the highest degree of tension which they were able to support, flung the paper from her, and, burying her face in her hands, burst into a flood of tears.

.   .   .   .   .

It was the Saturday following the murder of Mr. Mortimer. Chief Inspector Bramley, the Chief Constable of Oxford, two London detectives, and Mr. Barnes the Senior Proctor, Lecturer in Criminal Law and Fellow of St. Antony's College, were just rising from their chairs before the cosy fire in the Police office.

"It is difficult, sir," said Bramley, "to say what is the best line to follow in a set of cases like these, and I must frankly admit that I can't see *where* I am to begin. I accept, with gratitude, the compliments which you have paid the Force. And I can honestly say that, far-fetched as—I beg your pardon—I may at first have thought it, I begin to think that the plan which you have thought out is as good a one, in the peculiar circumstances, as could be devised. Foster—you've heard Mr. Barnes's plan. I'm going to do my best to give it a fair trial. I can't say more than that."

The Police officer shook hands with the plump little don, who beamed happily as he went down the steps into the street, having been taken, for the first time in his life, and by professional policemen too, as a practical detective. Perhaps some of his criticisms of the Force in the past had been just a little unfair.

CHAPTER XXII

An Arrest

THE days after the inquest upon the body of Mr. Horace Mortimer were big with excitement for Oxford. The City was as crowded as it could possibly be. For not only was Term "up," but the motor works were running at high pressure, executing orders obtained at the Olympia Show. The under-graduate journals, commonly facetious even in times of great national crisis, sounded a graver note than usual. For the personalities of the three victims of the murderer and the Master of St. Thomas's, who had so nearly been added to the tragic list, were all extremely popular in the University world. These papers took up, indeed, the cudgels in defence of the City Police and the Proctors against the destructive criticisms too often levelled at their heads in the columns of the big London dailies. To those who wrote for the bigger newspapers of the Metropolis the names of Professor Toogood, of M. Boissard and of Doctor Playford were but the labels of men prominent in the academic world. Of Mr. Horace Mortimer they had never heard at all before his sensational murder had brought his name into the limelight of popular notoriety.

To the young men—public schoolboys of not so many months back—who contributed to such papers as the *Isis*—each of the men, in his way, had been an honoured and respected figure. And for all of them not a few had feelings which were deeper and more enduring than those of mere respect. The world outside Oxford knows but little of the active parts which many of the

University's most noted members play in the affairs of the City in which they live. Some are its aldermen and its councillors. Some, like Professor Toogood, take the keenest interest in social welfare of the people of the town. M. Boissard had given lectures, when the work by which he earned his living was over, to those who could afford little, free, or for fees so small as to be merely nominal. His evening classes had been attended by youths and girls drawn from the industrial and commercial classes of the City. Mr. Mortimer, as well as being a private tutor to undergraduates up against fate in the persons of the Masters of the Schools, was a citizen and ratepayer, and had played an energetic, if not spectacular part in municipal politics. Pertinently, and with no uncertain voice, the scribes of the University papers, the leader writers of the *Oxford Times* and *Mail* had challenged their confrères of the larger outside journalistic world to suggest, out of their wider experience, some definite lines on which to advise the Police and the Proctors to tackle the strenuous task which circumstances had set them. To them each case of murder, and the occasion of the dastardly attempt to assassinate the Master of one of Oxford's most famous Colleges, was rather a personal matter than a mere opportunity of making partisan, anti-Polite capital. They knew, and realised far better than could, men sitting in their armchairs in Fleet Street, the difficulties of the tasks which confronted those charged with the prevention and detection of crime in the City and University.

"*It is easy enough,*" said the leader writer in the Oxford Times, "*to criticise the Police and the Proctors for their apparent inaction in dealing with the ghastly series of tragedies which have, during the past twelve months, stirred so deeply the feelings of the residents of the City and the University. It is more difficult to suggest, to those to whom we look for the safeguarding as much of our lives as of our property, a line of pursuit which is likely to be definitely fruitful in its results. We should like to state here, and without any fear of impeding the course of Law and Justice, that we are well aware that the Chief Constable of our City Police and the Senior Proctor of the University have never, from the time of the unfortunate tragedy which occurred last year in Wellington Square down to this last, and no less foul crime, which has affixed a melancholy and terrible reputation to the quiet pastures of the ancient Meadow which adjoins the confines of our ancient City, relaxed for one moment their endeavours to light upon a clue which will lead them to the final unmasking of the dastardly and cowardly criminal who is yet unpunished in our midst. It is no breach of confidence for us to say that conferences betweeen the respective heads of the Police of the City and of the University are not only of daily occurrence, but of long duration. Let us take off our hats to those who, in the defence of the citizens of this ancient City, are putting the best of their brains, the very last ounces of their energy, into the grim and difficult business which lies before them. Even as we go to press we are rejoiced to be able to tell our readers that, as the result of a particularly clever and ingenious scheme evolved by him who, for the time being, controls the working of the Proctorial machine, it is confidently expected that, not later than the middle of next week, and possibly before, an arrest will be made which will bring to the bar of Justice the mysterious assassin who has held us too long in his thrall. In the words of the greatest Latin orator of his age we say, 'Quousque tandem . . .?'"*

No less optimistic was the tone of the Editor of the *Isis:*

". . . The man in the street has got the idea fixed in his head that when a crime has been committed, once a fingerprint has been discovered, the detection of the criminal is a matter of days— of hours even. It became public property, not very long after the death of Professor Toogood last December, that a fingerprint had been discovered on some part of the victim's clothing, easily identifiable if a counterpart could be produced elsewhere. So far so good. 'οἱ πόλλοι' at once assumed that detection could not much longer be delayed. But the second—the more important link in the chain, is so far missing. It is at length rumoured that the progress of the chase has been speeded up by certain events which have recently taken place. We understand—it will be, by the time these lines appear in print, a 'secret de Polichinelle'—

that the much talked-of fingerprint system is at last to play a re-
ally effective part in the unravelling of the mystery. And the initia-
tive in the matter, we hear with satisfaction, comes from our Se-
nior Proctor. We—even the occupant of the editorial chair—have
at times had our differences with this Officer and his minions.
The time has come when we may, openly, and in all good faith,
say, 'Let the hatchet be buried.' The Proctors at this time have in
hand weightier matters than the combing out of prohibited cock-
tail bars, the fining of the undergraduate who walks abroad
'noctu—' and 'sine vestitu scholastico.' The hour is not, we firmly
believe, far off when citizens of Oxford and members of the Uni-
versity together may cry aloud, 'Vivant Procuratores!'"

One only of the big London dailies was inclined to be sympathetic towards Proctors and Police in their search for the
perpetrators of the series of revolting crimes which had, for the
time being, completely changed the focus of Oxford's claim to
notice in the eyes of England and the world.

"*We have heard,*" said this staid and rather pompous journal,
"*a great deal of censorious criticism levelled at the heads of the*
two bodies entrusted with the safeguarding of the two great sec-
tions of Oxford's population—we refer to the Police on the one
hand, to the Proctors of the University on the other. A little mature
reflection on the part of those who have sought to embarrass two
conscientious and hardworking organisations, in their unceasing
efforts to do their duty towards those on whose behalf their exer-
tions have been so unremittingly employed, would have, we feel
convinced, assured them that they were doing a great injustice.
Amongst the scores of proposed solutions of the mysterious and
untoward happenings of the past few months which have, some
in all seriousness, some in a spirit of ill-timed jest, poured in upon
both Police and Proctors, we can say, with full knowledge of the
facts of which we speak, that not one, even of the most promising
(and all have been considered and followed up with the best
resources and the greatest energy of which both parties are
possessed), has yielded the faintest shadow of a practical clue.
The nearest parallel which can be drawn to the present unhappy

series of crimes is the sequence of murders, many years ago, attributed to an untraced criminal to whom the fanciful and eerie name of 'Jack the Ripper' was applied. The whole forces of the Metropolitan Police, as then constituted, working ceaselessly and tirelessly over a period of many months, were unable to discover the slightest clue which could be of service in bringing the blood-thirsty miscreant to justice. There is little prospect that, at this late hour, the secret of this human demon's identity will ever be revealed. We should not like to suggest, with reference to what have come to be known as the 'Oxford Murders,' that a like result will attend the efforts of the forces now arrayed on the side of Law and Order. We merely seek to convince the public—which can know but little of the difficulties with which the Chief Constable of the City and the Senior Proctor of the University are faced in their search for the inhuman perpetrator of these recent crimes—that not the best brains of the detective forces of our own or of any other country can, without the element of luck, hope to achieve a successful outcome of their schemes. And this element of luck has so far, we must regretfully admit, been completely lacking."

Ignoring either criticism or praise, Chief Constable Foster and Chief Inspector Bramley and Mr. Barnes, the Senior Proctor, continued their work upon a plan which the University officer had devised and from which all three were at last hopeful that some positive success would result.

The Chief Constable's office was more crowded than usual, and, from its appearance, it might have been an annexe to the Examination Schools. For Foster's desk (not by any means a small one), and an extra table which had been installed, were piled high with heaps of the ruled, uncovered books so familiar to candidates sitting for various University examinations at the dread buildings in the "High". In addition to Bramley, Barnes, and Foster himself there were two or three dons of the University, wearing the gown and hood of the M.A. degree, each of whom carried yet further piles of books under their arms.

"There have been a lot of complaints, Barnes," said one fussy, plump, bespectacled little man, with watery blue eyes and the scholar's stoop. "I know the cause of justice must be served, but, at the same time, we examiners have our duty to do by the candidates, and I'm afraid I don't quite see the trend of your arrangements."

Bramley and his lieutenant and Foster and one of the Oxford inspectors were busily engaged in examining the books one by one with magnifying glasses. After a while each would put down the glass, and, in a gingerly way (each man wore a pair of white cotton gloves), would cut a small portion from the manuscript before him, write on its back the name of the candidate who had used it, and place it in a box before him, replacing the book itself in a neat pile of others which had been similarly mutilated, and, taking a fresh one from another heap, repeat the process. They went on with their work as if oblivious of the dons' presence.

"You see," said Barnes, "in a matter like this—of life and death— we can't stand by academic rules and regulations. You know enough now for me to tell you that it was that bit of gown that Bramley found in Doctor Playford's room that gave us the idea that a member of the University itself might be involved. Enquiries amongst the fellows and other graduates have been proceeding all the Term. But there was always, of course, just the chance that it was an undergraduate who was involved. It was quite impossible to conduct enquiries into the movements for the past eight or nine months of every single undergraduate in the whole of the University. So I devised a plan for obtaining the thumbprints at least of each man coming up for Examination in the Schools, without his knowledge. A thin film of an oily substance was placed on each of the pieces of blotting-paper which are put on the desk of each candidate. At some time during the course of each paper it was virtually certain that each man would take up his piece of blotting paper, and get part of this substance on his fingers—more particularly on his thumb—which was what the Police especially needed. Some of the candidates would wipe off the film with their handkerchiefs. But whether they noticed it or not, it was also pretty certain that at some time or other during the examination a print, faint or clear as the case might be, would be transferred to one or more of the sheets of paper in the books. The Police—" Mr. Barnes was glowing with obvious pride and breathing rapidly with his excitement as he approached the culminating point of his scheme, "the Police, as you know, have ways and means of developing even weak prints of fingers and on the least promising of materials. And paper is an admirable medium. My friend, Chief Inspector Bramley and his—er—coadjutors have been bringing out the prints. The examination for the first M.B. has yielded negative results. You gentlemen, in accordance with instructions approved by the House of Congregation, acting through the Hebdomadal Council have brought us the papers of candidates now being examined in several of the Groups in the Pass School of the Final Examination. These will take time, and I fear that the results will scarcely have been tabulated before the papers set by the Moderators in the Pass Schools are upon us?" He turned enquiringly towards Chief Inspector Bramley.

"No, sir. This sort of work, if it's to be done properly and with any hope of getting any useful results, must be done with *very* great care.

The examiners, having besought the detectives to mutilate as little as was humanly possible, the papers for whose safety they were responsible, bade them adieu and left them to their work. And Mr. Barnes fussed around them like a hen which fears for the safety of her chickens.

.　　.　　.　　.　　.

The porter of Somerset College was feeling much relieved. The term had ended the day before, and the ceaseless tramp of scouts and out-porters from the railway stations, with the trunks and boxes of undergraduates leaving Oxford for the Christmas vacation, had at last come to an end. A few men were still up, having still their *vivas* to face or some other of the hundred and one odd reasons which often crop up to prevent one or two undergraduates of each College from observing exactly the limits of the academic term.

It was not long after ten in the morning—the slackest morning he had known for a week—when a tap on the glass panel of his Lodge attracted his attention. He looked up from the latest Edgar Wallace which he was reading, and started violently when he recognised in his visitor the Chief Constable of the City Police, accompanied by a tall business-like looking man whom he did not know.

"Sorry to bother you, Mr. Neale," said Foster. "But do you happen to know if this man is in the College this morning?"

The Porter readjusted his glasses and read a name written on a slip of paper which the Chief Constable handed to him.

"Yes—as a matter of fact he is. I saw him come in about half an hour ago. He's not a member of this College."

"I know," said Foster, looking towards Bramley who had left him and was glancing round the first quad from the entrance archway. "But I believe one of your men is a friend of his. I expect he's visiting him."

"Ah yes, I daresay you're right. But what, if I might——?"

Foster put his fingers to his lips and slightly shook his head.

"I'd just like you," said he, "if you would, to direct me to his friend Mr. Drayton's rooms."

.   .   .   .   .

About ten minutes after the Chief Constable's interview with the porter, Barbara Playford passed the entrance to Somerset College on her way home from Somerville to St. Thomas's. She noticed a taxi drawn up at the pavement outside. Towards it, from the Porter's Lodge, came Chief Inspector Bramley and the Chief Constable. Between them walked the African student, Septimus Konti, of St. Antony's.

The police officers both recognised Barbara and raised their hats politely: they were not in uniform. And it crossed the girl's mind that it was odd that Bramley should use his left hand. She glanced again and noticed that the Chief Inspector's right hand was handcuffed to the negro's left.

CHAPTER XXIII

An Unexpected Turn

"THANK God he's gone at last!" exclaimed Reggie Crofts. "Have another one—a small one?"

He took the stopper from the square cut-glass gin decanter on the rickety Madeira table, and poured a generous measure of the spirit into a cocktail glass, the sides of which he had previously deftly coated with the requisite amount of Angostura. He had become learned in the manners and customs of "The Coast."

"Can't stick the blighter at any price," growled Daddy Dawson, in shorts and bush shirt, comfortably stretched out in a deep chair on his host's veranda.

His remark was punctuated by the soothing sound of the sparklet syphon as the Assistant D.C. finished mixing his drink for him.

"Nobody ever expects *you* to say the right thing at any time—I've learnt that much, if I've learnt nothing else!"

"And if they *do* expect it," said the old Coaster truculently, "they'll be damned well disappointed—every bloody time! Chin chin!"—and the major portion of the gin and bitters went the way of many a predecessor.

The rainy season was on, with its wearying succession of damp, dismal, dreary days, when not even a game of tennis could be had to while away the leisure hours on the hard mud court. Constructed by unskilled prison labour, its surface was reduced by the constant downpour, to the consistency of sodden, sticky porridge. Reggie Crofts, who had to spend the working hours of the day in the office with Mr. Commissioner Prescott, when his chief was not out on one of his regular tours of the District, had not been too pleased when the fussy little man had dropped in for a drink before dinner—a thing he would not have been permitted to do had the vigilant Mrs. Prescott been out with him.

Reggie had not been feeling too well. Successive "goes" of slight fever in the West African rainy season knock a good deal of the stuffiing out of the strongest and healthiest man. But, in his relief at the departure of his unwelcome guest, he felt as if he had taken on a fresh lease of life. His worries about Barbara and her uncle had been, to a great extent, set at rest by the last Reuter's, which had made it pretty clear that the Oxford police, aided by their more experienced London colleagues were really nearing the time when an expected arrest might safely be made, and the city's reign of terror brought to a definite end.

It was the first time for some months that the official news had been so definitely encouraging, and Reggie felt pretty confident that the series of tragedies, which had aroused the interest of the whole of the thinking world, had at last come to an end, and that the cunning criminal, who had so long and so skilfully evaded justice, was at last to be brought to book.

He looked round his bush hut veranda, and for the thousandth time during the past few months, compared it mentally with his comfortable digs in Oxford. Comfortable, at least, they seemed to him now, though the thought came back to him now that he had, not once, but many times, criticised them none too favourably to his friends. He had refrained from doing so in front of the formidable Mrs. Leary, who, for what she herself described as an insignificant sum, had conceded him the privilege of living in them. Mrs. Leary's *cuisine* had had its faults. But when he compared it with the efforts of Alimami, his Mendi cook, he began to think that some of his criticisms had been a trifle hasty.

Mrs. Leary's soup had at least never tasted of kerosene and her omelettes, though not such as a Parisian chef would have lauded, offered less resistance to the cutting edge of the ordinary table-knife than the black cook's similar productions.

Stone bungalows, built by the Public Works Department, had been promised the officials stationed at Baoma, "as soon as the revenues of the Colony permitted." But as Reggie had only twenty-seven more years to serve before retiring on pension, he decided that he had best reconcile himself to the idea of living permanently in the mud, native-built type of structure which he now inhabited.

After all, when the rains were over and it did not matter whether there were holes in the thatched roof or not, it had its advantages. It was ever so much cooler than the pretentious European-built bungalows which he had seen in Edwardsville. The scene was really rather beautiful, thought Reggie, as he looked out from his deck-chair, over the low mud wall of the veranda, towards the Police barracks and the native village a mile or so away beyond the belt of graceful oil palms, silver-leafed in the bright rays of the rising tropical moon.

"There's a good deal more," said he to his guest, "to be said for the wild beauty of Africa than anyone has yet written."

Daddy Dawson gave a contemptuous grunt, swallowed the rest of his drink.

"What's made you see the beauty of the ruddy place all of a sudden?" he growled.

Daddy Dawson, for reasons best known to himself had seen fit to spend more than thirty years of life at the lonely little village of Mapunga. So he must have seen *something* in it which he was not prepared to admit. But he could never be got to say a good word either of the country or of its people.

"You don't know these Africans as I know them, Crofts. You can't conceive the villany, the brutality, the loathsomeness which exists down there under the quiet moon and those gently waving palm-trees. I——"

"Aren't you just a bit unfair?" said Crofts, interrupting the older man. "I should say you could find all the same things only multiplied a hundred-fold, in quality *and* in quantity in London, Paris,

Berlin, New York—*any* big white man's city you like. The only difference, so far as I can see, is that you've electric light in place of moonlight, and that *these* people *have* the excuse of not having the advantage of the civilisation we white men have got. I suppose," he changed the subject, as old Daddy Dawson appeared to be about to burst into invective, "you know old Chief Konti came to the office this afternoon to see Prescott?"

"Aye—it's not often I miss an item of news like that," said Dawson.

"And do you happen to have heard what he came about?" said Crofts,—a suspicion of mischief in his voice. For as the old man had not interrupted him with an account of what had transpired at the interview, he knew well that the news could not have yet reached his ears.

"No, I haven't—*yet*," he said, rather shortly. "I *shall* hear it all to-night though, when I get back to Mapunga. Meanwhile—it's a thirsty walk back in the moonlight, and——"

Reggie supplied the needs of his guest.

"Would you like to hear *my* version *now?*" said Reggie, not displeased at for once being able to frustrate old Dawson, who took such pride in being usually much better informed about local matters than the Government officers in charge of the District.

"May as well," said Dawson, ungraciously. "Maybe I'll be able to correct it later, and fill in a few of the gaps."

He would not admit complete defeat, especially before a first-timer.

"Well, old Konti came in to beg an interview with the D.C. . . . As he was practically sober, I guessed that he thought the matter serious. I showed him in, and Prescott asked me to stay and hear what the palaver was about. For he's off again on tour, collecting some odd travelling allowance, I suppose, for there's nothing much outstanding at present to attend to, and he thought I might as well be *au fait*. Well, it was what we said just now, comparing Africa and Europe, that made me think of it. *He's* as nervous as a cat about this 'piccan' (*child*) of his, as the interpreter calls him, at Oxford. Seems to think he's in some sort of danger of his life from the man who's done in these three dons and tried to bag a fourth. Says his son *must* come home at once, and asked Prescott, as the D.C., to use his influence with the Government, and get him out of danger before it's too late."

Old Daddy Dawson lay back in his chair puffing at his pipe with a sardonic smile on his face which grew in intensity as Reggie went on with his story. As the Assistant D.C. came to the end of his tale the old trader burst into a harsh laugh.

"That's good," he said, "that's good! The young man *is* in danger—I've guessed that for some time from reading between the lines of what I've seen lately in Reuter's and the papers. But it's not quite the *kind* of danger that his respected Papa suspects."

"But what can *you* know about it?" said the young man in amazement. "I thought you'd never been to Oxford and knew nothing about it?"

"No more I have, Crofts, and no more I do," said Daddy Dawson, thoroughly enjoying the young man's bewilderment. "I know nothing at all of Oxford and its dons, and don't want to. But I know a damned sight more of 'the Coast' than you or a good many others I could name. And it's *that* that happens to matter for the moment." He became serious, and leaning forward with his pipe in his hand, said: "Would you like to hear *my* theory of all these murders and things which have been upsetting the whole world these last few months?

Crofts was completely mystified by his strange guest's words. But he was keenly interested, for he knew, from the experience of many evenings he had spent either here at Baoma or in the shack at Mapunga in Daddy Dawson's company, that the old man never talked for the mere sake of talking, and that good sound common sense was one of his most prominent qualities.

"Go on," said Reggie eagerly, "I'd be only too glad to hear *anything* that would throw some light on these awful shows in Oxford. I've been absolutely worried to death over them for months."

"Very well," said Daddy Dawson: and he settled himself down to talk. "You've heard all this rumour of Leopard Murders in this

District? You've learnt, by now, that old Chief Konti has been for a long time suspected as being the real power behind the scenes? His position has forced him to pretend to be on the side of the Government, and against the men who have been committing these crimes. You know that the reason that members of the Society commit these murders is not, nowadays, anyway, because they hanker after eating human flesh for mere love of its taste? They murder their victims in order to acquire new virility and all the waning powers of the body. That's why they almost always choose *young* victims—the sort of people who have got the very powers and youth and vitality which are beginning to grow feeble in their own bodies, exhausted as they are by their excesses all round. You know that this young blighter, Septimus Konti, who went to Oxford last year, is a son of this old devil of a cannibal chief. You know you told me that you knew, before you came out here, that the young fool's brains were not equal to getting him through one of the simplest exams on the way to getting an Oxford degree? You will have noticed, in the papers, the kind of men who have been the victims of the murderer: men who were exceptionally clever in the very subjects in which young Konti was unable to succeed. I asked you, one day, what were the subjects in which most people would have to pass in order to be successful in what you called 'Pass Moderations.' They were— you must check me if I am wrong—Latin, French, English and Logic."

"That's right," cried Reggie, excited beyond measure at Daddy Dawson's words.

"Now just consider, for a minute, the subjects for which the victims of the murders and the attack were most known. The first, Professor Toogood, was the Professor of Latin. The next victim was the leading French scholar in Oxford. Even an old 'Coaster'— an ignoramus like myself, has heard of the reputation of Doctor Playford, the Master of St. Thomas's, as a master of subjects connected with English literature. And, thinking what I did, and knowing what I thought, I was not surprised when I read the obituary notice of poor old Mortimer in *The Times* you lent me and found that, amongst his activities was the coaching of men for the Pass Examinations in Logic, on which he'd written a book which had been widely sold." He paused to take breath and to have another sip at his drink.

"Go on," said Reggie Crofts breathlessly, as he leant forward, his excitement showing in his eyes.

"Don't you remember," said Daddy Dawson, slowly and impressively as he waved his pipe at his hearer, "the thing which so puzzled the Coroner and the police in each case—the attempt to drill a hole in the *brain*—the presence, in the case of each murder, of *some* attempt to injure the *skull?* Konti came from a part of the country where Human Leopardism and its theories are rife. From childhood he has heard tales of how men can acquire or revive their *physical* powers by eating certain parts of the flesh of young and vigorous victims. He goes to Oxford. He has some education—some powers of reasoning. He fails, in every legitimate way, to acquire the necessary knowledge of the subjects in which he has to pass his examinations. Physical powers can be acquired, according to the beliefs of this disgusting Society, by material means. By a transition of thought and the substitution of *brains* for *flesh, why not also intellectual?* It *is* true," said the old man, raising his voice, "as his father thinks, that Septimus Konti is in danger." Dawson leaned forward, a grim smile spreading over his features, his voice husky with excitement, "but the danger to him comes, *not* from the murderer—but from Law and Justice, from the *police!"*

CHAPTER XXIV

Paddington

AND so it came about that, by the efforts of Mr. Barnes, Fellow of St. Antony's College, Lecturer in Criminal Law in the University of Oxford, and Senior Proctor, and of "Daddy" Dawson (whose Christian name no one knew), of Mapunga, in the Baoma District of the North Western Province of a small Colony in British West Africa, the guilt of the three tragic murders, and of the unsuccessful attempt on Doctor Playford, Master of St. Thomas's College, was clearly fixed in the eyes of the police officers into whose hands the conduct of the case was entrusted.

When the thumb marks on the Pass Moderations papers had been developed, photographed, and compared, as also had been those produced from former papers in the Schools, with the thumb print on Professor Toogood's hat, it became abundantly plain to the experts who were conducting the proceedings that, unless an absolute miracle had happened, the person who had last handled the dead man's hat was Mr. Septimus Konti, the African second year undergraduate of St. Antony's College.

But much work remained to be done by the detectives before an arrest could be made. Konti's "wives" were interviewed as to the movements of their "husband" on the night of the Professor's tragic death in the garden in Wellington Square.

He had dined with them in their lodgings that night instead of in the Hall of the College, where, by the rules, each student had to dine so many nights a week during Term. The women remembered clearly because they had had that night, as a special treat, a stock native dish of the West Coast of Africa called "palm oil chop," a mixture of meat and vegetables of various kinds, stewed in the heavy red oil of the West African oil-palm.

Konti's father had sent him home a case of bottles of this oil, by a steamer which had arrived at Liverpool a day or two before, and the occasion had been honoured by the broaching of the gift.

In their excitement at enjoying a dish fresh from their native land, the three, who usually plied knife and fork as easily as any European, had reverted to type and employed their fingers in dealing with the viscous stew. Septimus had rested awhile after the meal, which had, as customarily, been washed down with bottles of beer. He had gone out for a short time, and had returned at about nine o'clock. The women had gone to bed soon after ten, leaving their husband downstairs. He had expressed the intention of remaining at the lodgings all night instead of returning to his rooms in College.

He had seemed somewhat excited, and had referred, more than once, to the difficult character of the Latin papers set in the Pass Schools, and he had emphasised his dread of having to return home without the coveted degree on which he had set his heart.

Miatta, one of the women, had next seen him early in the morning from one of the back windows, going down the garden in his slippers, still fully dressed in his day clothes, with what looked like a grey felt hat tightly crumpled up in his hand. This he had put into the dustbin—placing over it some straw or paper: for the receptacle had no lid.

Regina, the "civilised" wife, said that when she came down next morning, she had noticed signs which seemed to show that some- one had lighted the gas fire in the sitting-room. There were lots of matches about, and Konti was not a smoker. And Septimus had been very cantankerous and irritable when questioned on the matter.

"Luck favoured us there," said Bramley to Foster after the interview and their return to the Police Station when Foster, on the facts he had. ascertained, had sworn an information before a magistrate for the arrest of the African student. "The heavy oil which the beggar had not washed from his fingers stuck tight to the material of the hat. And though the petrol took most of the obvious stains out, it wasn't rubbed in enough to take away *all* marks of the thumb, which were brought out pretty clearly by the experts at the Yard. It seems to me pretty clear that Konti, having done in the Professor, when there was no one about in the Square, nor anyone likely to be at that time of night, and in the rain, and wanting to do some kind of operation on the skull for some reason we don't know yet, took off his hat and hung it on the railings, When he'd got safe home, he remembered the hat some time afterwards. He'd heard all about finger-prints and their use in tracing crime, and he knew it was the only part of the Professor's clothing he had handled. So he crept back and retrieved it, between the time Merriless went away and returned with the doctor. "And I suppose," added Foster, "he meant to try to burn it. But that wasn't easy to do with only a gas fire, and someone in the house might have smelt it and interrupted him. So, as it was still very early in the morning, he thought the dust-bin would do as well. Fortunately the thing had no lid and the wind blew the hat away down the lane when the servant put it outside for clearance in the morning. As it fetched up opposite the backdoor of one of the other houses, it was especially noticed by the dust-man on his rounds, and he put it aside for sale. That wicked-looking length of rubber hose-pipe, weighted with plenty of lead, would be sufficient to do in most men. And this African is a pretty hefty fellow."

The magistrate had granted the warrant on the facts which he had deemed sufficient to justify its issue, and the arrest of Konti in Somerset College had followed.

The African had at once retained the services of a solicitor and, at the first hearing in the Police Court, a remand had followed the giving of evidence of arrest only.

So far, so good. But there were many links still missing in the chain, and it was the question of *motive* in particular which so sorely puzzled the officers in charge.

On hearing the news of the event, and much impressed by the theory which Daddy Dawson had unfolded to him, before any one else in the Colony had suspected the identity of the mysterious Oxford assassin, Reggie had cabled to the Chief Constable of Oxford that he had secured important information in connection with the Konti case and stated that he was writing fully in a letter. The remand was twice extended at the request of the prosecution and, in the meanwhile, the whereabouts of the African student at the times of the murders of Professor Toogood, M. Boissard and Mr. Mortimer, and at the time of the attempt upon the Master of St. Thomas's, were established by various witnesses. In the St. Thomas's case, it was clear that Konti having watched his opportunity, had got in by the front door of the Master's lodgings, whilst the front door was open, the passage dark, and Reggie and Barbara clearly not likely to take particular notice of anyone but themselves. He had, seeing that he had not after all managed to get in unobserved, dashed out through the open French window into the quadrangle beyond. There he had waited, concealed in one of the many passage ways, until the household had retired to bed, and, coming out of his hiding-place, forced the window, and attained the Master's study. Being interrupted in his plan, he had gone downstairs again and made his escape by the dining-room window. All he had to do then was to remain hidden until next morning, and make his exit from the College as if he had come in earlier still through the Lodge gateway. His escape was made the easier as he had an Indian friend whom he often used to visit, and the porter knew him well by sight. This man had stated that Konti came to him on some pretext or other, at about ten on the morning after the attempt. He had gone out with him through the Porter's Lodge actually whilst the detectives were in conversation with the porter. Being so well known to old Sawyer, his exit would pass unnoticed, and, even had it been perceived, the porter would naturally assume that he had come in some time earlier in the morning, when he had not happened to be looking. He had carried his gown with him, though it was not actually required in vacation, as a proof of his *bona fides* in case he had been stopped by any one in the College the night before and asked to explain his presence.

But so much depended on the setting up of a motive. The case, which was rather weak in the absence of a reason for the wholesale commission of brutal murders, with quiet, inoffensive scholarly men as their objects, would be immensely strengthened if only a motive could reasonably be established by the prosecution. And there seemed little hope that such a point could be cleared up without external assistance. When Reggie's letter arrived, giving in full, Daddy Dawson's startling theory, a new hope dawned and a conference was held at Scotland Yard at which Chief Constable Foster was present. The solicitor for the defence was beginning to make considerable capital at his client's court appearances out of the law's unaccountable delay, and prompt action was becoming daily more necessary.

It seemed clear that the presence of some European who had had some experience on the spot of the activities and mentality of the Human Leopard Society, which the experienced old trader had sensed at the bottom of the business, must be secured. And the Colonial Office promptly cabled to the Governor. Less than a week after the receipt of the cable, Reggie Crofts, who had seen a great deal of the Society's methods in cases in court before Prescott, and himself, was detailed by Mr. Resident Fielding, as the Commissioner could only be spared at the cost of great inconvenience to the Administration, to proceed home at the request of the Colonial Office, and left the Colony on the homeward voyage in the Elder Dempster liner *Accra*.

.   .   .   .   .

It was a gloomy January day. The fog had filtered through from London without and hung in billowing clouds under the glass roofs of Paddington. It was only just midday but the roof of the station might have been made of cast-iron for all the light it admitted. The arc lamps glowed like copper-coloured balls of fire in the choking murk. But Barbara Playford's heart was light within her, and she would not have changed the miserable gloom for the brightest day of the summer that was past. For, after a separation of seven months, seven months which, for her, had dragged out the length of seven years, she was to see her lover, safe and sound again after his adventures in West Africa. With the arrest of the negro student of St. Antony's who seemed, without a doubt, to have been the murderer of Professor Toogood, M. Boissard and Mr. Mortimer, the assailant of the Master of St. Thomas's, her fears for the safety of her uncle had vanished. She felt that she could sing for joy, and looked with pity at the coughing, shivering porters who awaited the arrival of the *Accra's* overdue boat special from Plymouth. All the weary, lonely, anxious days seemed to have been worth while now. If Reggie had never gone away, she would never have had the pleasure of welcoming him back. She hoped that Konti's trial would be protracted, for she guessed that Reggie would not be able to return to Africa until it was over. And there was always the hope that he might be able to find something better to do elsewhere than in West Africa. For the pictures of life there, which he had drawn in his letters to her, were not supremely inviting and attractive. And did she also consider the possibility of this meeting, perhaps, some day, on another boat another Mrs. Driver, with results more lasting than had been the case before? The suspicion, she felt, was unworthy of her, and she brushed it quickly away, remembering too, that her own ill-fated encouragement of Lord Ruislip, which had had most disastrous results, might have been misinterpreted to Reggie by someone who had witnessed it.

Would the train never come in? It was past noon and there were still no signs.

Suddenly the waiting porters, coughing more noisily than ever as the fog thickened, rushed over in a body to Platform II, and she saw, dimly through the gloom, the massive funnel of the huge Great Western engine.

.   .   .   .   .

"Dear! You mustn't! It's foggy—I know. But lots *can* be seen, even in a fog!"

Her further protests were smothered on her lips—literally on her lips. Reggie looked bronzed and well: and he was much more handsome, she thought, than he had been even before.

"And that," said Reggie, as he released Barbara at last, "doesn't come any too well from a girl who once accepted a proposal in a public room in a tea-shop!"

EPILOGUE

THE cosy room in St. Ambrose's College, Cambridge, looked cosier than ever as the servant pulled the heavy curtains and shut out the dark, January evening. It was tea-time, and Sir Martin Brasted, the distinguished Latin scholar, had asked his friend Professor Green to join him. The two elderly men munched their crumpets and drank their steaming tea with evident enjoyment.

"Have you seen," said Green, as he unfolded a copy of the latest London evening paper and spread it out on his knees, "the extraordinary theory put forward by the prosecution, at the instance of some quaint old beach-comber in West Africa, to account for the Oxford murders?"

"I have," said Sir Martin, who had never got over the defeat he had sustained at the hand of the Oxford professor in the columns of the *Classical Review.* "Apparently it is suggested that poor Toogood's assailant sought to acquire from his victim some *intellectual* power. I must confess that that is the last motive I should have suspected!"

THE END

Lightning Source UK Ltd.
Milton Keynes UK
UKOW031810020713

213152UK00016B/719/P